Damned
When I Didn't

by

Cherie Colyer

This is a work of fiction. Names, characters, places, and incidents are either the product of the author's imagination or are used fictitiously, and any resemblance to actual persons living or dead, business establishments, events, or locales, is entirely coincidental.

Damned When I Didn't

COPYRIGHT © 2020 by Cherie Colyer

Cover Art by *Diana Carlile*

The Wild Rose Press, Inc.
PO Box 708
Adams Basin, NY 14410-0708
Visit us at www.thewildrosepress.com

Publishing History
First Champagne Rose Edition, 2020
Trade Paperback ISBN 978-1-5092-3333-5
Digital ISBN 978-1-5092-3334-2

Published in the United States of America

"You're the one who pissed off the Queen of the Damned," he countered.

I twitched a shoulder. "I still can't stand how you smell right now."

"Fine!" He grabbed me just under my butt and lifted me over his shoulder. I screamed. He held my legs, keeping me from falling.

"What are you doing?" I grabbed his waist from my upside down position.

"You think I smell?"

"Reek. And you said I do, too! Now put me down!"

"Let's fix that."

He marched to the bathroom with me slung over his shoulder. The next thing I knew we were standing in the tub. He continued to hold me like a sack of rice.

"Cole?"

He slid me down his chest so I stood in front of him with his arms keeping me from moving.

"Cole?"

He reached behind me.

I glanced up at the showerhead, then to the knob next to me. "You wouldn't!"

"Want to bet?"

Praise for Cherie Colyer

2012 SCBWI Crystal Kite finalist
for her debut novel, *EMBRACE*

~*~

"Cherie Colyer has done it again, hitting another 5-star homerun with a new YA supernatural [*CHALLENGING DESTINY*]."

~Kate O'Sullivan, author

~*~

"Colyer's *EMBRACE* grips you from page one and doesn't let go until the end."

~Kate Evangelista, author

~*~

"Colyer writes some of the strongest and most authentic teenage characters in a YA fiction."

~RoloPoloBookBlog

~*~

What readers say about Cherie's books:

~*~

"Great world-building."

~*~

"I stayed up all night because I couldn't put it down."

~*~

"Action unfolds throughout the pages with a very developed and descriptive writing style that is just amazing."

Dedication

To the dreamers who never give up

Chapter 1

It wasn't the things I remembered that scared the crap out of me. It was the things I didn't.

Take that night, for instance. I knew I'd been at the same party as my fifteen-year-old sister. She'd been laughing at something her friend had said. Caleb Higgins, the guy I'd been crushing on senior year, had come over to talk to me. I remembered feeling panicked at some point during the party and hearing my friends' heart-stopping screams. But my strongest memory—the one that haunts me even now as I run my hand over the smooth skin on my stomach—was of the sharp pain that had pierced my body just below my rib cage. I'd thought I'd died. Thought I'd glimpsed the Bright Light. But soon after, I wasn't sure of anything. Like how I'd ended up at the hospital. There was no mistaking that's where I was. I recognized the curved wooden reception desk in the waiting room from the time my sister had broken her arm.

I stood near the closed double doors leading into the emergency room, wearing dirty jeans, baby-blue flip-flops, and a too-thin, pale-rose tank top, freezing my butt off. Why were hospitals always so cold? Seriously, there were sick people there. A little heat might have done them wonders.

A disbelieving giggle bubbled up my throat. The temperature in the waiting room was the least of my worries. I rubbed my arms and scanned the area around me for clues to why I was there. A middle-aged man seemed to stare right through me. A few seats down from him, a mother coddled a toddler girl. There were others there, also, but no one I knew.

A woman in a navy pantsuit, carrying a silver tablet and a pink stylus, approached me.

"Avery Caroline Williams," she proclaimed.

She wasn't asking me if I was Avery, more like telling me she knew who I was in a tone that sparked my curiosity.

I glanced around one last time but still didn't recognize anyone. "Yes?"

"I need you to come with me."

Not sure what else to do and too embarrassed to admit I didn't know how I'd gotten there, I did what she asked. I managed a step before my legs turned to rubber.

She grabbed my arm to steady me. Her big hazel eyes met mine. "Careful. You may feel a little off for a while."

I swept a hand through my hair. My fingers snagged on a curl at the back of my head. I tried again to recall how I'd gotten there and once more came up blank.

No longer caring what she might think of me, I asked, "What happened to me?"

Cautiously, she released my arm. When I didn't crash to the floor, she said, "Any questions you have will be answered once you arrive at your destination. Please, follow me."

I opened my mouth to thank her but noticed she wasn't wearing a nametag.

She glanced down at her jacket and back up at me. "I'm Chloe."

Chloe led the way through the double doors and past the nurses' station. The emergency room buzzed with activity. I hurried to keep up with her quick stride. The fluorescent lights revealed shimmers of red in her silky auburn hair, and I caught the scent of honeysuckle when she turned her head. She smiled and waited for me to catch up.

My loss of memory was weird because I remembered choosing my classes for freshman year of college in the morning and stopping by Justin's house in the afternoon. I also remembered coming home to a full-blown argument between my sister and our parents. They'd been in the kitchen.

"Oh, he's a senior," Dad had remarked sarcastically. I'd figured Gracie had a new boyfriend who Dad thought was too old for her.

Then Mom had spoken up. "Gracie, you're not going to a party at a senior's house."

Gracie had begged me to come with her to the party, so Dad and Mom would let her go. In exchange for my help, she'd promised to stop taking my clothes without permission. Before I'd agreed, I'd made her cross her heart and hope to die if she didn't keep her word. I hadn't told Gracie I'd have most likely ended up there anyway because my best friend wanted to go. Gracie must have had her fingers crossed when she'd made the promise because the first thing I'd noticed when I'd gotten to the party was Gracie kicking the toe of my favorite pair of cowboy boots against the wooden deck out back.

"Stay close to your guide, and you'll be fine,"

Chloe said, pulling me out of my reverie.

"You're not my guide?" At that moment, I saw my mom standing next to the half-drawn curtains in one of the examining rooms. Her back was to me. "Mom!"

Chloe caught my arm, keeping me from sprinting to my mom. "We're expected elsewhere."

New questions invaded my thoughts. Who was behind the curtain? Dad? Was I here because Mom had asked me to meet her? Instinctively, I patted my side where my purse should have been if I'd driven myself to the hospital. My finger slid through a hole in my tank top as a small amount of reason told me Gracie would have been with me if that had been the case. My vision blurred, causing a bout of vertigo. The next thing I knew, Mom was gone. I wasn't sure if I'd imagined her. I reached next to me and let my fingers skim the smooth surface of the wall for a second or two. When the hallway in front of me came back into view, I asked, "Did I hit my head?"

"That's a possibility." Chloe opened a door at the end of the hallway.

I staggered past her. "Are my parents here?"

The door closed behind me with a *click*. Chloe was gone.

"Hey!" I tugged at the handle, but it was locked.

A sinking feeling filled me. I shouldn't have followed her. I rested my forehead against the cool, white door and cursed my stupidity.

Movement in my peripheral vision had me spinning around. I was in a white corridor interrupted by doors the color of glistening snow. A tall, lean guy had his back pressed against the wall not far from me. He was nineteen—maybe twenty—and a few hairs

4

short of six feet tall. He wore a nice pair of jeans and a short-sleeved shirt.

"About time." He dragged a hand over his raven black hair and pushed off the wall. "Ready?"

"For what?"

He smirked devilishly, indicating with a sideways jerk of his head for me to follow him.

"I'm not taking another step until someone tells me what's happening." I crossed my arms over my chest and waited.

"I only know what I've been told, which was to take whoever came through that door"—he pointed behind me—"to Lilith. That was over three hours ago." When I continued to stare at him, dumbfounded, he sighed and added, "Surely, you know why you're here."

I shook my head. "I don't even know how I ended up at the hospital or if my parents are here or where my sister is." I had a nagging feeling that if I was at the hospital, then Gracie should be as well.

"Seriously?" His mouth opened. Closed. After a moment, he replied, "I don't think I'm the right person to explain." He told me to follow him. "I'm Cole, by the way." I was just about to tell him my name when he asked, "What's the last thing you remember?"

"Ah…being at a party with my sister, Gracie." I squinted, trying to see what lay beyond the black void of an open door, but I couldn't tell if it was a room or another corridor. A stale breeze brushed my bare arms, sending a chill through me.

"Did you have fun?" he asked.

I tore my gaze away from the darkness. "What?"

He slowed so that I could catch up. "Maybe talking about the last thing you remember will jog your memory. Was it a big party or more of an intimate get-together?"

"Big. At least forty people."

"And your sister was there."

"Yeah." Gracie had been thrilled about being invited to the party. She'd spent over an hour choosing her outfit and then just as much time fussing with her long chestnut hair.

"That's something. The rest will come back to you." He held out an arm, indicating that I should turn down a dimly lit hallway, then pulled his phone out of his pocket. "Next left and we're there."

I racked my brain, trying to recall what had happened at the party as his fingers flew over the screen of his phone. I kept seeing Gracie, her eyes wide in shock. Cole and I came to a T-intersection. I opened the door in front of me, barely registering that the temperature had risen.

"No!" Cole grabbed me around my waist, forcing me to come to an abrupt stop. A flip-flop flew off my foot and down a canyon in front of me. Dry heat slapped my face and feathered through my hair as my toes curled over the lip of an insanely hot ledge. My gaze traveled down rock and earth to a bubbling river of fire some twenty feet below. Countless red hands reached up from the molten liquid, fingers grasping at air and rock. Featureless faces bobbed above the surface, mouths open. Their inhuman screams of agony caused a surge of panic to claw its way down my spine.

"I said *left*." Cole locked my back against his chest and yanked the door closed.

I sucked in breaths of smog-filled air and choked on the sickening stench of rotten eggs and burning hair.

Through a veil of my dark curls, I took in the crimson hue seeping under the door in front of us.

My mouth opened, but no words came out. I wanted to ask, "What was that, and why is it connected to a hospital?" But all I managed was a few disbelieving grunts. I couldn't suck enough air into my lungs to form coherent sentences.

Cole placed a hand on my shoulder. "You need to calm down before you hyperventilate, which would be stupid since you don't need to breathe anymore."

I stopped gasping long enough to tilt my head to the side. Cole's hauntingly blue eyes peered back at me through my bangs.

"I don't what?"

"Need to breathe." He tucked my hair behind my ear. "You're doing it out of habit."

"I'm breathing out of habit?" I parroted back to him.

"You really don't remember anything, do you?"

"No."

He exhaled heavily. "You met Chloe, right? She's a reaper for the northeast part of the United States. Looks as if she's in her mid-thirties, about your height, auburn hair, bored expression, never travels without her tablet and stylus."

My mind only registered one word. "Reaper? As in mythical creature that schleps souls to the afterlife?"

"Yes."

I ran a hand along my rib cage and mumbled, "The sharp pain was real?"

But it couldn't have been. I felt fine. Yet, I wasn't. I mean, there was a chunk of time I couldn't account for, and if my mom was really there, she should have heard me. I lifted my fingers, knotting them in my hair. Mom heard everything, and I mean everything. Her hearing was that good.

"No, no, no. I can't be." I paced away from Cole. "I was at Jared's. Caleb was telling me…telling me what?"

"Ah, excuse me, but we're already late," Cole said, interrupting my meandering thought process.

I spun on my heels and faced him. "Am I dead?"

"Yes," he said, obviously relieved I'd figured it out on my own.

Still in a state of disbelief, I pointed a shaky finger to the glow seeping under the door in front of us. "And that?"

"River of Souls."

"They're on fire!"

Cole rubbed the back of his neck as he let out a low whistle. "I'd assumed Chloe would have prepped you for this." He paused. "Short version—you didn't go up."

The heat. The fiery river. The stench. "Am I in Hell?"

"Technically, you're between Hell and Earth. The Nether, to be exact."

I leaned against the wall next to me and concentrated on inhaling and exhaling, which—despite being told I no longer needed to breathe—seemed to be the only thing I could do.

I'd died and gone to Hell. But why? I wasn't cruel or evil. I hadn't sinned. Much. Something else had to have happened in the last minutes of my life to warrant a one-way trip down. I knocked my knuckles against my skull. "Think!"

But the moments leading up to my death weren't what I dwelled on. I'd never see my family again. I wouldn't attend college. I'd taken my last stroll along a moonlit beach, and it wasn't even with the guy of my dreams. Megan—my crazy, amazingly spunky best friend—and I were supposed to spend two incredible weeks this summer at her parents' condo in Key West. I'd already bought a new bikini for the trip. I wasn't ready to leave my life. There were things I needed to do. Stuff I wanted to talk to Gracie about. I'd thought I had time.

Cole's hand came to rest on my arm. "I hate to cut this pity party short, but Lilith will have my head if we're not back soon."

I pulled my hair away from my face. It was the second time he'd mentioned that name. "Who's she?"

"My boss."

"There are bosses in the Afterlife?" I pressed my fingers to my temple to ease the pressure building there. "Please tell me you're not taking me to meet the devil." No way did I want to chat with Satan himself. Cute demon or whatever Cole was—fine. Beelzebub—I'll pass.

"Of course not."

I glared at him, trying to determine if he was being honest with me.

"If it makes you feel better, she's an angel," he added with a cautious smile.

That did ease my worries some, and crazy as it was, I felt safe with Cole. My gut told me he wouldn't put me in harm's way, and at that moment, my instincts were all I had.

"What's an angel doing in Hell?" I asked.

"Probably thinking up ways to make my life miserable for keeping her waiting." He gave a light tug on my arm. "We have to go. Lilith isn't someone you want to make angry."

We took the next left. Me hobbling along now that I'd lost a shoe. This hallway was mauve with dark wall sconces giving off a strange amber glow every ten feet or so.

"There are far worse places in Hell than where you're being sent," Cole said.

I glanced at him. "You mean there are different types of Hell—like really, really bad places and just medium-bad places?"

He chuckled. "Something like that. In any case, the sooner you accept where you are, the sooner you'll be allowed to return topside."

I stopped, not sure I'd heard him correctly. "Wait a second! I'm going back, as in to blue skies and green grass? Not a wooden box six feet underground?"

"You have to return, or you'll grow weak. Lilith will explain."

Cole motioned for me to keep moving. I clung to the promise of getting the heck out of the maze of corridors and back to my family as I let myself be led onward. Every other step, I felt cool slate under my now-bare foot. The awful smell from the fiery river faded, and in its place came the sweet fragrance of flowers. It was pleasant, like my grandma's garden.

"So, do you have a name, or should I call you Gracie's sister?" Cole asked.

"Avery."

"Nice to meet you, Avery."

Cole didn't wait around for me to say anything

else.

I stuffed my thumbs into the front pockets of my jeans and entered an awe-inspiring living room with a vaulted ceiling. Sunlight streamed in tall windows.

"Lilith enjoys the finer things in life and in the afterlife," Cole said. "We aren't actually above ground, though. What you see through the windows is an illusion."

I trailed behind Cole farther into the room, stopping next to the sofa. A woman with long blonde hair and ruby lips thumbed through a magazine with bored interest.

"You're late," she snapped. Her frigid gaze fell on Cole.

He nudged me forward. "Avery was held up in processing." I took Cole's word for it, seeing as I still couldn't account for several hours of my day. He continued, "She doesn't remember much. Is that normal?"

Lilith set the magazine aside. "Quite."

"How did I die?" I asked, sure if I knew the answer to that question, I'd remember everything.

"That will come to you in time." Lilith sat up, legs crossed in front of her.

"Why can't you just tell me? I mean, I know I was with my sister—" At least I was eighty-nine percent sure of it. "—and I have this bad feeling." It was a deep-in-the-gut pang that urged me to find Gracie. Maybe that was why I was being sent back to Earth. Maybe I had unfinished business.

Lilith tapped her perfectly manicured nails on the couch. After a moment, she said, "I've been down here long enough to know a human's mind often blocks memories when the soul can't handle them. Now that I have you, I don't need you falling apart."

"Fall apart? Why would I—she didn't…she's not…" Oh God, my poor parents would be alone. Both of their children ripped from their lives in one night. My knees threatened to give, but I forced the last word past my lips. "Dead?"

Lilith sighed and seemed to consider how to respond. I worried my bottom lip between my teeth and prayed Gracie was all right. Cole had said I was being sent back. While I didn't know how or why, that knowledge was enough to stifle worries about myself. But I was supposed to watch out for Gracie—keep her safe. What if I had failed?

"That will come to you when the rest of your memories do." Lilith rose to her feet. Her floor-length dress hugged her slender frame as she sauntered closer. "It's been a long time since I've acquired such a young specimen."

I winced, not liking to be referred to as a science project, but the promise of home gave me the strength to hold my tongue.

"You're very attractive," she noted.

Cole elbowed my side, causing me to squawk out a "Thank you."

Lilith was absolutely stunning: porcelain skin, rosy complexion, and the figure of a super-model.

Why's an angel slumming it in Hell? I thought.

Lilith's eyes narrowed as Cole groaned. Their reaction made me realize I'd asked the question out loud.

"I'm sorry. I didn't mean any disrespect," I quickly said. Upsetting a superior being who had the power to send me home wasn't my intention.

One corner of Lilith's mouth quirked upward. "Being called an angel isn't an insult, even here. That's just not a term many use when they talk about me."

Cole bent close to me and whispered not so quietly, "She fell."

"Fell?" I studied Lilith. She had an angelic smile, gentle eyes, and a creamy complexion that seemed to shimmer with light just under the surface. She appeared to be one of Heaven's creations. "But you said she was an angel."

"Technically, she is, but that's not how those of us in Hell usually refer to her."

"What do you call her?"

Lilith—obviously unfazed at being the topic of conversation—surveyed Cole.

"Queen of the Damned," Cole replied with a slight bow of his head.

"I prefer to rule the damned rather than to have someone else tell me what to think and do," she explained with a dismissive wave of her hand. "Besides, I revel in life's little pleasures and simply do not have the time to spare regretting the choices that led me here." I couldn't blame her. Her living arrangements were far from horrible. Her gaze fell to my feet. "What happened to your other shoe?"

My toes curled against the cool slate floor. "I lost it."

"River of Souls," Cole added.

She nodded as if shoes flew into the fiery river every day. She circled me with the grace of a lioness. "Not too busty. What are you, a 34C?"

I folded my arms over my chest. She was right, but

Cole didn't need to know that.

"Tiny waist and alluring, violet eyes." Lilith clapped her hands together. "You'll have the boys eating out of your hands."

That image did nothing for me.

Lilith eased a hip down onto the arm of the sofa. "As a succubus, you'll lead a charmed existence—as long as you remember to feed regularly—and you live amongst humans. Because of your age, though, you'll be leaving here with Cole. He'll show you the ropes and help keep you out of trouble."

The living amongst humans I could handle. "I'm sorry, but what's a succubus?"

"Female demon, of course." She gave another little wave of her hand. "One who survives on the companionship of men, preferably the purest of the species."

"I don't understand," I confessed.

"Nice guys," Cole said. "You know, the ones who finish last."

I could hang out with nice guys. Hell wasn't nearly as bad as I had thought. But one glaring question plagued me. "Why Hell?"

I hadn't been a saint when I was alive, but I hadn't been a monster, either. Something horrible had to have happened in the last minutes of my life to have damned my soul. I'd been drinking. We all were. Gracie was having fun. Megan had been chatting with the guy she swore was her soon-to-be boyfriend. Things got loud. Time froze, or did it speed up? I wasn't sure, but that bad feeling—the one about Gracie—grew. Her wide eyes staring at me in shock pierced my heart.

Lilith frowned. "Avery, the mind is a delicate

wonder and can easily break. For that reason, it's important that you figure these things out on your own."

"Fine," I said as if I couldn't care less that she wasn't talking. I did care, but I couldn't drag the information out of her. "At least tell me why I'll be a succubus."

"You have Eddie Grenier, Adrian Bloom, Frank Lutz, Tom Cooper—to name but a few—to thank for ending up in my care."

Eddie Grenier was one of the teen counselors at the summer camp I went to when I was fourteen. Adrian, Nathan, and Tom were guys from school.

"What do they have to do with any of this?"

Lilith let out a high-pitched cackle. "Promiscuous girls hardly make desirable angels."

But I hadn't been promiscuous. Not really, anyway. I had met Eddie the summer between eighth and ninth grade. He'd been the totally hot counselor that all the girls at camp had been crazy about, me included.

One day, I had an unexpected visit from my monthly girl-thing. None of the female counselors had been available to drive me to the store to pick up feminine products. Mortified, I had no choice but to ask Eddie. I'd told him I wanted to surprise my cabin-mates with munchies for the movie that night, but I think he knew the trip was for more than potato chips and sodas.

Our return to camp hadn't gone unnoticed. A couple of the girls from my cabin had seen me getting out of his car. They'd assumed we'd snuck off camp grounds to fool around. I didn't correct them. My fake-sleeping with the hottest counselor at camp had earned me instant fame with the girls in my cabin. They'd hoped Eddie would pay them "extra" attention, also, so they'd kept their assumptions a secret from the rest of camp. In their minds, there would have been more competition if others had found out Eddie was into younger women.

That little white lie had led to the next one a few months later. A group of us had been playing spin-the-bottle in Donny Sullivan's basement. I got sent to the closet for Seven Minutes in Heaven with Adrian Bloom, who at that time had just so happened to be my best friend's secret boy-crush. As cute as Adrian was, I just couldn't make out with him. It would have devastated Megan. So we talked, instead. It turned out Adrian liked Megan but was too shy to ask her out. I spent my Seven Minutes in Heaven setting up my best friend with the guy of her dreams. Adrian and I agreed not to tell anyone except Megan the truth. I guess we'd both behaved extremely guilty when we came out of the closet because everyone assumed we'd gone further than just kissing. I told them to believe what they wanted. At the time, it only mattered to me that Megan knew the truth.

The next two guys were similar stories. The rumors of what had happened were far more exciting than reality, and the more I denied them, the more people thought I had something to hide. Not to mention, guys treated me differently when they thought I'd done *it*. They invited me to more parties, and they included me in their group outings. My social life improved several notches with each lie. Could I be blamed if the list of guys I'd allegedly slept with kept growing?

"I'm a virgin," I stammered.

Lilith let out a whimsical laugh. "Aren't we all? You stick with that story, and you'll have guys flocking to you."

"But it's the truth. Shouldn't an all-powerful creature such as yourself know what transpired between me and those guys?"

"Yes, and so does the court that determined your soul should be placed in my care. You weren't as innocent as you like to believe." Lilith picked up her magazine, apparently done with the conversation. "Dinner's at seven. Cole, show Avery to the guest room upstairs. She'll find everything she needs to freshen up."

Cole motioned for me to follow him.

"And Cole," Lilith added without glancing in his direction. "Don't be late."

Chapter 2

You'd think one had the right to know how her life had ended and why she'd been cast into damnation like the scum of the Earth, but apparently, the leaders of Hell felt differently. I would have freaked out if hellhounds or horned beasts had strolled by or if Cole had led me through a dismal wasteland littered with souls of the condemned, but there seemed to be some mercy in my sentencing.

I followed Cole up a winding staircase. My fingers trailed over the polished railing as I admired the crystal chandelier that dangled above the slate foyer below and the breathtaking sunset seen through the windows. And speaking of awe-inspiring, spending eternity ogling Cole wasn't exactly punishment. He had a natural swagger that made it hard not to notice that his jeans hugged his butt nicely.

"This place is incredible," I commented as we passed an enormous bedroom.

"Looks can be deceiving." Cole opened a dark wooden door halfway down the hallway. "Don't let the décor suck you in."

A large four-poster bed with an azure-blue comforter occupied the center of the room. Against a wall was a wardrobe half filled with clothes that could've been plucked right out of my closet at home. The other half was stuffed with guy's jeans, shirts, and shoes. I ran a hand over the fabric, causing the hangers to clink as they hit each other.

"Lilith put them there for you—well, the girl stuff, anyway," Cole said. He made himself comfortable on the bed.

Was I dreaming? At any moment, would I wake to find myself at home, laughing at my weird imagination? My gaze fell on two black-and-white glass penguins. They stood motionless in a gliding position on the nightstand.

Cole closed his eyes but not before pointing to the door next to the wardrobe and saying, "Shower's through there."

The fresh scent of the sea wrapped around me as soon as I stepped into the pearl-blue bathroom. A tall, clear jar was filled with white sand. Smooth, black stones dangled from a rope wrapped around its neck. Not far from that was a flat bowl of seashells and a pile of clean, white towels. The place screamed oceanside resort. My fingers grazed the edge of a soaking tub. A bath would have been wonderful, but I didn't know how much time I had, and Cole was waiting for me in the next room.

I dropped my stained clothes, letting them land in a heap next to the pedestal sink, and stepped into a shower big enough for two. A curved glass divider separated it from the rest of the bathroom. On the far wall, a large selection of body wash in tantalizing fragrances such as strawberry daiquiri, coconut-lime, and mint-infused stood like enticing soldiers. There was an equally impressive selection of shampoos and conditioners. I chose mango body wash and raspberry-vanilla shampoo, hoping the sweet scents would help me relax.

Cole had said that the sooner I accepted my fate, the sooner I'd be allowed to return to Earth. The first thing I planned to do was call my parents and ask about Gracie. I'd tell them I wasn't gone forever. Instead, I was dead-turned-demon.

I rolled my eyes at how my God-fearing parents would take that news and figured I had a little time to work on the wording.

My senses reeled in delight as the sweet scent of mango lather washed away the last of my human aches and fears. Being dead didn't have to be the end. Not if a succubus got to live on Earth with her family and friends. It seemed too good to be true. I made a mental note to ask Cole what the catch was as I closed my eyes and let the beads of water flow over me, rinsing the suds from my hair and body.

"I knew you'd feel better after a shower."

I froze, hands on my head ready to push the last of the conditioner from my hair. Please tell me I didn't just hear Cole's voice as if he were standing in the same room. That had to be my imagination. I opened one eye but couldn't see anyone or anything through the steam on the glass wall. Quiet surrounded me. After a second or three, I exhaled a sigh of relief and even managed to giggle at myself for daydreaming that Cole was in the bathroom with me. He was everything I liked in a guy: sexy, muscular, kind, and not a leering creep.

Hello! My conscience knocked on my brain. *Cole's a demon! Bad boys are SO not your type.*

"Want me to wash your back?" Cole asked.

I did *not* imagine that.

"Don't you believe in knocking?" One hand flew

to cover my breasts as the other did what it could to hide my lower parts. A fig leaf would have done a better job than my skinny fingers. A quick glance around the steam-filled shower showed I'd forgotten to grab a towel. I cursed under my breath.

"I'll take that as a no," Cole said, not bothering to hide the chuckle in his voice.

"I'm okay, thanks." I opened the door wide enough to stick my arm out and prayed the glass walls would remain frosted with stream. "Can you please hand me a towel?"

"Sure."

Yet plush terrycloth didn't touch my fingers. I peeked out, one arm still covering the girls. Cole leaned against the sink, jeans hanging low on his hips and feet crossed at his ankles. His bare chest confirmed he was all muscle. He held a towel out in front of him.

Did he think I'd prance over to him *au naturel*? More importantly, why were his shirt and shoes off? Flabbergasted at seeing him, I failed to form a witty comeback.

"Can you bring the towel closer?" I asked, feeling the heat of embarrassment warm my cheeks as Cole's eyebrow rose in a questioning way.

"Don't tell me you're shy."

"Just because I'm not willing to sashay around naked in front of a guy I just met doesn't mean I'm shy." I stuck my chin in the air. "It shows I have dignity and self-respect."

He smiled wickedly. "Sashaying is optional."

"The towel." I wiggled my fingers in a come-closer way. I would have stomped my foot, but the glass was clearing and I was using my leg to help cover my lower region. To my relief, Cole took two small steps forward, his eyes not straying from mine.

"Thank you," I said a moment too soon.

Cole released of the towel just as my thumbs brushed cotton. It fell in a cozy pile outside the shower. He smirked as he slid back to the sink.

Okay, an eternity with him might drive me to do something that would be Hell-worthy. I'd actually earn my sentence.

"Very mature." I bent down and snatched the towel off the floor as quickly as I could without slipping on the wet tile, then covered up.

"Why are you half dressed?" I asked as I wrapped the towel around me.

"It takes me a few days to acclimatize to the blazing heat down here. I'm hoping not to stay that long."

See, he has a perfectly logical explanation for taking off his shirt and shoes.

I stepped out of the shower and grabbed a second towel to use on my hair. "Speaking of our, uh, existence, I'm confused. Are you a succubus, too, and is it true that we live with humans?"

"Only females can become one of those. Males are incubi. We live on Earth *near* humans. We wouldn't be able to survive if we didn't."

"Why's that?"

"We feed on their touch. Without it, we can't function. We might as well be dead."

"We are dead." Although, I had to admit I'd never felt better.

"We're immortal, which means that unlike most dead people, our souls still occupy corporeal, nondecaying bodies."

Definitely a plus.

I raised a brush to my head and paused. The girl staring back at me had changed in subtle ways. My hair was an inch or two longer than it had been the day of the party, and my violet eyes were even brighter than usual. The pimple I'd had on the side of my face was gone, and my complexion was smooth and tan. It was like staring at a different person, only with the old me just under these new features.

"And we absorb energy from being around humans? How does that work?" I imagined we were giant sponges absorbing excess power from the people we hung out with.

"Not *around* humans, *with* them—as in intimate," Cole said.

My dazed astonishment at seeing a new me turned into a whole new bout of panic. The brush fell from my hand and landed on the floor with a clatter. My eyes met his in the mirror.

"You survive by sleeping with girls?"

"Their gender doesn't matter, but I usually renew with girls. Any sexual act will have their life force flowing into you, including long, meaningful kisses."

I tipped my head to the side as my mind processed what he'd said. No matter how I tried to put a positive spin on it, the end result was always the same.

"I died and became Hell's personal prostitute?"

He shrugged. "That's one way to view it."

My gaze shifted back to my reflection. The new and improved me wouldn't have any problem luring guys into bed.

I couldn't breathe. My palms landed on the cool

sink, keeping me upright. Sure, I'd dated, and sure, we'd kissed, but that was with guys I knew and liked. Even then, I hadn't gone much further than making out and being felt up. If being loose with guys I'd just met was my only hope for survival, I was as good as dead— this time for real.

Cole's strong hands gripped my trembling shoulders from behind. "Controlling the amount of life you siphon from humans comes naturally. You won't have to kill your partners if you don't want to."

My reply came out in a combination of mortified huffs and *I'm-going-to-be-sick* grunts. Cole wrapped his arms around me, pulling me closer presumably to stop my shaking.

"It's not that bad," he said into my hair.

"Ha!" I wanted to believe him, but things couldn't possibly get worse than my survival depending on me making out with random guys.

He leaned to the side until he could see my face in the mirror. "You know, you're doing it again."

"Doing what?"

"Hyperventilating. You don't actually breathe anymore."

Easy for him to say. I forced myself to relax enough to stop gasping. In doing so, I became very aware of my back pressed against Cole's rock-hard chest. I didn't move, though.

"What does Lilith get out of us slutting around?"

"Souls." He paused. "The process of who is sent where is determined by the choices one makes while he or she is alive, and it takes more than a few petty sins to damn a soul. Which region of Hell a person ends up in should they go down is predetermined by his or her first major sin, if one is committed, that is. Are you familiar with the seven deadly sins?"

"Yeah—pride, lust, greed, envy…"

"Wrath, sloth, and gluttony," Cole added when I couldn't remember the last three. "If a person steals, for instance, then greed leaves a mark on their soul. A person who acts as if he's above his fellow man is marked by pride. With me so far?"

"I think so. You're saying that our sins leave a stain on our soul, and if we commit enough to earn a one-way ticket to the pit, then our first sin determines where in Hell we end up because there are bad places and really, really bad places."

"Right. Your flip-flop ended up in the lower level, by the way."

"The section where the more evil of the condemned end up."

"Yes. Incubi and succubi"—he pointed to himself and me—"are drawn to people who are faithful. If a guy who's never cheated on his girlfriend *and* whose soul has yet to be marked by another sin kisses you, his soul becomes branded by lust. In a way, we're like recruiters, only we aren't asking people if they'd like to join our cause."

"And what's in it for us?"

"Besides a life back on Earth—we become stronger. Once you feel that kind of power flowing into you, you'll have to have more. It's worse than an addiction to drugs because you literally need it to survive, like humans need food and water."

I took a moment to absorb this information, and then asked, "When you said, 'control the amount of life we siphon,' did you mean we steal months off an innocent person's life span with just a kiss?"

"Yes."

"We slowly kill people?" I asked to make sure I understood.

"That will only happen if you tap the same source repeatedly."

"So the choice is to become either a floozy or a murderer." Neither appealed to me. "I won't do it."

"If you neglect your succubus duty—which is to increase the number of souls marked by lust—Lilith will punish you for being disobedient. You'll be begging for a second chance, and Lilith can be creative when she wants to be. She'll pick who you get your energy from."

The thought of being told who to date had my stomach turning in disgust.

Cole spoke softly, as if afraid to scare me more than I already was. "Trust me, the alternative is far worse than spending a night with a person of your choosing."

I clutched my stomach, breaths coming in short, painful pants again. "I'm going to throw up."

Cole draped my arm over his shoulder and bent forward to reach behind the back of my knees. He lifted me off my feet and carried me to the bedroom, where he set me on the edge of the bed.

"Put your head between your knees."

I did and then asked, "Why?"

"I'm not sure, but I've seen people do it when they feel sick."

I couldn't help the smile that crept across my face, despite the anxiety coursing through me. I said into my knees, "People do that to keep from hyperventilating and passing out."

"It seems to work; you stopped shaking."

I tilted my head so that my cheek rested on my thigh. "Why are you being so nice to me?"

Cole could've been a lot of things: angry that he'd been pulled away from his life on Earth to babysit the new demon, annoyed that he'd been saddled with the responsibility of showing me the ropes, wary of my reaction to all of this. Instead, Cole was sympathetic and patient and a perfect gentleman. I wasn't sure how I felt about the last one. There I was, alone in a bedroom with a guy who oozed sexy, and he hadn't even tried to kiss me. And while the old me wasn't homely, the new me was gorgeous.

His fingers gently brushed my long bangs away from my eyes. "You need rest. We have time before dinner. Close your eyes."

"We don't need to breathe, but we need sleep?"

"I suppose you could stay up all night, but you'd use up more energy that way and would need a fix from a human sooner. Besides, imagine how long the days would be if you never slept."

Too long, I decided. I lay down on the bed—hugging the towel close—and let sleep claim me.

Chapter 3

I had another surprise when I woke. My once dark-brown, incredibly curly hair wasn't only longer, it was also shiny, straight, and a deep auburn color. I couldn't say I hated the new look, especially since it came with no frizzy flyaways that insisted on doing their own thing, but I did feel like I was losing the old me, the one that had been human.

"I trust the accommodations are adequate," Lilith inquired when Cole and I joined her in the kitchen.

"The room's lovely. Thank you." My gaze roamed over the stainless steel appliances and dark wood cabinets.

Supposedly, like sleep, eating was another thing I could do without now that I was a succubus, but no one had told my stomach that. It promptly responded with a loud growl the moment I smelled the freshly baked bread cooling on the counter.

"If we eat, does that mean our bodies function like they did when we were alive? I mean…" I felt weird asking, but curiosity had gotten the better of me. "Do we use the washroom?"

"Yep," Cole responded. "Think of it as one more thing that makes it easy for us to blend in with humans. Imagine if you spent an entire day with someone and never took a piss."

We stood near the island and watched Lilith dump

chopped romaine lettuce into a stainless steel colander. A light shake on her part tossed it together with baby spinach and shredded red cabbage.

Cole glanced around. "I like what you've done with the place. It's very Old World meets modern comforts."

"I so miss Athens," Lilith replied dreamily. The wistful gleam in her emerald-green eyes along with the white jeans and long, iridescent tank top she'd changed into gave her a youthful appearance. "Aristotle was quite the romantic. Most people don't know that about him."

"Aristotle, as in *the* Aristotle?" I asked.

"That's the one." She handed me the lettuce mixture and pointed to the sink. "To humans, his notable contributions were to philosophy and science. Aristotle had an incredible mind. Did you know he taught Alexander the Great?"

I shook my head. Cole must have heard this story before because he didn't appear interested in hearing more. He slid the cutting board closer to him and began slicing the tops off strawberries. He'd put on a linen shirt, which he left unbuttoned. The white material accentuated his tan abs. His faded blue jeans hung low on his hips, revealing rope-like muscles that invited the eye to travel downward. His mildly bored expression gave me the notion that his outfit had less to do with impressing anyone in the room and more to do with being comfortable in Hell's sauna-like atmosphere. I wondered if he'd always been so toned or if death had fine-tuned his body like it had done to mine. I didn't want to announce I'd been checking him out, so I didn't ask.

I'd chosen a denim miniskirt, a lavender cap-sleeve T-shirt, and purple flip-flops as my wardrobe. My hair was up in a high ponytail to keep it off my neck.

Lilith looked from me to Cole and smirked. "There's no rule against incubi and succubi hooking up," she said as if we'd been discussing the dos and don'ts of being Hell's servant. "But it won't sustain you, so a monogamous relationship is impossible."

Ohmigod! Was it that obvious I'd been staring at Cole?

I quickly stepped to the sink, but not before Cole's attention snapped to me. My cheeks grew warm, and I wished I'd left my hair down. It would have hidden my face from both of them.

Lilith chuckled and then went on about how lovely Athens had been. I rinsed the greens. If someone were to have seen us, they'd have thought we were a happy family preparing dinner.

When I could stall no longer, I brought the over-rinsed lettuce to Lilith. She tossed the ingredients together. Once seated around the table, she placed a napkin over her lap and said, "You'll return to Earth with Cole, either work or register for classes at College of Dupage—"

"Why can't I attend Orange County?" I interrupted.

She served herself and held the bowl out to me. "How will you explain being back from the dead resembling a woman who vacationed in Crete?"

When I didn't take the salad from her, Cole did.

"No one's going to notice my skin is a shade darker," I said. "And they certainly won't care how I'm alive; they'll just be glad that I am." And if there was a God, he'd see to it that Gracie was as well. When I got back home, I'd tell her about Justin. Ask her to be there for him. Maybe then he wouldn't end up like my old friend Krista.

"Your miraculous return would raise questions you wouldn't be able to answer." Lilith stabbed a forkful of strawberry and lettuce. "Besides, you no longer age, and that's something people will notice. The colleges near Cole are reputable schools."

"That's not fair!" I protested.

"Death isn't fair, my dear," Lilith replied.

I slammed my fists on the table, causing Cole's and my silverware to bounce. I pretended not to see his shocked expression and asked, "What's the point in going back if I can't see my family? Why bother with college if I can't be with my friends?" And how was I supposed to find out how I'd died and if Gracie was okay?

Lilith swallowed. "Do not forget that you are, for all intents and purposes, dead. If I hadn't stepped in, you could've ended up someplace different. You wouldn't set foot on God's green Earth."

"You're such a—"

Cole kicked me under the table and mouthed, *Shut up!*

Lilith sipped her lemonade. "You now serve me, and I decide what you will and won't do. You're a succubus whether you like it or not. Succubi feed on human touch, so you must live amongst them, but to live with the ones you knew when you were human will only cause confusion for both them and you. As far as college, it would behoove you to continue your education so you don't spend eternity as an idiot."

While I didn't think of myself as stupid, my IQ

wasn't the point at that moment. I glanced down at my tanned arm and then ran my fingers through my ponytail, pulling it forward so I could see the shimmer of red in the dark auburn locks.

"I have a new look," I argued. "They won't recognize me."

"You have nothing you couldn't obtain from a day at the spa," Lilith countered.

"So change my features even more." If she could clear up my skin and change my hair color, surely she had the power to make me a blonde with light brown eyes and a willowy figure. "I don't care if I'm thin or fat, as long as I can be with the people I love!"

"And how will you explain your eternal youth?"

I served myself dinner as I thought that one over. I supposed it would be too much to ask Lilith if she could stop by every five years and magically age me. Not wanting to push my luck I said, "I'll figure something out."

She studied me a moment. Out of the corner of my eye, I saw Cole open his mouth. This time, I kicked him under the table to keep him from saying anything.

"No, because you'll know things you shouldn't about the people around you." She took a dainty bite of her dinner as if the conversation were over.

"I'm a great actress." Since I hadn't taken drama in school, I didn't know if that was true, but I was winging it. "I swear no one will find out it's me."

Lilith's brow rose in challenge. "You'll be able to act as if you don't know your best friend's likes and dislikes or how your father takes his coffee or your mother prefers tea?"

She didn't mention Gracie, but I refused to think

the worst. I had to focus on getting back before I could begin to find answers.

"Absolutely!" I replied, although I had no intention of letting the people I loved continue to think I was gone. Given the options, I was sure they'd rather accept me as I was than lose me forever.

"And you'd have no problem making Cole leave his apartment and friends so that you can try to fit back into your old life? Or knowing he'd need to siphon years from these same people to survive himself?"

Of course I wasn't okay with Cole slowly killing my family and friends. "Maybe Cole and I could keep in touch. We could video chat. I'll check in every day. Twice a day, if you'd like."

We ate in silence. This would work, I just knew it. I'd live in Warwick, New York, pretend to be new to the area, and sign up for a couple of Megan's classes. We'd become instant best friends again, I just knew it. I'd have to find a way to run into my parents—and Gracie, if…no, because she had to be okay—but I figured that wouldn't be hard.

It'll work. I silently willed my thoughts to sway Lilith's decision.

She chewed slowly, glancing at me every few seconds. Cole said nothing, but he jabbed at his salad with enough force to let me know he wasn't on board with my plan. Too bad. Lilith's slight shake of her head and sincere smirk hinted that she didn't totally hate it.

I can do this.

Lilith patted her ruby red lips with her napkin.

She will say yes.

"You'll be returning with Cole," Lilith announced.

"What? But I won't know anyone!"

"That's the point." Lilith leveled me with a glare that had me swallowing my next rebuttal with an audible gulp. She continued in a tone that sounded sweet but was definitely laced with poison. "It may take a day or even a year, but if you're around the people you love, something will go wrong, and then I'll have to clean up the mess. Not another word or I'll be your mentor instead of Cole."

Cole rested a hand on mine. "Avery, I'm begging you, drop it before you really upset her."

His comment about the alternative being worse than being a succubus came back to me, along with his warning that Lilith wouldn't hesitate to choose our victims for us if we didn't follow her rules.

A single tear escaped the corner of my eye. It followed the contours of my cheek as it ran down the side of my face. I now understood what made the part of Hell I'd landed in so terrible. On top of the expectations of a succubus, I was expected to live with the memory of the people I loved yet not see them.

"I'll leave it up to you, Cole. You can say either that Avery is a cousin who's come to stay with family or a friend of a friend who needed a place to live due to some tragic event." She got up and left me at the table with my tear-streaked face. "I have business I must attend to. An incubus needs a new alibi, and two succubi are fighting over the same city. You're welcome to stay the night. It was a pleasure to see you, Cole." She bent down and kissed him on the forehead. His fingers curled into fists, and his body quivered. When Lilith stood, the healthy glow Cole had about him was gone. "I'm holding you accountable if she screws up."

Chapter 4

"Who does she think she is?" I demanded the moment Cole and I were back in my room.

Cole sank onto the corner of the bed. "Queen of the Damned."

"Bitch on a power trip is more like it." I kicked the wall as hard as I could. Pain shot up my big toe. "Ow! You'd think being immortal would mean I'm indestructible," I grumbled as I hobbled over to the bed to examine the damage.

"We're low on the totem pole of demons. Our strength comes from humans, and until you feed, you'll be susceptible to the same weaknesses you had before you died," Cole replied softly.

"Great." I plopped down next to him. "I'm a lactose-intolerant demon with a swollen toe."

Cole didn't spare a shadow of a smile. His hands gripped the bedspread as he focused on the deep blue carpet in front of him. Upon closer inspection, I noticed he looked a little gray.

"Are you all right?" I rested the back of my hand on his forehead like my mom used to do whenever I'd been under the weather. His skin felt clammy.

"I'm fine." He fell backward onto the bed and rubbed his eyes with his palms. "I hate coming here."

"I can see why." Lilith wanted to play gracious host, but her polite chitchat ended the moment you challenged her orders. I lay on my side, propped up on an elbow next to Cole. "What happens now?"

"We journey home. I just need a minute."

I didn't have a home anymore, but I didn't say this to Cole. I didn't want to start my new life by upsetting the only being I knew. For a demon, he was sweet.

His eyes closed. I would have thought dinner was poisoned, but I felt fine and we'd eaten the same thing. I brushed a strand of Cole's black hair from his forehead. I had so many questions I wanted to ask him. What had he done when he was human to land him here when he'd died? How had he died? How long has he been a demon? How many of us lived amongst humans? Did he live alone or with other demons like a mock family? Had he killed anyone?

Well, maybe I didn't want to know the last one. I sort of liked thinking of him as the good guy, and good guys didn't murder people.

"Where's home, again?" I asked, trying to remember if Lilith had told me that.

"Woodridge," he replied without moving any extra muscles.

I'd have to double-check on a map, but I didn't think Woodridge was all that far from Warwick. Maybe I'd be able to see my friends, after all. I held onto that hope as I stroked the side of Cole's face, moving the hair that clung to the sweat on his temple and letting my fingers rest on his cheek. He leaned into my hand. A gentle tingling sensation traveled through me. My vision went fuzzy, and I became dizzy. Before I could decide if these sensations were agreeable or not, my wrist was locked in Cole's ironclad grip.

In the next moment, he shot off the bed and across

the room. "Grab what you want, and let's get out of here."

I pushed myself up into a sitting position.

"Did I do something wrong?" I asked, not sure what had just happened and starting to wonder if I was the reason Cole felt ill. Maybe he hated being stuck with the new succubus. Maybe he'd thought he'd grab me from processing, deliver me to Lilith, and be back home seducing girls by sunset. He probably hadn't expected a roommate. I bet having me around would cramp his gigolo-incubus style.

He didn't answer my question. Instead, he stood as far away from me as he could and waited for me to grab my things. My gaze swept the room. Nothing was mine. Not one outfit in the wardrobe. None of the shoes or the makeup. I wandered into the bathroom. The pearl blue toothbrush was now mine. I picked it up along with the mango body wash and raspberry-vanilla shampoo and returned to the bedroom with these things clutched to my chest.

"Ready?" he asked, not commenting on my selection of items to take with me.

I nodded. "How do we get topside?"

I envisioned an express elevator to civilization and a Learjet waiting to whisk us back to Cole's life. Or maybe we'd have to click our heels together three times Dorothy-style. Only for us, ruby slippers would be optional.

In the time it took to blink, we were suddenly standing next to a tattered leather sofa, sweating as if we'd just climbed out of the bowels of Hell with an anchor strapped to our ankles.

"How?" I uttered.

We were in a small living room. To my right, navy vertical blinds hung in front of sliding glass doors. To my left, two mismatched stools were pushed up to a breakfast nook. Through a five-foot opening, I could see a gas stove.

Cole let out a sigh. "Lilith gave us permission to depart. At that point, leaving was as simple as saying we were ready. Welcome to your new home."

He sounded about as thrilled with the new living arrangements as I'd been to find out I was a soul-sucking demon.

A small flat-screen television rested on top of old crates that housed various items including a football, a baseball mitt, DVDs, and a stack of car magazines. The breakfast nook separated the living room from a galley-style kitchen. Through one of two doors behind me, I could see a bathroom sink and a faded black hand towel.

Cole grabbed a military-style jacket off a hook near the door. "Make yourself at home. Knowing Lilith, she'll have stocked the fridge with your favorite snacks."

"You're leaving?" I asked in shock.

"Stay here." He slammed the door on the way out, leaving me standing in a strange place clutching a toothbrush, body wash, and shampoo as if these things were my only friends. Which they were, but he didn't have to rub it in.

My gaze traveled over the couch. A Chicago Bears throw blanket draped across one arm with a matching pillow propped against it. Three remotes sat in a neat row on the coffee table. The view out of the patio doors revealed a playground complete with swings, a brightly colored jungle gym, and benches for parents to sit on while watching their little ones.

I looked back at the door Cole had exited through. I couldn't believe he'd left, but then again, that meant I wasn't being supervised. I rushed to the phone on the wall between the kitchen and the living room, dropping my personal belongings onto the counter below it. Lilith had forbidden me to go home, but I had to know if Gracie was all right. I hit the power button and put the phone to my ear. Nothing but dead air greeted me, telling me Cole didn't have a landline.

Disappointed, I slammed the handset back onto the cradle and frowned at the dark screen of the television. The image of Cole hanging out with friends while I sat by myself flipping through channels popped into my head. Did he think I'd be a buzz kill if I went with him?

"Screw this!" If I had to learn to blend in, then I wanted to do it right away, and I planned on telling Cole this. My palm grazed the doorknob a moment before I yanked my hand back, yelping in pain. Tentatively, I tapped a finger against the scalding hot metal. If I hadn't known what Cole was, I'd have thought he was standing on the other side, holding a blowtorch under it.

I didn't like being thrown into his life any more than he liked having me here, but since we were stuck with each other, I was willing to try to make it work. Okay, more liked forced to deal with it. Point was, Cole shouldn't have run out on me the moment Lilith wasn't around.

"Wait until I see him," I said to myself.

Shaking off the stinging in my palm, I rushed to the kitchen and flung open cabinets and drawers, only to slam them shut again. I found a bunch of towels under the sink. I folded a dark red one into a thick square and covered the doorknob. Heat seeped through the terrycloth. Not wanting to take a chance on the towel bursting into flames, I quickly opened the door.

"Take that, demon boy!" I said with a nod of satisfaction. I tossed the towel on the counter and left.

It wasn't until I reached a large window that I realized I'd gone the wrong way down the hall. I had a decent view of dumpsters and the edge of the parking lot. Over the trees, I could just make out the setting sun. There was no way I'd catch up with Cole if I didn't hurry downstairs, so I sprinted to the other end of the building, happy to see the elevator. I punched the down arrow and bounced on my toes as I waited.

The little round light above the elevator stopped on the number six, and the doors slid open. I stepped into a smoky-mirrored compartment and pushed the number one. I'd only descended two floors when the elevator came to a stop. A guy in his early thirties joined me. I pretended not to notice his eyes travel from my head to my toes and back up. I moved farther into the corner, tugging my short skirt a whole centimeter lower.

Creep.

He smelled like cigarette smoke and cheap body spray.

Thankfully, when we reached the lobby, he hurried down the hall away from me. I headed out into the night. A cool breeze had me wishing I'd changed into jeans and sneakers before rushing downstairs. Then I remembered I was wearing everything I owned. Rubbing my arms in an effort to fight off the night's chill, I took in my surroundings: dimly lit parking lot, vacant road, and a whole bunch of open land. Cole was nowhere to be seen.

"Jerk."

Deciding to return to the apartment to do some research or snooping—depending on what options were available to me—I tugged on the door handle at the front of the building. The door, however, remained shut.

My existence sucked.

With my arms wrapped around my waist, I sat on the curb and waited for someone—anyone—to arrive and let me back inside. I realized I was probably locked out of Cole's apartment also, but waiting inside a warm building beat being stuck outside on a cool summer evening sorely underdressed for the weather.

When the door behind me opened, I jumped up only to pause when I saw it was Creepy Dude from the elevator.

"Need a lift?" Creepy Dude asked as he lit a cigarette.

I glanced from him to the door to the road and back. The old me would have politely said no and ignored the guy until he left, but I wasn't that person anymore. Why not be a little reckless? My afterlife couldn't possibly get any worse.

"Yeah. That'd be great," I said, ignoring how his eyes wandered over the length of my body again. I'd prove to Cole, Lilith, and any other demonic beings that I didn't need to be shown the ropes. I'd manage fine on my own.

"It's kind of cold for that skirt, isn't it?"

"I'm fine," I lied.

Cole would be lucky if I came back. Really, what

reason did I have: a toothbrush and shampoo? I could easily replace those things. I followed Creepy Dude down a row of parked cars.

"I'm Rick."

"Avery."

"Nice to meet you, Avery." He tossed his cigarette on the ground and snuffed it out with the toe of his work boot, then unlocked the doors to a blue compact car with a click of the remote. Once we were seated, he asked, "Where can I take you?"

That was an excellent question. If I wanted to prove I could make it on my own, then I'd need somewhere to stay. Only one place came to mind: home. And, okay, that would mean I technically wouldn't be making it on my own, but I'd be making it without Cole's help. I'd also be proving to Lilith that living with my family could work. The question now was how did I get from Woodridge to Warwick with no money?

"If you could drive me as close to Warwick as you're going, that'd be great," I finally replied.

Rick started the engine and blasted the heat. "Is that the name of a subdivision?"

"No, it's a town. Can't be more than an hour from here." I tried to remember if Woodridge was east or west of my house. "It's off Route 94."

His forehead creased. "Where do you think you are?"

"Woodridge, New York." *Is he on drugs?* "Where do you think you are?"

"Woodridge, *Illinois*." He burst out laughing. "You must have had one hell of a night if you don't know what state you're in. Whose apartment did you come

42

out of?"

"Excuse me?"

"If you don't know where you are, it's a safe bet you don't live here. That would mean you were visiting someone."

Sounded logical. "Cole."

"From six?"

I nodded.

"He doesn't usually bring people outside of his inner circle home." Rick backed out of the parking space.

"You know him?"

"He helped me out a time or two. Guy's a genius when it comes to electronics."

Cole had probably been around since television was invented, so that didn't surprise me.

Rick circled the parking lot, heading toward the exit. "I know where he works. How about I drive you there?"

Had he rushed to work? If that was the case, though, why wouldn't he have said so? "I don't think he's working," I replied.

"He usually works on Sunday nights."

My head fell against the headrest. I hated Cole for leaving me stranded in a strange place with nothing but the skimpy clothes on my back and a pair of flip-flops. "I'd prefer not to see him." Ever. "How about the train station?"

I could only hope the conductor or driver would take pity on a stranded teenager with no cash.

I tried to imagine my parents' reaction to their dead daughter showing up on their doorstep. I'd have to convince them I'd been given a second chance. Maybe

I'd say the powers that be decided it wasn't my time. I might even be able to throw in one of my dad's favorite sayings: "Don't look a gift horse in the mouth." I knew, deep down in my heart, my parents would want me home. Maybe they'd be so happy to see me they wouldn't ask questions. Maybe I could tell them to view my return as a miracle. They'd assume that meant divine intervention. I just wouldn't correct them.

Rick stopped the car and twisted in his seat so that he faced me. "I am not leaving a half-dressed girl like yourself alone at the train station this late at night."

"I'll be fine."

"And I'm not spending the rest of the night wondering if you're okay." He sighed. "Avery, I've got to get to work myself. Your options are to stay here and wait for Cole or hang out with him at his work where, by the way, it's heated and there are plenty of things to eat and drink."

I folded my arms over my chest. "Fine, his work."

With any luck, it would be near the train station.

As it turned out, Cole worked at a pizza place located in the middle of a small strip mall between a dry cleaner and a bait shop. Unfortunately, there was no public transportation in sight. Cole's manager told me I'd missed him by fifteen minutes. "Something about a family emergency and he needed the night off."

Since I had nothing but lint in my pockets, I strolled down to the burger place not far from there and sat at one of the outside tables.

Lilith had one sick sense of humor, sending me back to Earth and sticking me smack dab in the middle of nowhere, hundreds of miles from my family with no money. A group of guys joked around at a table not far from me. I guessed they were a year or two older than I was. A guy with short brown hair noticed me watching them. A minute later, he sauntered over carrying a tray with two sodas and a bag of fries. His dark-gray hoodie was embroidered with a skull and crossbones, and his jeans were baggy. He reminded me of the stoners at school. He turned a chair around and sat on it backward.

"Don't tell me your friends ditched you." He smiled, revealing a row of straight, white teeth.

I shrugged. Technically, I had been ditched.

"Their loss, my gain." He handed me a soda. "What's your name?"

"Avery."

He pushed the fries so they were between us. "You live around here, Avery?"

"I do now," I replied, my words laced with contempt.

"You don't sound happy about it." He drank from his cup. His gorgeous copper eyes studied me.

"I liked my old home," I admitted, taking a lukewarm fry.

"Grab your drink." He stood. "I'll introduce you to my friends."

I ate another fry and then replied, "I don't even know who you are."

"Sean. Come on." He motioned with a sideways jerk of his head to follow him.

I took a long sip of cola as we made our way over to his friends. It seemed flat—like there was more syrup than soda water in the mix.

Sean told me everyone's names, but they didn't stick, so I silently gave them each a nickname. The guy with greasy hair and a chain dangling from his belt loop to the wallet in his back pocket was Chain Man. Next to him was Stains, named after the dingy white undershirt he wore. And the guy wearing a baseball cap backward with a mouth full of metal became Grill.

Sean seemed nice enough, but his friends kept staring at me as if waiting for me to do or say something exciting. It was weird.

Whatever. I'd only joined them to pass the time until I came up with a plan. I took another fry. My focus shifted from Sean's friends to the keys sitting in the middle of the table. I could drive to New York if I had a car. The key ring included a clicker similar to my dad's. It let me know the car had an alarm, one that would beep when I hit the button to unlock the door. If I played nice with Sean and his friends, I could slip the keys into my pocket, excuse myself, claiming I needed to use the restroom, and bail on them and Cole. What was the worst thing that could happen? I'd be arrested for grand theft auto and have to give the police Cole's address. Cole would be pissed when he found out, but I was willing to bet he'd post my bond.

Feeling better, I nibbled on fries and sipped my drink as I pretended to be interested in the conversation. They were crude, but I didn't let on that their comments bothered me. The keys to my getaway car remained in my peripheral vision the whole time.

Sean scooted his chair closer to mine. "How old are you?"

"Eighteen." For eternity. How sad was that?

Chain Man coughed, "She's legal," from behind me. Someone else hissed, "Shut up."

I jerked my head to the left to see who'd said it.

The restaurant swam in front of me in a blur. I gripped the chair to steady myself. I should've asked Cole if demons could eat and drink any kind of food. Maybe the sugary soda or greasy fries had a bad effect on me now that I was immortal.

"Where are your girlfriends?" I blinked, hoping to clear my vision, which kept fading in and out.

"No one's desperate enough to hang with them," Sean said, poking fun at his friends before running a hand down my arm. His smile blurred, and for a moment he appeared to leer at me. I squeezed my eyes shut and felt the world tilt. Sean's arm snaked around me. "How about we get out of here?"

I twisted out of his grasp. My mind went fuzzy. I couldn't remember why I was with Sean or how I'd come to be at the restaurant. I pushed back the panic that gnawed at my conscious and forced myself to think. I'd walked here from Cole's apartment. No, I'd gotten a ride—but not from Sean. And I was headed somewhere. A small part of me knew it was important to keep moving, but I couldn't recall where that was. Something inside me screamed, *Get out of there!*

"I gotta go," I said, my voice distant to my own ears.

"I'll drive you." Sean pulled me to my feet, wrapping an arm around my waist when I stumbled. His lips trailed down my neck, sending a warning alarm to my sluggish brain. "My place is right down the street."

Some of my bearings came back to me, enough to put a few inches of air between Sean and myself and to take a critical look into his eyes. What I saw was a soul already destined for Hell. How I knew that was beyond me, but it stirred foreign urges deep within me. I kissed his collarbone and a tingly sensation tickled my stomach. Something feral in me snapped awake. He was filled with life essence, and I wanted it. I had to have it. And not just from Sean, but from his schmuck friends, too. I licked my lips in anticipation, but when I pivoted to get a better view of them, everything around me spun. Sean tightened his grip once more.

"What's wrong with me?" I leaned heavily on Sean just to remain on my feet.

Surely Lilith and Cole would have warned me if I had to be on a special diet, and from what I could tell, the meal we'd shared was normal, everyday food.

"I got you," Sean assured me a split second before I was yanked from his grasp.

"Now you don't." I broke into a fit of giggles, not fully appreciating the trouble I was in. One little me against—my finger bounced in front of me as I counted four, no—five of them. Plus, of course, the guy who currently held me. He smelled nice. I peered up. Cole's set jaw and narrowed eyes sobered me enough to stop laughing. "Hi." I smiled, and a new wave of dizziness came over me.

"Son of a bitch," Cole growled, sweeping me into his arms and giving Sean and the others a glare that had them backing up several feet.

Sean held his hands in front of him. "Cole, I didn't know she was with you. Honest. I never would've—"

"Don't bullshit me," Cole snapped. "You're just sorry I showed up when I did. If you lay so much as a finger on her again, I'll kill you." Cole's tone said he wasn't speaking figuratively.

I rested my head on Cole's shoulder. He was warm and familiar. I could get used to a knight in shining armor coming to my rescue. I ran a hand over the pocket of his jacket. *Knight in olive green cotton*, I thought with a snort.

"I told you to stay in the apartment," Cole said. I didn't remember getting in his pretty black sports car or putting on a seatbelt.

"Yeah, well, I didn't like being ditched." I held my forehead in my hands. "Why is my brain floating in the clouds?" It was sort of a fun sensation. I had a sudden urge to skip, but the doors locked and Cole peeled away.

"Because they slipped you a roofie."

"Are you kidding me? I died, became a demon, and I'm still sujectible—subspetible—susceptible to date-rape drugs?" I burst into laughter at my inability to speak and the irony of the whole situation.

"It's not funny, Avery. You don't have to sleep with the scum of the Earth to survive. The fix you'd receive from them is minimal and will leave you needing more thirty minutes later."

"Sounds like Chinese food." I held in the rest of my laughter. "How'd you find me, anyway?"

"A co-worker texted to tell me you'd stopped in. She saw you wander toward Burger Palace and knew those creeps liked to hang out there. She didn't want anything bad to happen to a friend of mine."

Like Mr. Can't-Get-Away-From-Me-Fast-Enough cared. "I can take care of myself."

He pulled into the apartment's parking lot. "You were doing a bang-up job of it." He cut the engine and shifted in his seat so that he faced me. "Tell me something—could you have lived with yourself if those guys had gotten their way with you?"

Once the drugs wore off, I was sure the answer to that question would be no, and I hated that he was right. "Why am I not stronger? Shouldn't I be immune to the things that can hurt humans?"

"You'll become stronger over time." He exited.

I had to focus on putting one foot in front of the other—like you do when walking on a balance beam. Keeping my arms out to the side helped a lot. I was actually proud of myself when I made it to the rear of the car without falling on my face.

"If you don't put your tongue back in your mouth, you'll bite it off when you trip." Cole scooped me up for the second time that night.

"Will not." But he was probably right, again.

"Next time I tell you to stay in, try listening."

"Next time don't leave me behind."

He shook his head. "You're going to be impossible to live with."

And maybe I was.

Chapter 5

I woke the next morning in a queen-size bed wrapped in a soft cotton sheet. My head felt as if a hundred dancers did a shuffle-hop-step as they tried to tap their way through my memories, which made the endless banging of pots and cabinet doors in the next room true torture.

"People sleeping here." I grabbed the pillow next to me and covered my head with it. At the scent of sandalwood, my eyes snapped open. The dresser across from me had a man's watch, wallet, and two bottles of cologne on it. The jacket Cole had worn the night before hung from the closet's doorknob. The realization that I was in Cole's bed had me scrambling from underneath the warm covers. I scooped my hair out of my eyes. One glance at the oversized Chicago Bears T-shirt and pink panties I wore sent a wave of dread through me.

Slowly, last night came back to me. What stood out the most was how comfortable it had felt to be in Cole's arms while he'd carried me into the apartment and how I hadn't wanted him to put me down. But he had, and I'd been fully clothed when he did.

I tiptoed forward, tripping over Cole's jeans. The skirt I'd worn lay next to it. I groaned at what our clothes lying in a cozy pile implied.

Way to make the little white lies about you true,

Avery.

I bent to pick up the skirt and paused, my attention locked on the black cell phone poking out of the front pocket of Cole's jeans. I bit my bottom lip and glanced at the door. I was still alone.

One call and I'd know how I died. I'd know if Gracie was okay. And I'd be able to tell her the things I should've a long time ago.

I snatched the phone off the floor and quickly dialed her number. When I received a message stating the call couldn't go through, I dialed again, thinking I'd gotten a wrong number the first time. My hand trembled when a fast-busy blared from the speaker.

"No, no, no. She has to be alive."

I tried Megan next. Fast-busy. I tried my parents. Same.

Relief flooded me. Something had to be wrong with Cole's phone. To be sure, I scrolled through his contacts and hit send to call the local Chinese restaurant. When it went through to their answering machine, I assumed Lilith had managed to block calls to my family and friends.

"Bring it on," I whispered, determined more than ever to show Lilith that she didn't own me. Not being able to call from Cole's phone was a small setback. I'd find another phone, and I'd reach someone from my past.

After stuffing Cole's phone back into his pocket, I picked up my skirt, but it was shorter than the T-shirt I now wore, so I decided it wasn't worth trying to be modest by slipping into something that showed even more leg.

The noise coming from the other room reminded

me that the details leading up to my death weren't the only thing I couldn't remember. Cole had to be cooking. The aroma of fresh-brewed coffee dared me to join him.

Instead of heading to the kitchen, though, I crept to the doorway and peeked around the corner. Thrilled that Cole wasn't standing there waiting for me, I darted to the bathroom.

This isn't so bad, I silently told my reflection. *Nothing happened between you and Cole.*

Although, my tousled hair and mascara-stained eyes begged to differ. After washing my face, I took an extra-long time brushing my teeth. What if I had lost my virginity? That would be so my luck. A big event in a girl's life—afterlife—whatever—that was supposed to be special, and I did it while drugged and with a guy whose only reason for being nice to me was because the Queen of the Damned had ordered him to be.

But did I sleep with Cole? No way did I want to barge into the kitchen and accuse my new roommate of foul play without proof. Plus, I was embarrassed to admit I had no recollection of what had happened after we got back to the apartment.

If I brushed my teeth any longer, I'd wipe the enamel off, so I switched to rinsing my mouth with water for a minute or two before taking the eight steps needed to reach the stool next to the kitchen counter. Cole had his back to me. He wore pajama bottoms matching the top I was drowning in. I groaned inwardly, no longer believing nothing had happened between us.

Cole turned to face me.

"I was wondering when you'd wake up." He placed

a steaming cup of coffee in front of me. "You hungry?"

"Starving."

He cracked two eggs directly over a skillet. "Sunny-side up okay?"

"Yeah." I spun my cup around on the counter as he took plates from the cupboard. Should I say something about my behavior the night before? "About yesterday—we…um…it was a one-time thing. I was upset you'd left me here, and my guard was down or else those guys would never have been able to do that to me, and the drug made me all loopy." *Ugh! Stop rambling.* "I don't want it to affect our relationship."

He paused—an egg balanced on the spatula—one eyebrow raised. "We have a relationship?"

"Of course we do, with all the succubus/incubus stuff. And I know it has to be hard, having me thrust into your life, but I think we need to have boundaries."

He slid two eggs onto a plate next to a couple of slices of wheat toast, set it in front of me, and then repeated the whole process. The newly cracked eggs sizzled when they hit the hot frying pan.

"Go on," he encouraged.

"We should set some type of rules so what happened last night doesn't happen again."

"Fine by me. From now on, you do as I say, and I won't have to worry about you getting gang-raped."

I shuddered at the thought of what had almost happened with the guys at the restaurant. "Thanks for showing up and saving me. And I appreciate everything you've done for me, but that's not what I meant."

"So you won't to listen to me." He put his eggs between two slices of toast and ate standing up. "I'm curious, what was the plan? I mean, you had no ID, no money, no cell phone. Hell, you didn't even grab keys. Were you planning on coming back?"

"I thought I'd catch up to you."

I would have, if I hadn't burned my hand on the doorknob, and if I hadn't had to find something to wrap around it just so I could open the damn door. "Besides, I don't have any of those things, remember?"

"The pink key chain's not mine." He indicated with his chin to the set of keys hanging from a hook near the door. Dangling from the silver ring was a crystal-covered pink strap.

I glowered at him. "Maybe if you'd taken a minute to show me around, I would have seen them."

"It's a one-bedroom apartment. You can see the whole thing from the stool you're sitting on."

"I know that now." No thanks to him.

"You didn't think Lilith would give you a new life yet not provide you with the basic things you'll need to live it, did you?"

"She's a demon. Why wouldn't I think the worst? Besides, you have a job, so she must not give you everything you need."

"I have a job because I like to keep busy, and I like to earn my own money." He ate a bite of his breakfast. Chewed. "Were you planning on coming back?"

I jabbed at an egg yolk with a corner of toast, causing yellow to ooze onto the plate. "When I saw that you not only ditched me, but must have run to your car—"

"I didn't run."

I ignored his interruption and continued as if he hadn't spoken. "I decided to head to New York."

I ate a bite of breakfast just so I wouldn't be sitting

there staring at him.

"Why'd you stop by my work, then?"

I stabbed egg white instead of answering. He'd already ticked off the list of reasons why I hadn't made it more than a few miles from the apartment.

"Lilith knows where her demons are at all times. Trust me, she won't let you get within two states of New York without her permission."

His statement confirmed my theory about why I couldn't call anyone—*yet*. Lilith might be good, but I planned to prove to myself that I was better.

He ate while I mulled over my situation. I did trust him. Probably because he was the only person I knew and because he'd saved me from those guys, Lilith's wrath, and the fiery river I nearly fell into. He really was a knight in shining armor. But that didn't change the facts.

"I'd just gotten here. I don't know anyone, except you. You could've asked me if I wanted to come with you."

"No, I couldn't."

"Wouldn't." I slathered butter on my toast to avoid his gaze.

He was in front of me before I even knew he'd put his sandwich down. His placed his palms flat on the counter between us, his face inches from mine. His eyes were the blue of the ocean at sunrise, and they burned into me.

"Lilith drained my energy before we left Hell, and you still reek of human essence. It took every drop of self-control I possess to go against my very nature and not steal that from you."

Cole had lost his healthy glow after Lilith had

kissed his forehead. At the time, it'd seemed like such an innocent gesture. That's why he hadn't wanted me touching him. He didn't loathe my presence. Seeing as we now lived together, that was a relief. "Why'd she take your strength?"

"To force me to pilfer from humans sooner than I may otherwise have needed. Lilith doesn't make us tap the same source until we kill them, but she likes it when we knock a decade or more off what might have been a long, healthy life."

"So that the condemned arrive in Hell sooner?"

"Exactly."

"And demons can steal energy from each other?"

"Once you burn through what you're currently running on, the only way you and I can share energy is if we choose to give up some of what we've siphoned from humans." He backed up, running a hand through his hair.

"So you were off getting laid?"

He shrugged. "I do what I have to do to survive."

That might not be a problem for him, but I saw it as only a matter of time before I withered to nothing. Getting laid wasn't on the list of things I was willing to do with random guys. Maybe, just maybe, if I grew weak, Cole might share some of his energy with me. But then I'd have some girl's essence running through me. *Ew!* I shuddered involuntarily. That wasn't going to happen.

"Thank you for not taking what's left of my energy." That must mean we didn't sleep together last night. I lifted a piece of toast to take a bite. Paused. "How long do I have until it's gone?"

"A couple of days," he replied through a mouthful

of food. "Eat regularly, and you might be able to stretch it to four."

Wonderful.

Cole continued to eat. I studied him. The color was back in his cheeks, and he did appear healthier than he had when we'd left Hell. His bare chest and pajama pants reminded me of what we'd been talking about before the conversation had gotten sidetracked.

"About last night and what I was afraid might have happened between you and me."

"Between us?" His eyes widened in what I took as realization of what I thought. "I don't have to drug a girl to get her in bed."

"I never said you did, but…" I glanced down at the T-shirt I wore and then his pajama pants, wondering how I'd gotten out of my clothes.

"I helped you change and tucked you into bed. That's all," he said in reply to my unspoken question.

"Thanks. I think." My cheeks warmed, wondering how much help I'd needed, but I was too self-conscious to ask. I also realized I was constantly thanking him. I'd have to make sure I didn't put myself in any more situations that would require him to rescue me.

He sipped his coffee. "You think we're a bad idea?"

Had we been back home—my home—I would have been dancing with delight to have a guy like Cole paying even the slightest bit of attention to me. But I wasn't home, and Cole wasn't just a guy. "Under the circumstances, yes."

He nodded, then grabbed the frying pan from the stove and placed it in the sink.

It wasn't like I was in Cole's apartment because

he'd invited me. We hadn't met through mutual friends, discovered we had a lot in common, and decided to hang out. I knew absolutely nothing about him. Except that he slept with girls and siphoned months off their lives, and he didn't trust Lilith. Not that I could judge him on the first—being that I was a succubus and in the same shoes as him. Only, unlike Cole, I was figuratively screwed, because my survival depended on me doing something that went against my morals. I'd deal with that when the time came, though. Regarding the latter item—I didn't trust Lilith either.

"If you and I"—he pointed to each of us in turn—"sleep together, it will be your doing. Not mine."

Flirting with one of Hell's gigolos was not going to happen. "Don't hold your breath waiting for me to ask you to, you know. I'm saving myself for true love."

The silence that fell over the kitchen gave me time to realize that, as a succubus, finding true love was fruitless. I was a demon. A relationship with me would literally kill a guy. I still didn't plan on hopping into the sack with losers just to replenish my strength. I wondered how long it would take Lilith to discover my disobedience, and how long I could survive without human contact.

"Get dressed," Cole said when I shoveled the last bit of egg into my mouth. "You can shower first, and hurry or we'll be late."

"For what?"

"A visit to the zoo."

"The zoo?"

"I'm a huge fan of snow leopards."

My eyes narrowed as I tried to decide if he was serious.

Noticing, he added, "We're meeting some of my friends. It's better than sitting at home all day watching bad TV." When I still didn't move, he said, "You wanted to get out, right?"

I did—to a mall. Of course, that took money. I'd settle for a thrift store. A garage sale. Raiding the neighbor's closet. Yeah, I was desperate.

"I have nothing to wear. Remember? New in town, arrived with a toothbrush and some shampoo."

"Lilith supplied you with a wardrobe. Check the closet." He picked up my plate. "And don't dawdle, because if you're still in the shower when I'm done with the dishes, I'm pushing you aside so I can get under the water."

I choked on the coffee I'd been drinking. "You wouldn't!"

He paused—a dirty dish in each hand—and gave me a look that challenged me to take my time and find out.

I scurried to the bathroom, figuring I didn't want to waste one second checking to see if there really were clothes for me in the closet. I took a speed-shower. I'd just finished wrapping a plush black towel around my body when the door opened. He wasn't kidding about pushing me aside.

"Not bad, for a girl." His hands went to the drawstring on his pajama pants.

"At least let me get out of here." I turned sideways to squeeze past him, accidently bumping into his hand as I stepped into the hallway. The contact managed to move the towel enough to show the smooth skin of my hip and cause my heart to pound a little quicker. Certain that the sudden increase of my pulse was due to nerves—it had been a weird twenty-four hours—I hurried to the bedroom.

His laughter bellowed out of the small bathroom. "Seeing as we live together, you might want to loosen up."

"Says you!" I called back.

The shower started, but he'd left the door open. "Succubi are supposed to be promiscuous. Not shriek at the sight of a naked man."

"Well, I'm not most succubi, and you're not a man," I retorted.

My jaw dropped when I opened the closet and found it stuffed with clothes. The things on the right were obviously Cole's. A hint of his cologne wafted from them. The left side, however, was crammed with juniors' jeans, skirts, tops, sweaters—everything I could possibly want and not department store knock-offs. Designer brands that I used to dream of owning.

I fanned through the various items, wishing I had time to try them all on. If Megan knew the road to Hell was stocked with the best clothes, she'd purchase a first-class ticket.

"So I'm not a man?" Cole asked from behind me.

He leaned against the doorframe, wearing a towel that conveniently hung low enough to emphasize his six-pack abs and the muscles leading to…you know. He didn't bother to dry off either. His chest glistened with water droplets.

"I have parts that beg to differ," he added, sending mixed signals. I didn't know what to do with them.

At breakfast, he'd made it perfectly clear he wouldn't touch me by choice, and now he was flirting with me. At least, I think that's what it means when a guy stands around practically in the buff, telling you about his parts. The room suddenly became hot, or maybe it just felt that way because all my blood had rushed to my cheeks.

"Men are old," I said, recovering from the temporary shock of seeing him dripping wet, wearing only a towel. I made sure my own towel was securely in place. "You're a guy who'll never age into a man." Which made me a girl who'd never age into a woman.

"Don't be so sure." Cole's tan skin turned pale and creamy right before my eyes. Waves of blond replaced his dark hair as bright red seeped into his baby blues. I watched in awe as his eyes glowed brightly for a fraction of a second. Then a pair of crystalline maple-brown eyes stared back at me. Cole's muscle definition waned, and his body became huskier as he finished morphing into a guy in his early twenties.

"Whoa! How'd you do that?"

Effortlessly, he turned back into the Cole I knew with thick black hair and an ocean-blue gaze. "Once you're chock-full of human essence, you'll be able to do it, too. You can only age five years from the age you were when you died, though."

I thought about that a moment. "So the oldest person I can turn into is a twenty-three-year-old?" Would I receive an ID to match?

"Or you can become thirteen again."

"I'll pass." Middle school was something I only wanted to experience once. I rifled through my choices of bottoms and asked, "We got superpowers to pair with the demon status?"

"We're given what we need to survive. Hell gave incubi and succubi the ability to change our appearances. We can find out the type of person a potential partner is attracted to and then become that person."

Hell really did think of everything.

Cole went on. "Having the ability to step into a new body whenever we choose works to our advantage in another way. We can be one person in front of our friends and a completely different person to brief acquaintances."

I took "acquaintances" to equal "victims." Superpowers or not, I still wasn't about to start making out with random guys because Hell said so. There had to be a way around this whole feed-on-the-life-essence-of-poor-unsuspecting-people-because-I-need-a-fix thing.

As if he'd read my mind, Cole said, "Eventually, you'll accept what you are."

So he kept saying.

He reached around me and grabbed a pair of light gray cargo shorts. "The sooner you relinquish your human inhibitions, the sooner you'll be able to embrace your new life."

That was a goal I wasn't in a hurry to achieve, and no way was I giving up my human side. It was what made me who I was.

"Why five years?" I asked instead of replying to his comment. "Wouldn't it be easier for us to blend in if we could age a little each year until we reached a ripe old age?"

"Only Hell's top incubi and succubi are granted that kind of mojo."

"The ones who kill?" I asked, sure that was what it took to become one of Team Lust's best.

"Yes."

I held up a silky, crimson sleeveless top, decided it was a bit dressy for the zoo and returned it to the closet.

"You draw?" Cole asked, holding out a sketchpad he'd picked up from on top of the dresser.

"Not since my art teacher told me I suck." Damn near two years ago. Although, when bored, I still doodled on the edges of my notebook paper and on napkins.

"Hmm." He dropped the sketchpad, opened the dresser drawer, and pulled out a pair of violet panties. "These have to be yours."

Omigod! We even shared an underwear drawer. That made me forget about being a succubus.

I snatched the unmentionables out of his hand. "I'd appreciate it if you didn't handle my underwear."

He shook his head and grabbed a pair of boxers from his side of the dresser.

Cole got dressed in the bathroom—thank goodness. Since I didn't know how long I'd have privacy, I put on the violet panties and a matching bra, grabbed a pair of jean shorts and a rose-colored top from the closet and quickly put them on.

Lilith had thought of everything: blow-drier, makeup, jewelry, and a decent selection of shoes. There were even a couple of different purses to choose from, and best yet, some money inside the wallet. If this was Hell, how much better could Heaven be?

I'd just secured a fine silver chain with a dangling heart around my ankle when Cole returned, looking as hot as ever in a tight cream T-shirt, shorts, and gym shoes. I pretended not to notice how his wet hair hung in tendrils over his piercing-blue eyes.

"Ready?" he asked.

To be a demon amongst humans? Not really, but it wasn't like I had a choice.

We're hanging out with Cole's friends, I reminded myself. At the zoo of all places. Zoos were safe. And Cole hadn't mentioned anything about hooking up with humans to feed on them.

He's not slowly killing his friends.

If that were the case, he wouldn't change his appearance when he prowled for victims. Right?

Right.

Butterflies invaded my stomach—normal will-Cole's-friends-accept-me-into-their-group jitters. I'd never been so happy to have such a human reaction to meeting new people.

I grabbed a small cross-body handbag, stuffed my wallet inside it, and replied, "Yep."

Like it or not, day one of my new life, here I come.

Chapter 6

We got to Brookfield Zoo around ten, and even though I had forty dollars in my purse, Cole insisted on paying for the both of us. We entered through an underground tunnel that led to the main entrance. Images of ostriches and lions watched us pass as we followed the crowd to the turnstiles.

Cole handed a heavyset guy in a blue uniform our tickets and then held his hand in front of him. "Ladies first."

"Thanks." I tucked my hair behind my ear and asked, "Are you sure your friends won't mind me tagging along?"

During the drive over, I envisioned Cole's friends as a group of unruly demons. I couldn't believe I hadn't asked him what to expect when he first mentioned getting out of the apartment. When I voiced my concerns to Cole, he let out a loud guffaw. A minute later, he assured me there wouldn't be a demon in the bunch, except for us. He also told me that Luz was psyched to meet me. She was tired of being the only girl in the group.

Cole and I headed toward a large water fountain at the center of the zoo. A boy wearing a lion sun visor held his little hands up as if they were paws and roared. His sister—who was about half his size—screamed. I couldn't help but laugh. Then I remembered Cole's comment back at the apartment.

"Are you really a fan of leopards?" I asked.

"Snow leopards," he corrected. "They're smaller than other wild cats, but they're graceful, cunning, and exceptional survivors."

I got the feeling he related to them on a personal level. Cole had said incubi were low on Hell's totem pole of bad asses.

"What's your favorite animal?" he asked.

I tapped a finger to my lips. "Hmm—"

He jumped in front of me, walking backward with a bounce in his step. "Don't tell me. I'll guess."

I giggled. Cole's behavior was so human it was hard to believe he was a demon. But then again, so was I.

"You'll never guess."

He tipped his head to the side. "Is that a challenge?"

"Maybe," I replied with a smile.

He slowed, avoiding bumping into a stroller even though his back was to it.

"How'd you know they were there?" I whispered, fully expecting to be told that demons had the radar-like senses of a shark.

"Reflection in your sunglasses." He wiggled the ones he wore.

Darn on the supernatural radar, or lack thereof.

"Where were we?" he asked.

"You were about to admit there is no way you'll guess my favorite animal."

"You think so." Cole smirked. "Let's make it interesting…winner sleeps in the bed tonight, his choice if he wants to share."

"Or hers, and just so you know, I'm not sleeping in the same bed as you."

"You did last night."

"I was passed out due to being drugged. It doesn't count."

I hadn't given much thought to the fact that Cole and I shared everything in a one-bedroom apartment. "Does the couch pull out into a sofa bed?"

"Nope. I usually don't have company sleep over. I discovered last night you're a cover hog."

Since most mornings I woke tangled in the sheet, I knew better than to argue with the latter statement. "Don't you have girls over?"

"Definitely not. Except Luz, but she's a friend and doesn't stay the night." His expression became serious. "No bringing work home. House rule."

I didn't plan on hooking up with anyone, so that rule was fine by me. "Deal."

His lips curved upward into a devilish smirk. "Which one: you won't bring strange guys home, or you're willing to risk losing dibs on the comfy mattress?"

I began to think Lilith had purposely paired me with Cole as a way to add to my own personal Hell. He was seriously charming and—had we been human—the type of guy I went for.

But he's not human, and the only reason you find him charming is because he's the only person you're still allowed to talk to.

Even Gregory Davis—the geeky brain from school with thick black glasses and a never-ending supply of sweater vests—would look appealing when you're staring down eternity and he's the only person you know.

I shook my head to clear my runaway thoughts and replied with confidence, "Both."

"Be prepared to lose." He turned and fell in stride with me. In a low voice, he said, "Luz, Nick, and Dylan are human. Hunter's something else."

I stopped. "What's Hunter?"

Cole didn't answer. Instead, he bumped fists with a tall guy with straight brown hair wearing a *Save the wolves* T-shirt. I found out shortly afterward that the guy's name was Nick. Luz was a cute Colombian girl who greeted Cole with a hug and a "What's up?" She wore a yellow tank top, white shorts, and denim sneakers. The other two guys—one with short, dark brown hair and the other with golden blond hair, both wearing cargo shorts and T-shirts—gave Cole a slight nod as their hellos.

"This is Avery," Cole said, stepping a little closer to me. "She's staying with me awhile."

I waved. "Hi."

"Cole let another girl set foot in his castle?" Nick jested.

"Shut up." Luz smacked him with the back of her hand. "You're just upset he won't let you bring any of your hoes there."

"I don't date hoes!"

The guy with short, brown hair stepped in front of them and extended his hand, effectively blocking Nick and Luz's argument. "I'm Dylan."

I shook his hand.

"And I'm Hunter," the blond said. "You'll have to forgive Cole. His introductions tend to be one-sided."

"Whatever, dude." Cole indicated with a jerk of his

head for us to follow him. I got the impression he was the head of their little group.

Where Cole goes, they shall follow.

As we strolled toward the big cats, I found myself constantly glancing at Hunter, trying to figure out what he was. It helped that Dylan, Cole, and I had ended up behind the others. If Hunter was an incubus, Cole would have said so. Hunter sauntered confidently next to Luz. He was cute, but not in the unearthly way Cole was cute. Girls noticed him, though, almost as much as they noticed Cole. Two brunettes tripped over a trash can, rubbernecking, and I caught another group of girls trying to decide if Luz was with Hunter or Nick. Not that the girls used their names. Their conversation went more like "Think the short girl is with Adonis" (which I guessed was Hunter because of his blond hair) "or Sexy?" (Nick was no slouch himself.)

Considering I didn't have an encyclopedia of supernatural beings, I came up completely blank on what Hunter could be.

The others stopped to watch the tigers. I went with Cole two exhibits down.

"What is he?" I asked as soon as we were away from the others.

Cole had his forearms on the railing as he watched the snow leopards prowl around their habitat. "Who?"

"Hunter!"

For a guy who seemed to be in tune with everything around him, he was clueless about how much curiosity a statement like "Hunter's something else" would incite.

Cole gave me a sideways glance. I moved closer to him, half watching the animals and half watching him.

"He's a cambion. His mom's human, and his father's demon. Hunter doesn't see much of him."

"I bet demons are the poster children for deadbeat dads."

Cole shook his head. "It's not like that. If Heaven or Hell discovers Hunter exists, they'll kill him. No questions asked."

I gasped. "Why?"

"Demons aren't supposed to procreate. Both sides frown upon it. It's one of the few things they agree on."

I glanced back at the others. Hunter pointed at something in the tiger exhibit. He didn't give off an evil vibe. "He seems nice."

"He is," Cole said. "But cambions are born with the ability to sway human minds, an ability that helps them live rather comfortably. Plus, they're stronger than humans, almost strong enough to defeat a low-level demon or angel in a fight."

I blew out my cheeks, slowly letting the air escape my lips. Someone who could put ideas into other's heads could easily become the leader of a nation or head of a company.

Cole shrugged. "Hunter rarely uses his gifts. It's how he manages to stay under the radar. And his father doesn't come around often enough for other demons to question his visits."

"Aren't the higher-ups worried about incubi getting some poor human pregnant or succubi having children?"

He shook his head. "Only high-level demons can have children. We're sterile."

While I hadn't given much thought to having children, I'd thought I had time to decide if I wanted a family or if I wanted to be a career woman. I think I would have wanted both: a job that allowed me to enjoy the finer things in life and a family to share it with. My husband would have an amazing job, too. This way, once we had kids, I could stay home with them until they were in school. At first, I felt Lilith had robbed me of that choice, but then realized that particular future had died when I had.

"How'd you guys meet?" I asked.

"When I first moved here, I was supposed to be sixteen. It wasn't old enough for me to be living alone, so I stayed with Raymond. He's a mid-level demon. He introduced me to Hunter."

I nodded. When the leopards found a cozy spot in the shade and lay down, Cole whistled to the others. We headed to Pinniped Point and then continued through the habitats. His friends absorbed me into the group as if I were a long-lost friend, which was cool. When we stopped to admire the giraffes, I got the feeling Cole would guess that this was my favorite exhibit. Instead, he sat on one of the benches. I approached Luz, who was watching the animals munch on tree leaves.

"The guys know I love giraffes," she said. "Saw that one being born." She pointed to the one with russet-colored spots closest to us.

"Dylan and the others seem nice."

"The best friends a girl could wish for." She smiled, revealing an adorable dimple on her left cheek. Right then, she reminded me of my old friend, Krista, who'd had an identical indentation at the end of her smile. I wondered if Krista was in Heaven and if I would have seen her had my soul gone up.

"How did you and Cole meet?" Luz asked,

breaking into my reverie.

The Queen of the Damned introduced us. But I couldn't say that, so I replied with the cover story Cole and I had gone over during the drive to the zoo. "Our moms are friends."

"Cole's the big brother I never had." Luz gave me a sideways glance. "In case you were wondering. We're just friends."

"Yeah, of course." I rested my arms on the railing. "So are we."

"Ah-ha." Her lips tipped upward into a grin. "I see how you look at him. He doesn't have a girlfriend, you know." She said the last part in a singsong voice.

"We're just friends," I repeated. And I happened to know Cole had lots of girlfriends. He just wore a different face when he was with them. For all Luz and I knew, she could've slept with him. Besides, the only reason I'd kept looking at him was because we'd been talking.

"Where are you from?" she asked.

"New York." I figured it would be better to tell the truth and not have to remember a lie. "Things happened, and I needed a place to stay."

"If I had to crash somewhere, Cole's would be my first choice. He can cook." She leaned closer to me. "Tell him you're in the mood for pizza. He won't order takeout."

"But he works at a pizza place."

"I know, and they have delicious pizza, but Cole's a total health freak. He makes this veggie pie with a honey wheat crust." She moaned. "It's scrumptious."

I laughed. "I'll have to remember that," I replied, even though I was hoping not to be staying with Cole long enough to find out.

The muffled sound of an upbeat pop song began. Luz dug her phone out of her purse as she said, "Oh, and ask him to make you one of his crazy fitness shakes. You'll swear you're drinking strawberry ice cream." Her fingers flew over the screen, replying to a text. "My mom," she said in way of explanation.

I nonchalantly peeked over my shoulder to where the guys were chatting. Maybe Cole's tight body had nothing to do with being Hell's servant and everything to do with hard work. I made a mental note to watch what I ate.

"Can I make a quick call?" I asked when Luz went to drop her phone back into her purse. "I had to leave mine back home."

"You're kidding me!" She handed me hers. "That's just cruel." She shuddered. An actual shiver that started in her shoulders, traveled down her back, passed her hips, to her legs.

I smiled. Luz was cool.

Cole, however, was not. He'd have a problem with me ignoring Lilith's order to forget my old life. I turned my back to him, hoping he wouldn't see the phone to my ear.

I got a busy signal when I called Gracie.

Megan.

Mom.

Dad.

And Jared—who I really didn't want to speak to, but I was desperate to contact anyone from my past.

Lilith—two. Me—zero.

I'd find a way around the gag order.

"Can you do me a favor?" I held the phone out to

Luz. "Dial a number for me?"

Her eyebrows pulled together questioningly, but she did it. "Fast busy. Are you sure that's the right number?"

"Guess not." But it was.

We followed the guys to the next exhibit. I shouldn't have been surprised that I'd been blocked off from my old life no matter whose phone I used. I was dealing with powerful forces. If Hell could snatch me from the grave and plop me back into the world, why shouldn't it be able to control what I could and couldn't do?

If I thought about all I'd lost, I'd cry. So instead of allowing myself to dwell on it any more that day, I asked Luz, "How'd you meet Cole?"

"Hunter introduced us. I've known Hunter, gosh…" She paused. "Since grade school."

"And you've never dated him or any of the other guys?"

She slowed her pace so that the guys moved several feet ahead of us. "Dylan and I went out sophomore year. It didn't take us long to figure out we made better friends." She dropped her voice to a whisper. "And I made out with Hunter once. Don't tell anyone. I shouldn't have let it happen, but we were drunk and—well, have you seen him?" She gave a slight jerk of her head in Hunter's direction. "You could bounce a quarter off that ass."

"Luz!" I whisper-shouted.

We burst into giggles, which earned us four over-the-shoulder glances from the guys.

"I don't want them to think I'm one of those girls." Luz made finger quotes when she said the last two words.

I turned an imaginary key in front of my mouth in the universal gesture that her secret was safe with me. It wasn't until we reached the bears that Cole dropped back to walk with us.

"Avery and I have a bet going," Cole told Luz. "Mind if I borrow her so that I can win it?"

Luz let out a boisterous guffaw. "You made a bet with him. Not smart. The guy never loses."

"He will this time," I said, thinking that Cole was about to guess my favorite animal was the polar bears.

Cole winked at Luz, grabbed my hand, and pulled me along the path. When Dylan yelled that we'd missed the reptile house—which according to him and Nick was the only building worth entering—Cole told them we'd meet up later.

"Where are you taking me?" I asked.

"To say hello to your favorite inhabitants. Close your eyes."

When I hesitated, he crossed his arms over his chest. I scrunched my face in an effort to be difficult. He waited.

"Fine," I said with mock exasperation and squeezed my eyes shut.

He laced his fingers through mine. "No peeking."

"I'm not."

I held onto his arm with my free hand to make sure I stayed close enough to him that I wouldn't walk into anyone or anything. We stopped, cold air caressed my bare arms and legs, and then we were indoors. The air conditioning was a welcome break from the morning's humidity. The murmur of conversations drifted around us, and the sound of my flip-flops slapping tile echoed through the mystery building. I breathed in deep, hoping to catch a scent that would tell me where we were, but the only thing I smelled was overpowering perfume, and I highly doubted this zoo had an exhibit of old women.

A few seconds later Cole said, "Open your eyes."

We stood in front of a glass partition. Deep-blue water sloshed against the viewing window as a plump penguin swam gracefully by us. Another jumped off the icy ridge that lined the back wall into the frigid water below. Cole was dead-on about my favorite animal, which wasn't an animal at all. I was too surprised to worry about losing the bet.

"How'd you know?" I asked.

"I saw you staring at the glass ones when we were at Lilith's home. I guessed she had them put there for you."

I slapped his arm. "Man! I can't believe you're that observant. Are you sure you aren't using some devil-mind-reading trick?"

"You were gawking at them. It was sort of hard to miss."

A family of five moved on to the next exhibit, leaving Cole and me alone.

"Is Lilith always so welcoming?"

"She believes a happy demon is a productive demon. Cross her though, and you'll wish you'd been sent to the fiery bowels of Hell and not to her."

The penguins waddled along the ice as I pondered my future. How was I supposed to appease the Queen of the Damned without losing the person I strived to be? For a dead girl, I really didn't have it bad. My soul occupied my body, I lived on Earth, had a roof over my head, a closet full of clothes, and even money in my wallet. I was very much like the baby penguin that glided through the water discovering its world. But I was no longer human, and I was expected to follow the rules of a fallen angel. Let's face it, if Lilith's intentions were morally sound, she wouldn't have been cast out of Heaven.

My father used to say, "Don't compromise who you are, Avery. As long as you're true to yourself, you'll be happy." At the time, I hadn't realized just how right he'd been.

"What are you thinking about?" Cole asked after a few minutes.

I smiled, but I'm sure it was a sad sort of smile. "When I was little, my father would end our zoo visits with a trip to the penguins. 'I saved the best for last,' he'd say each and every time. Cie-Cie—that's my nickname for my sister—and I would race to the glass for a better look. Did you know penguins have solid bones?"

Cole shook his head.

"It counteracts their buoyancy and helps them zip through the water better." I took a deep breath and swiped at a tear with the back of my hand. "I miss them," I whispered. Two days and I missed them so badly it hurt. How could I survive eternity?

"See that one?" Cole pointed to a small penguin that had waddled to the edge of the cliff and was now watching us. "He misses you."

I bumped his shoulder with mine. "I meant my family and friends."

"I know." He paused. "As hard as it is to accept, they'll be okay, and so will you."

"I didn't get to say good-bye."

"Then go say good-bye," a voice said from behind me.

I wiped the tears that ran the length of my cheek with my fingers and turned. Hunter stood behind us, his hands stuffed into the front pockets of his shorts.

"It's not allowed." Cole's gaze bored into Hunter. "You know that."

"What Lilith doesn't know won't hurt anyone." Hunter observed me. "You're new. I can tell." He tapped the side of his nose. "How long ago was it?"

"A couple of days," I replied. The last forty-eight hours seemed like a dream. I think that was why I hadn't completely fallen apart and become a blubbering mess of tears. I kept expecting to wake up to the sound of Gracie and my parents arguing.

"Perfect." Hunter clapped his hands together. "You can attend your funeral."

"I can?" I tucked my hair behind my ear and glanced at Cole. A red flush crept up his neck. He was obviously pissed that Hunter had suggested it.

"Like the doppelganger of the person in the casket visiting the funeral home won't freak anyone out," Cole said sarcastically. I noticed he didn't say it would be impossible for me to go. Hope surged through me. Cole continued, "I was the one who collected her from Judgment. With the exception of appearing as if she's been out in the sun, her appearance hasn't changed."

"So she becomes a blonde, loses a couple of inches in height, increases her cup size." Hunter held his hands in front of his chest as if we didn't understand his meaning.

"Cole, you could show me how to shift. No one

will know it's me." It was such an easy solution. I couldn't believe I hadn't thought of it the moment Cole had turned into a blond hunk with light brown eyes.

"You'd have to be chock-full of human essence," Cole said.

"Look at her." Hunter held out a hand as if to invite Cole to stare at me. "She's gorgeous. She could make out with any guy in this room. Hell, they'd do her in the restroom if she let them."

Heat rose in my cheeks. I wanted desperately to see my family and Megan again, but… "I'm not 'doing' anyone in the bathroom!"

"You're a succubus. No one will judge you," Hunter said.

"The guy will," I pointed out. And so would Luz, Nick, and Dylan if they saw me entering or exiting the restroom with a guy in tow.

"He'll be busy getting his rocks off. He won't care if you're a nun or a slut."

I cringed, covering my ears in an effort to block the rest of Hunter's words. It didn't work.

He continued, unfazed by my behavior. "And once a guy has you, all he'll be able to think about is being with you again. Your touch is addictive to humans."

"La la la la la." I stared at the light blue tile on the floor.

"What's with her?" Hunter asked.

Cole's eyes narrowed as if he was considering something. After a moment, he said, "She hasn't embraced her immortality yet."

"What's to embrace? She just has to be herself."

I lowered my hands. "Yeah, well, myself doesn't kiss just any guy!"

"Right," Hunter replied with a wink.

My fingers curled into a fist. Just because fate had turned me into a succubus didn't mean I had to change my beliefs. Cole cupped my hand in his, stopping me from punching Hunter in the nose.

"You'll only hurt your hand," Cole whispered, but I was pretty sure Hunter heard also. Louder, Cole said, "Lilith won't let her near New York. You know that."

Right, cell signals wouldn't be the only technology Hell could control.

Hunter's gaze dropped to our hands. I slid mine from Cole's. A smirk flittered across his features. "Then don't ask for permission."

"Hunter," Cole said through clenched teeth. "We don't have the ability to hide from the Queen of the Damned."

"Then why bring up going?" I asked. My gaze bounced between them. "Unless you know someone who can hide me from her." That had to be it. Hunter's devious grin and Cole's set jaw confirmed it. "I promise I won't do anything to upset Lilith."

"Going will piss her off," Cole countered, shifting his weight from one foot to the other.

"Besides that." I needed his help to pull this off. "I just want to see that Gracie made it and that my family and friends are okay."

"Why are you so convinced something happened to your sister?" Cole asked at the same time Hunter said, "You know he can do it."

My gaze locked on Hunter's dark licorice-colored eyes. I was dying to know who *he* was, but I needed Cole to understand why this was important to me. With great effort, I tore my attention from Hunter and faced

Cole. "The last thing I remember is Gracie's eyes bugging out of her head. Yeah, she's easily excitable. And yes, she can be a bit of a drama queen, but this was different. And then there's this feeling deep in my gut." I wrapped my arms around my midsection. "It keeps telling me to find her and talk to her."

I needed to remind Gracie of the very thing I was trying to cling to: don't become someone else just to make others happy.

Cole pinched the bridge of his nose.

I grabbed his arm and pressed on. "Please, Cole, I promise not to let anyone know what I am."

His skin grew warm under my fingers. I might have thought I imagined it, but there was no mistaking the red hue that overtook his ocean-blue eyes. I didn't back away, though. Cole might be angry, but I trusted he wouldn't hurt me over wanting to see my family one last time.

"*Who* I am," I added reluctantly, because I knew it wasn't enough to promise to conceal what I'd become. I had to agree to hide that I was back on Earth living life as if I hadn't died. I'd figure out if I'd keep my promise once I got there.

I stepped closer to Cole. So near I could see each long, dark eyelash framing his bewitching eyes. My fingers curled more desperately around his biceps.

"Please," I pleaded.

"Absolutely not." Cole raked a hand through his hair. "I happen to like not burning in the River of Souls for all of eternity, and there's a spectacular chance that's exactly where we'll end up if you don't forget this stupid idea right now."

"Dude, you know Lilith wouldn't toss you in the

river," Hunter said.

"Maybe not, but she will punish us," Cole shot back.

"She won't find out." I addressed Hunter. "This friend will be able to make sure of that. Right?"

"Yes."

Not a muscle in Cole's body twitched. What I wouldn't have done to be able to read his mind. I fought the urge to fidget and gave him my best sad-puppy-dog expression.

"I'll help you even if Cole won't," Hunter said.

Cole moved between Hunter and me. "You're not becoming her new best friend."

"Does that mean you'll help me?" I asked.

Cole cursed. "Do I have a choice?"

The gleam in Hunter's eyes gave me the impression he'd known that if he pushed Cole, he'd say yes.

Now that Cole was on board with the plan, I couldn't wait to find out who had the ability to pull one over on the Queen of the Damned.

Cole glared at Hunter. "You're asking him for the favor." He cursed, again. "The guy's already a smug bastard. No way do I want to be in his debt."

"Whose?" I asked.

"He won't do it for me." Hunter held his hands in front of him. "He despises my very existence."

"What?" My gaze bounced between them. "Why?" If this person loathed Hunter for being half demon, he was sure to detest Cole and me.

"You're the one who brought him up," Cole said to Hunter, either not having heard my questions or choosing to ignore me.

I jumped between them and practically shouted, "I'll ask him!" I'd get down on my knees and beg if I had to. "Just tell me who you're talking about."

Hunter opened his mouth—the name on the tip of his tongue, I just knew it. But before he could say it, and as if sent from Hell itself, Luz, Nick, and Dylan showed up.

Chapter 7

The discussion between Cole, Hunter, and me ended as abruptly as a party raided by the police. Part of me was surprised the others didn't know Cole and Hunter weren't human, and another part of me called myself an idiot for thinking an immortal went around advertising his demonhood.

Cole checked the New York obituaries on his phone while we finished our tour of the zoo. He only found mine, something he shared with me on the sly, leading us to believe Gracie was alive. Knowing this eased some of my worries.

I'd have to wait until we were back at Cole's to find out who Hunter and Cole had been talking about. As much as I liked his friends, I was more than relieved when only Hunter returned to the apartment with us. Cole paced from the sliding glass doors to the breakfast nook and back, over and over. Hunter slouched against the wall near the television. Me, I walked circles between them, too excited to sit.

He turned out to be a nephilim named Wyatt. I learned that nephilim were the offspring of humans and angels. Apparently, these children were extremely uncommon compared to the number of people in the world who were the result of a demon and a human hooking up, and cambions like Hunter were rare.

So far, all I knew about Wyatt was that his father

was a powerful angel, he was homeschooled by his human mother, and he was an entitled prick. Truthfully, I didn't care what Wyatt was, as long as he could sneak me into Warwick, New York, under the radar of the Queen of the Damned.

"How exactly is it that Wyatt can help me get home without Lilith knowing?" I asked.

Cole breathed in deep. "I need a drink."

His sudden desire for alcohol could have been because we were plotting my trip to the one place Lilith had forbidden me to go, or it could've been because he hated admitting there were things Wyatt could do that he couldn't. I knew it was one of those two reasons by the way his jaw clenched whenever New York or Wyatt were mentioned.

I waited for Cole to grab three beers from the fridge. He held a bottle out to me and replied, "Wyatt has the ability to hide his signature from both Heaven and Hell."

"And unlike me, the lucky bastard's strong enough to extend that gift to conceal a friend when he wants to," Hunter added as he grabbed the beer Cole offered him.

"Great, I think." I stopped my aimless meandering and leaned against the couch. "What's a signature?"

Cole drank deeply and then answered, "All immortals have one. It's the energy we give off. Once you're stronger, you'll notice it, too."

"You mean once I'm chock-full of stolen essence."

Just one more thing that got better after I accepted my new existence. I wasn't sure if I should be excited to know I would gain another superpower or upset that I couldn't invoke this power right now.

After a moment, I said, "A person wanting to hide from Hell and its demons I understand, but why would the son of an angel need to hide from Heaven?"

"Because Heaven despises the existence of nephilim more than it despises the existence of cambions. Hell does, too, but for different reasons." When my eyes narrowed questioningly, Hunter added, "Heaven expects angels to guide humans, not sleep with them. They consider the act unholy."

"Let me get this straight…" I set my beer on the coffee table. "Your idea to send me back to New York is to pair me with a person who's hated by both Heaven and Hell more than demons and cambions combined?"

Cole rubbed his temple as if warding off a headache. "His idea is to pair you with someone who can't be found by Heaven or Hell unless it's intentional."

"Because he can hide his supernatural beacon?" I asked.

"Right," Cole confirmed.

That had to be a positive thing. And Cole must trust Wyatt if he was willing to introduce me to him. Unless this was Cole's way of getting rid of me.

I pushed that thought aside. Cole would be in as much trouble from the Queen of the Damned as I would should I be discovered.

"So what happens if Heaven discovers that one of theirs fathered a child?" I asked. I pictured a jail cell made of gold located on a lonely cloud.

"They destroy the evidence," Hunter said with a low, disgusted growl. He downed his beer.

"Destroy?" My head tipped to the side. "As in…" But surely Heaven wouldn't do something so horrible.

"Kill the child," Cole said with a frown, confirming my unspoken thoughts.

"But Heaven is good," I replied, unwilling to accept what they'd said.

"It is." Cole lowered himself onto the couch. "But you have to understand that angels aren't supposed to have the same needs as humans."

"That's bull," Hunter interjected. "If angels were the perfect, emotionless creatures some believe them to be, none would fall and none of us would be here now."

"Whatever, dude. We aren't debating their virtue." Cole threw the Chicago Bears throw pillow at him and then said to me, "The point is that angels don't like to leave behind proof of their indiscretions. Since they consider nephilim to be abominations, they don't have a problem destroying them. Luckily, nephilim have the natural ability to cloak their signatures."

"Their angelic creators don't know they're fathers," Hunter said almost enviously. "It's a built-in defense mechanism that's turned on at birth."

"Almost as if the Almighty doesn't approve of his angels smiting children," I said.

Cole got up and stood near the patio window. Hunter had taken a seat on the coffee table. Once the shock had faded of finding out that an angel's wrath over the birth of a child was worse than a demon's, I realized Hunter and Cole had started a new conversation. My gaze bounced from one to the other as they debated who'd be the one to call Wyatt. It didn't take long for it to become obvious neither of them would volunteer.

I threw my hands in the air. "You guys are worse than my fifteen-year-old sister and her friends. And trust me when I tell you they can be the biggest babies."

They gawked at me, apparently stunned into silence.

"Text him at the same time," I said.

That was the solution I'd given Gracie when she and her two best friends couldn't agree on who'd invite the cute boy to their pool party. Simultaneous texts became their trademark move.

Cole and Hunter typed two words into their phones—*meet-up, apartment*—and had me hit send to ensure that neither of them only pretended to text Wyatt. It became apparent there was very little honor amongst demons and cambions.

Wyatt must have lived close, because less than twenty minutes later a loud static-ridden buzz screeched through the apartment, startling me off the couch. Hunter burst out laughing.

"It's the intercom," he brayed. "Brave, aren't you?"

I pushed him off the coffee table. "Shut up!"

Cole buzzed Wyatt in.

If you lined Cole, Hunter, and Wyatt up against a white wall and asked me to pick out the guy with angel blood flowing through his veins, I wouldn't have pointed to Wyatt. He was average in height and build with shaggy brown hair, thick eyebrows, and a goatee, but that's not what made him appear less than angelic. It was the way he studied me—like I was a freak of nature—and how his lips froze in a wily smirk. I started to scoot closer to Cole, who'd taken a seat on the couch but stopped myself. Wyatt could help me see my family and friends again, and I wanted that. Badly. What I didn't want was for Wyatt to realize he intimidated the heck out of me. Besides, he was part angel. How bad could he be?

"Since when do we meet up?" Wyatt asked with extra emphasis on the words *meet up*, apparently not concerned with introductions.

"It was Avery's idea," Hunter said dryly as if he wasn't the one who'd suggested we contact Wyatt in the first place. Hunter was seriously more immature than Gracie on her worst day.

"Hi," I said with a half wave. "I—"

"You're a succubus," Wyatt said, interrupting me.

Did I have *Hell's Slut* stamped across my forehead? I resisted the urge to run to the bathroom to check and instead cocked my head to the side and regarded him a moment, hoping to see some sign that he wasn't human—a halo, a white glow about him, the hint of wings—but all I saw were candy-brown irises and a five-o'clock shadow.

"I was going to say, I wanted to ask you for a favor."

Cole's jaw muscle twitched when I said *favor*.

"This should be good." Wyatt squeezed between me and Cole, which meant I had to move over so he didn't end up on one of our laps. "What would a succubus need my help with?" His pointed glare moved from Cole next to him on the coach to Hunter on one of the kitchen stools. "Better yet, what is it I can do and they can't?"

"I knew he'd gloat." Cole got up. "I need air."

He opened the patio door but didn't actually step onto the balcony. Since there wasn't much of a breeze, he didn't get much air, either.

I explained what I wanted to Wyatt, ignoring the

way Cole kept shaking his head every other sentence. I already knew he didn't like the idea of me planning a trip back home.

"Will you help me?" I asked Wyatt when I finished.

"That depends. You said you need to deliver a message to your sister. I want to know what that is and how you plan on doing it because she can't know you're you. And if you say she never returned a top she borrowed or that her new hairstyle makes her look fat, the answer is no. She'll figure the trivial stuff out on her own."

I didn't want them to think Gracie was a cruel person, because she had a big heart. But she'd wanted so badly to fit in with who she felt were the cool girls that, after the cheerleaders and their entourage invited her to sit at their lunch table, she'd shunned some of her own friends. "She's been sort of ignoring a mutual friend of ours. He's a kind person but suffers from depression."

"A lot of people do," Wyatt pointed out.

"True. If you figure out a way to help every last one of them, I'm all ears, but for now, I'm focusing on the person I can help." I heaved out a breath. "I've known Justin most my life. He's like a brother to me, and he's had it rough. His parents divorced when he was young. His mom took off, so he and his younger brother lived with their dad until he fell ill and died. Their grandparents ended up moving into their house. Then, less than six months after Justin's dad was buried, his grandfather suffered a heart attack and didn't make it. Justin hasn't been the same since. Not many people know this."

Gracie did, but she didn't know that there were times when Justin's depression swallowed him whole or that his grandmother would call me, knowing I'd come over and talk to him. Sometimes he'd cry. Sometimes he didn't say a word for a very long time. No matter what, though, I'd always been able to help him find his way back.

"Gracie and I are the ones he turns to when he feels like giving up."

"And with you gone and Gracie ignoring him, you're worried about what might happen to him."

It sounded dramatic, but Justin's problems were big enough that his grandma had him seeing a therapist. Gracie knew he liked to come over to talk, but she didn't know just how important it was to Justin that we listened. "He needs Gracie, and she needs to realize there are more important things in life than who she eats lunch with. If her new friends can't accept her old ones, then they aren't worth knowing. And as far as how I'll get that message to her, I can pretend to be a friend of Justin's. I'll tell her I'm worried about him."

Wyatt strummed his lips with his finger thoughtfully. "This trip is because you're trying to make a difference in two people's lives?"

"Their happiness is important to me."

Wyatt chuckled low and deep. "You know, you and Cole don't live up to the heartless, evil image that one tends to associate with demons."

My shoulder rose. "I wasn't cruel when I was human, and I don't intend to change now that I'm a succubus."

Wyatt scrubbed his face with his hands. "Avery, you seem like a nice person, but this trip will be harder on you than you think." When I opened my mouth to argue, Wyatt raised a hand and went on. "Your family won't know who you are. You'll be an outsider at your own funeral."

Only if I don't tell Gracie or Megan that I'm alive. If one of them were in my shoes, I'd want to know the truth. I'd accept them for what they'd become if it meant they weren't gone forever.

But what if seeing them and revealing my identity put other people in danger? Would Lilith punish me by punishing them?

I massaged my temples. Could I stop by my funeral and not let anyone know who I was? Would Gracie want to talk to someone she'd never met? Would Megan?

"Stop trying to talk her out of it," Hunter said.

I glanced at him.

"Going might offer you some closure, Avery." He got up and strolled over to the patio doors where Cole stood. "This is probably the only chance you'll get to talk to your sister. But hey, maybe if I couldn't have my cake and eat it, too, I'd pass also."

Cole shook his head. I swore I heard him mumble, "Subtle."

Three sets of eyes studied me. I couldn't let them know I had an internal debate taking place. Cole would pull the plug on the plan before it started, and Wyatt was already skeptical. Hunter was the only one a hundred percent on my side. Unfortunately, his opinion held the least amount of weight. I had time to decide if I should or shouldn't tell Gracie or Megan my secret. Right then, though, I needed Wyatt's help and Cole's support.

"I want to do this. Wyatt, will you help me?"

Wyatt pursed his lips. "Because you're trying to make a difference in someone else's life, and because my agreeing will annoy Cole to no end"—he grinned at Cole—"yes."

"You're an ass," Cole said.

"Yet you still called me." Wyatt stroked his goatee. "Even with my abilities, the trip will be risky."

"No shit." Cole plopped down on the chair and glared at Hunter. "This wasn't my idea, and if it weren't for a certain person sticking his nose where it doesn't belong, we wouldn't be having this discussion."

Hunter flipped Cole off. I didn't bother to ask why the trip was risky. I already knew Lilith would be beyond upset if she found out I went against her wishes. *Hell has no fury like a queen betrayed.*

"Cloaking your signature won't be enough. You'll have to look different," Wyatt said.

"I'll learn how to change my appearance."

"Her wake's on Friday. That gives us three days to prepare," Cole said. "Avery, if we do this, you have to throw your mild manners out the window."

I swallowed but said nothing. I was a succubus now. I sure hoped that gave me the guts to sashay over to a stranger and start a conversation. Determined, I told myself I could make a cute guy want to kiss me. My head bobbed up and down in confirmation. Cole might have thought I was saying *okay,* but really I was convincing myself I'd be able to siphon months off an unsuspecting guy's life to sustain my own.

Wyatt clapped his hands once. "Then it's set. We'll take an early flight out of O'Hare Airport Friday morning, pay our respects, and leave."

With the details on how I'd be traveling worked out, all that remained was for me to stock up on human essence and learn how to shift into a different person. After that, I'd be on my way to home.

What could go wrong?

Chapter 8

Weird is sitting at a U-shaped booth in a dimly lit restaurant as two guys you've known for less than ten hours select the stranger you should make out with. Not something I'd recommend to anyone. In the nineteen minutes and thirty-seven seconds we'd been there—not that I was counting—the only thing I wanted to do was to eat my dinner in peace.

Rock music from about two decades ago played in the background. I sat squeezed between Hunter and Cole wondering why I agreed to this. I shifted in my seat, peeling my thighs from the vinyl cushion. We had a clear view of the bar and most of the dining area.

"That one has a pure soul." Wyatt used his chin to point to the middle of the restaurant.

I followed his gaze. There were three occupied tables in the general direction he'd indicated. Two women chatted at one of them, a young family was finishing their meal at another, and a man with a buzzed haircut picked up the menu at the third. He had teenaged boys with him. Their backs were to me, so I couldn't see their faces or tell just how old they were, but I guessed they were a couple of years younger than me. I stared at their heads. One had light blond hair, and the other had hair as shiny and black as oil. I guessed they were friends and not brothers.

"What do you suggest I do?" I asked sarcastically.

"Plop down in the chair next to the father and decide who I want to kiss?"

Wyatt's gaze met mine. "Kiss them both for all I care."

Cole was the only one who hadn't tried to pimp me out, which I found funny, since he was the reason we were there.

"If you insist on taking this trip, which I want noted I'm still against, then you need to build your strength quickly," Cole had said just after Wyatt had agreed to the plan. "Grab your purse. We'll eat dinner at Old Time."

Hunter and Wyatt had insisted on coming with. Hunter claimed to have a craving for a bacon burger, swearing Old Time Bar and Grill not only had the best burgers, but they put a fried egg on top. Wyatt had calmly shrugged and said he could eat. They didn't fool me, though. They'd come to watch the new succubus make a fool of herself.

The restaurant turned out to be an hour away. Less chance that Cole would run into someone he knew.

"How about him?" Hunter asked, pointing to the businessman sitting at the bar. He had pretty eyes, neatly combed hair, and a slender build, but that's not what jumped out at me.

"Ew! He's old!" I blurted.

"He's in his late thirties, maybe early forties," Wyatt said through a mouth full of food.

"Yeah, well, I'm eighteen, and I'm not making out with a guy twice my age."

"Hell's going to love her," Wyatt said, lifting his soda as if he were saying a toast.

I scrunched up my nose and made a face at him. It

wasn't my fault I'd died young, and I knew Lilith was banking on me marking young souls for her team. No way could I approach a businessman—even one who resembled my favorite movie star—and swap spit with him.

I dragged a curly fry through ketchup as I contemplated my afterlife. Was this what it would be like—an eternity hunting for someone who could give me a precious few months of life? Did I even want to live if this was what was expected of me?

Cole reached over me and grabbed the salt. His mere presence made me think I had to at least try. I didn't know what he'd done to end up an incubus, and I wasn't so sure I wanted to know. The Cole next to me was sweet and a bit protective. He'd found a way to make what he'd become work without turning into a jerk. If he could do it, then maybe I could.

A shiver ran through me at the memory of the fiery river I'd seen during my brief visit to Hell. The alternative was horrific. I had to do this.

I shot down every guy in the restaurant. Even with my newfound determination to survive, I couldn't work up the nerve to make out with someone I'd just met. I stuffed a fry into my mouth to chase away the butterflies in my stomach and drank a sip of cola, hoping the sugar would help the lightheaded feeling that had crept up on me in the last hour.

Cole bent closer and whispered, "You need to relax. Your stress over this is causing you to burn through the last of your human energy."

My eyes grew wide.

"How about the redhead by the door?" Wyatt asked. "He's around our age."

I tore my gaze from Cole to check out the new prospect. The guy was lanky with pasty-looking arms and legs. My first thought was that he shouldn't have worn green shorts. My second thought was that he should give the orange sneakers back to whatever clown he'd stole them from. Then he turned.

"His face is a road map of pimples," I replied, knowing deep down I shouldn't judge a person on looks alone, but we were talking about me kissing him without getting to know him.

Cole snagged a fry from my plate and pointed to a dark-skinned guy in a high school football jersey. He stood at a tall table with two guys—both taller and bigger than him—watching sports on one of the television sets in the bar area. "That's who you should talk to."

The guy was too small to be a linebacker. Wide receiver, maybe. Quarterback, probably. He had short black hair and dark almond-shaped eyes. His gaze flicked to mine and then back to the news.

"Why him?" I asked.

"He's seventeen or eighteen, his soul's pure, and he keeps checking you out." Cole ate the fry he'd nabbed. "If you're lucky, he has a girlfriend."

I gawked at Cole. "How's that lucky?"

"You receive a bigger fix from humans who're being unfaithful. We went over this."

"Right." My new mission was to be a relationship wrecker. *Nice in life, bitch in the after-life. Who knew?*

Cole didn't give me a chance to object. He got out of the booth, pulling me with him.

"Glance at him on your way to the bar. He'll follow. And don't tell him your real name."

Cole sat back down before I could say anything, and he didn't leave room for me to slide in next to him. It was Wyatt's amused smirk that got my feet moving.

Just talk to him.

I breathed out slowly, squared my shoulders, and glanced at the guy as I weaved my way through the tables. He had gorgeous brown eyes and long curly lashes. I tucked my hair behind my ear and rested my forearms on the bar.

I wasn't old enough to be standing near the beer on tap. And now that I was there, I had no idea what to ask for. I still had a nearly full soda and half my food. I drummed my fingers on the lacquered wood, feeling rather stupid for letting Cole and the others talk me into doing this. Someone next to me said *hi.*

I swiveled on my heels and faced my cute target. "Hi."

"I didn't think I'd catch you away from your friends." Up close, he had smooth black skin, and I could see that his eyes weren't dark at all, but instead a beautiful tawny color.

I glanced at my table. I had to give it to my friends—even though I knew they were watching my every move, they appeared to be deep in conversation.

I'd never been good at talking to guys, which was ironic, considering the little white lies that'd spread like wildfire when I was alive and had subsequently followed me to the grave. I opened my mouth, realized I had no idea what to say to him, and closed it.

Cute Guy smiled.

He had to think I was starstruck. I would have hit myself in the forehead for being so lame, but that'd only made me look crazy and awed by his presence.

"I'm Marcus," he said, running a finger along the edge of the bar.

Cute, but not overconfident, I thought.

"Megan," I replied, saying the first name that popped into my head.

"Is one of those guys your boyfriend?" He pointed toward my table with his chin.

I caught Cole's gaze. He turned away as if uninterested, although his fingers curled into a fist. Or maybe I imagined that. Cole laughed at something Hunter said, hand relaxed again.

The bartender stopped in front of me. "Need something?" he asked. Not, *What can I get you,* like he'd asked his adult customers.

The exit. I smiled sweetly and replied, "Napkins, please."

"Me, too," Marcus said. He looked at me expectantly.

"They're just friends." I accepted a stack of napkins from the bartender.

Marcus's stance relaxed. "Do you live around here?"

"Yeah." Well, not around *here.* About forty miles away, but there was no point in giving him a fake name and then telling him where I lived.

Marcus rested an elbow on the bar. The shift put him close enough that I could see amber flecks in his golden brown irises. When I breathed in, a hint of mint filled my nostrils. His shampoo, I thought.

"I need to pick up my kid brother in a little bit, but maybe we could do something afterward." Marcus didn't sound annoyed at having to taxi his brother around, which made him sort of endearing. His eyes narrowed. "You wouldn't want to come with me, would you?"

It was my in. I could hang out with Marcus for an hour or so. He seemed nice enough. And Cole and the others would wait for me, I was certain of that. Marcus was one of the good guys. I'm not sure how I knew that. I just did. Cole had said the purer the soul, the greater the fix. Would one kiss steal three months from Marcus? Six? Twelve? Would that kiss give me the strength I needed to alter my appearance for a minute? An hour? A day?

I only needed enough to get to New York, see my friends, and return home. Was it possible one guy—and a nice guy at that—could provide that much energy?

Marcus rolled his stack of napkins in his hands, waiting patiently for my reply. As I gazed into his eyes, I realized I couldn't steal part of his life or be the one to mark his innocent soul as Lilith's property. Wasn't I proof that not everyone sent to her deserved the sentence they'd gotten?

"Thanks, but I should stay with my friends."

His shoulders slumped forward. "Yeah. Of course." He grabbed a pen from near the cash register and jotted down his number on a napkin, which he slid toward me. "Call me sometime?"

"Sure." I stuffed it in my pocket to be polite, but I had no intention of calling him. I wouldn't be the one who shortened his life. He smiled and headed back to his table.

"What was that?" Hunter asked when I scooted into the booth.

I shrugged as if I didn't know what he meant. I'd like to see him kiss a stranger.

I take that back. Someone like Hunter wouldn't have a problem with that.

Wyatt studied me through narrowed eyes.

I felt exposed, like I'd shown up naked at school without my homework. "What?" I snapped.

He picked up his drink. "Nothing."

Cole slid in next to me. "I wish I could say you don't have to go through with this, forget attending your funeral, and start your new life."

"But?" There was always a "but" to a statement like that.

"Your new life requires you to meet nice guys like Sport Goofy over there."

I'd hardly call Marcus *Sport Goofy*. Instead of becoming defensive, I said, "He's not my type." I sipped my soda. The sugar still didn't help the lightheaded feeling that had settled deep in my skull.

"Eat." Cole pushed my plate closer.

"I told you she should've gone after his friend," Hunter said.

"His friend's a player." Cole leaned back, arms resting on the back of the booth. "She can do better."

I took that to mean I'd get a greater fix from someone like Marcus. I could tell we would be there until I kissed someone. I sank lower in my seat and bit into my now cold hamburger. It tasted gross, but I ate it, anyway.

How badly do you want out of here? I asked myself. After several uncomfortable minutes, I said, "Excuse me."

Cole got up so I could scoot out of the booth.

"I have to use the little girl's room," I said in way of explanation.

If I thought there might be a window in the restroom, I'd climb out of it and hitch a ride back to the apartment. But really, how many public bathrooms had windows?

Marcus looked up as I passed his table. I indicated with a slight jerk of my head for him to follow me and continued toward the wooden plaque shaped like a hand. It read *Restrooms* in dark maroon letters. I didn't turn to see if Marcus had followed me until I knew I didn't have an audience.

I'd just settled against the wall, the sole of one shoe kissing red brick, when Marcus turned the corner. I inhaled deeply and told myself I had nothing to be nervous about.

"Thanks for following," I said.

Marcus stopped in front of me with his hands shoved in his jean pockets. "Change your mind about coming with me?"

"Not exactly." I had to be back here long enough for the guys to think I'd made out with Marcus. "I felt a little guilty."

"About?" Marcus coaxed when I grew quiet.

"About saying I'd call when I know I won't." Deep breath. "You're a nice guy, and five days ago I would've been happy to date you, but—"

"You like the guy you're sitting next to. The one on the end."

"What? No!" Cole and I were work associates and nothing more. "It's just that I've been through a lot lately, and I'm not ready to jump into dating, yet."

He nodded, but the way he diverted his gaze told me he didn't believe me. "It's okay. Keep my number, and if you change your mind, call me."

I'd have felt better if Marcus had stormed off pissed that I'd wasted his time. Instead, he added, "It was nice to meet you, Megan."

I almost asked *who,* but then remembered I'd given him a fake name.

"You, too."

We left the corridor at the same time. I waited to say bye until I was sure Cole and the others would see me talking to him. I even wiped my mouth as if my lips were wet from Marcus's kisses.

This time, Cole slid over when I returned to the table. I didn't sit, though.

"I got my fix. We can go now."

Hunter choked on the soda he'd been drinking. "Damn! Did you do it in the stall?"

"I'm not telling you the details!" Heat flooded my cheeks.

Cole's expression hardened. He and Wyatt exchanged glances.

Hunter laughed as if he was sure I'd dragged Marcus into the bathroom and jumped him. "Why can't I meet girls like you?"

"Because a succubus would know you're not one hundred percent human," Wyatt said dryly. "To them, it'd be like kissing a dead guy."

Not that I'd ever in a million years kiss Hunter—he was Cole's friend and too crude for my liking—but if I did, I'd know the difference between kissing him and kissing a corpse. For one, Hunter would kiss back. And arrogant as he might be, he was attractive, and he smelled like musk and citrus. All things a cadaver was incapable of.

"Can we please get out of here?" I asked.

"I got this." Wyatt glanced at the bill, threw money on the table, and stood.

Cole had said a succubus would become corpse-like herself if she didn't siphon life from humans. If I didn't find the courage to act like a succubus soon, I'd find out if he were right.

We left the restaurant. Cole unlocked his car with the remote and then grabbed my arm. His hand was warm on my chilled skin. Hunter and Wyatt passed us without comment. Cole stepped closer. The blue in his eyes was a few shades darker, like the ocean at night. Their intensity frightened me. I looked right back at him, trying my best not to squirm.

He scowled. "I hate liars."

"I didn't—"

His fingers dug into my arm, cutting off the rest of my words. He leaned in until the thinnest sheet of air separated his lips from my ear. "When you've kissed someone passionately, his energy flows into you, and your soul becomes brighter. After sex, your cheeks will be flushed with color."

"Cole, you're hurting me." I tried to pull away, but he only held on tighter. And while I could have taken a step backward to put some distance between us, I was too surprised at his anger to think straight.

"Right afterward, you'll even smell like him." Cole's nose brushed my neck as he inhaled. "You smell like a faded version of yourself. You're almost out of human strength."

I didn't know what exactly to say. So he'd busted me. I hadn't sucked even a minute of life out of Marcus. My actions hadn't hurt anyone but me.

"Avery," he said more gently. "You can't fake

your way through being a succubus."

"I have no intention of faking my way through it."

Cole's gaze bored into mine. "Lilith will burn you alive, and that'll be after she breaks your willpower."

I wet my lips and prayed my voice would sound braver than I felt. "Then so be it."

He froze. Every muscle in his body paralyzed for the briefest of seconds. His statuesque posture reminded me of Lilith's threat to him. She was holding him responsible if I failed.

"I'll make sure she knows it wasn't your fault and that you're an exceptional mentor."

"No." Cole released my arm and stepped back as if I were poisonous. "I won't let you."

"It's not your—"

Cole's lips pressed against mine, rough and venomous at first, but when his tongue coaxed my lips apart it was with so much fervor that mine obeyed. His fingers weaved through my hair and held the back of my head in a soft but firm grip as his other hand wrapped around my back and pressed me to him. *Choice* echoed in the back of my mind, finishing what I'd been about to say. I found myself kissing him back even though my arms hung at my side unsure if they should embrace him or push him away. While his hold on me remained ironclad, his kiss turned tender. My pulse raced as my body melted into his. Then the most wonderful feeling filled me, like liquid sunshine, warm and enticing. It awoke every nerve in my body. I wanted more, but too soon it stopped and all that was left was Cole with his arms around me and his lips against mine. He kissed me so passionately my knees buckled. He held me tighter, keeping me from falling.

"Get a room," Hunter called from somewhere behind us.

Cole broke our kiss. His dark eyes were now a dull steel gray. His kiss left me breathless, though I didn't need to breathe anymore. One day, I'd figure out how that worked.

"Try denying your true nature now that you've had a taste of human energy," Cole said, acid lacing each word. He turned toward the car.

"Secondhand essence won't be enough for her to shift," Wyatt said and climbed into the backseat.

I grabbed Cole's arm. "Wait! What did you do?"

"I give your body what it craved: human essence."

I scooped my bangs away from my face. "Why would you do that?"

"So that the next time you have a willing participant standing in front of you, your instincts will override that prudish mind of yours." He shook my hand from his arm, stepped toward the car, then stopped, shoulders stiff. With a sidelong glance, he added, "Welcome to Hell on Earth. As your conductor on this journey, I suggest you get your ass in the car before I throw you into it."

Chapter 9

I climbed into the back seat with Wyatt to avoid being near Cole. I couldn't believe he pushed energy he'd gotten from the last girl he'd been with into me. I felt dirty, as if I'd been a part of the act between this unknown person and Cole. More than that, I was furious, but I couldn't pinpoint the cause of my rage. Was it that Cole had given me a taste of what it felt like to have a human's life force coursing through my veins or that I liked how it fueled my lethargic muscles and awakened my tired senses? Was it that he'd kissed me without my permission or that I couldn't stop thinking about his skilled lips moving over mine? Then there was the cold hard truth that I didn't want to face: Cole had only kissed me to prove a point, and I hadn't wanted him to stop.

I bounced my head against the back of the seat. Wyatt said nothing about me stewing in my mixed emotions. Instead, he talked sports—mainly with Hunter, because Cole appeared to be having a hard time keeping his eyes open. His right hand curled and uncurled around a squeeze ball as if he needed something to keep his blood pumping or he'd fall asleep at the wheel. I knew the sudden drowsiness must be a side effect of giving away energy. He looked almost as bad as he had after Lilith had kissed his forehead.

"Serves him right," I mumbled. I hadn't asked him to do it.

Wyatt glanced at me. I huffed, not caring that he'd heard me.

The windows were down. An ever-changing bouquet of flowers, grass, and grilled foods wafted through the car. Scents I hadn't smelled with the same clarity on the drive to the restaurant. Everything was amplified: the sounds of traffic, the birds, voices of people in other vehicles. I felt wonderful. Like I could run a marathon or climb Mt. Everest, yet Wyatt had said secondhand essence wasn't enough to shift my appearance.

I stared at my left hand, focusing on my nails and willing them to be longer. When they didn't grow, I tried imagining blue nail polish on them. Nothing happened, which left the question of just how amazing would I feel if I pulled energy directly from the source?

I had a very strong inkling that Cole was right; now that I had a taste of life essence, I wouldn't be able to resist taking more from a human the next time the opportunity presented itself. It'd be like offering water to a person who'd been wandering the desert, lost for days.

At the apartment, Cole stopped behind a sporty silver coupe and a sleek black muscle car with windows tinted so dark it oozed danger.

"Later, dude." Hunter gave me a nod goodbye and got out. The taillights to the muscle car flashed, letting me know that was his.

"It was nice to meet you," Wyatt said.

"You, too," I replied.

Wyatt got out, and then leaned down and addressed

Cole, who had his forehead on the steering wheel. "Not everyone's been doing the dance for a century and a half."

I didn't know if Wyatt was referring to Cole or himself.

Cole groaned. "Close the door before I drive over your feet."

Wyatt laughed, light and amused. "You blew it, dude. Tonight, you confirmed your devil-don't-care attitude is just an act."

Cole glared at him. "The last thing I want to hear is one of your righteous speeches. Close the damned door before I run over your overpriced Italian leather bullshit."

"My boots are from Spain." Wyatt winked at me. "See ya, Avery." He shut the door.

"I can't stand that guy." Cole drove to the front of the apartment complex instead of parking.

I wanted to know who Wyatt had been talking about—himself or Cole. Maybe both? "Cole—"

"Got your keys?"

It was more like key, singular. *I'm sorry,* got stuck in my throat. "Aren't you coming in?" I flipped the front seat forward but didn't exit the car. I wanted to ask Cole how long he'd been an incubus. I wanted to apologize for wasting his time tonight. I wanted to know if he'd felt anything at all when we'd lip-locked. His kiss lingered on my mouth, and the feel of being pressed against his body left me utterly confused, my stomach fluttering, and my mind whirling. I didn't know if the succubus in me, the incubus in him, or something more had caused these new desires.

"I've got something I need to do." There was no

excitement in his voice, just exhaustion.

"Right."

Because I couldn't kiss one cute guy, you have to make out with whoever your quick-fix go-to girl is.

I wished he'd say something more. I'd take him calling me selfish over him staring at the dashboard as if not really seeing it. Guilt at taking his supply of energy settled in my gut.

"I'll see you when you come home?"

At this, he glanced over his shoulder. "You called the apartment home."

I had. It seemed right. It was *his* home, after all. "Cole, I'm—"

"Make sure you lock the door once you're inside." He shifted into gear. I took the hint and climbed out from the backseat.

The short walk to the elevator gave me time to decide that I'd forgive Cole for what he'd done. "That's nice of you," I said to myself on the ride up to the sixth floor. "Forgive him for caring about you. You're such a dork."

But had he shared the energy with me because he was concerned about my well-being or because he was afraid of what Lilith would do to him if he couldn't force me to be an obedient little succubus? I was still contemplating this when I turned the corner to our apartment and saw Wyatt leaning against the wall.

I hiked my purse higher on my shoulder. "Did you forget something?"

He shook his head and pushed off the wall. "Cole will be awhile. I thought I'd keep you company until he gets back."

"Thanks, but I don't need a babysitter." I unlocked

the door and slipped inside the apartment. My apartment. Home.

Still sounded weird to me.

I went to close the door, but Wyatt's hand stopped it from moving more than a few inches.

"What are you doing?" I asked.

"I told you." He stepped around me.

My hand flew to my hip. "What part of 'I don't need a babysitter' didn't you get?"

"I'm not here to babysit." He lowered himself onto the worn sofa and kicked his feet up on the coffee table.

I pursed my lips and appraised him. I wasn't happy to be alone with him, but nothing he'd done that evening could be remotely construed as coming on to me. Problem was, there had to be a reason Cole and Hunter both hated him. "I don't suppose, if I asked nicely, you'd leave?"

"Nope."

I heaved out a sigh. I wanted to be alone, but it wasn't like I had somewhere else to go. Unless I went to the park, but it stood to reason Wyatt would just follow me there. I was still having a silent debate with myself about what to do when Wyatt patted the cushion next to him.

"Sit a spell," he said.

I hoped he wouldn't try anything as I locked the door. I hung my key on the hook before making the short trek to the family room and sitting on the arm of the couch. Wyatt stifled a laugh, as if amused I hadn't plopped down next to him. It didn't make me feel any better about being alone with him. I drummed my fingers on my leg, trying to come up with something to talk about. When that didn't help, I scanned the ceiling as if there'd be a list of conversation starters taped above the television. My thoughts were single-mindedly on Cole, though. Maybe I could use that to my advantage.

"Why do Hunter and Cole despise you?" I asked.

"Did they say that?"

Not in so many words. "I can tell you aren't BFFs."

Wyatt shifted so that he could see me better and asked, "Was it your idea for both of them to text me at the same time?"

I nodded, immediately thinking of Gracie, who I might never see again thanks to my inability to kiss a stranger. I hunched forward, wishing I could be more like Megan and just go with the flow of things. She'd kissed plenty of cute guys she'd just met. "No way am I missing out on a chance to find out if his kisses are as hot as his ass," she'd once said at a party. I chuckled inwardly at the memory.

"What happened?" I asked Wyatt, needing to get my thoughts off my friends and family.

"Hunter hates me because I'm always right, and he's a dick. Being the spawn of a demon will do that to a guy." Wyatt added the last part as an afterthought. I wondered if being the offspring of an angel automatically gave Wyatt an elevated opinion of his own self-worth. "Cole hates that I can see through the person he wants everyone to believe he is. It threatens his demonhood or something." Wyatt shrugged as if he didn't understand it, but the glint in his eyes implied that he did.

"See through him how?"

The corner of Wyatt's mouth tugged upward, but

he didn't answer me.

Did Wyatt mean Cole was only pretending to be a nice guy? Was he sucking the life out of some poor unsuspecting girl as we spoke, leaving her corpse for her family to find? I didn't want to believe Cole was capable of such a coldhearted act.

"Cole's not a monster," I finally said, refusing to let my imagination get the better of me.

"I didn't say he was."

Wyatt studied me, his grin turning serious.

"You mean it literally," I said. "You can see demons' souls."

"I can see the color of everyone's soul, which allows me to see their true nature." He watched me as if gauging my reaction. "It's an unintentional gift from Dad."

I lifted my feet onto the couch and rested my elbows on my knees, interested in learning more about his kind. "Can all nephilim see a person's soul?"

"I don't think so. I've only met two others— twins—and they couldn't. Mom thinks I inherited the ability because my dad is a cherub."

"Your dad is Cupid? The fat, short guy in a diaper?" A picture of Wyatt hanging from a rope, wearing a cloth diaper and sporting a pink bow popped into my mind. I covered my mouth with my fingers in an effort to hold in the laughter that begged to burst from my lips.

He rolled his eyes. "That's the Hallmark version. Cherubim are second order angels, seraphim being the highest. In case you aren't familiar with how high up the chain that is, Satan was Heaven's top seraph before he fell."

If he was trying to impress me, it worked. "Cole said you never met your dad."

Wyatt shook his head. "Mom doesn't think he'd kill me, but she hasn't exactly told him he's a father, either." He draped an arm over the back of the couch and said, "You have an interesting soul."

I folded my arms over my chest, afraid of what Wyatt might see and hating that he'd used his supernatural mojo on me without my permission. "You shouldn't peer inside people. It's rude."

"It's not like there's an on/off switch."

"Fine, you can't help being a Peeping Tom. What does Cole's soul look like?" I asked, not wanting to discuss my own.

"Who's the nosy one now?"

I scowled.

Wyatt stroked his goatee thoughtfully. "Let's just say his picture wouldn't be in a yearbook next to Evil Bastard any more than yours would be next to Most Likely to Give It Up."

I rubbed my palms over my thighs. I hadn't expected my soul to have *virgin* stamped across it. Had that been the case, some higher power would have pointed out that I shouldn't be a succubus, and while I wasn't thrilled with my new identity, it had kept me out of the fiery river.

Wyatt watched me expectantly, so I blurted, "I'm not discussing my sex life"—or lack of one—"with you."

"It only takes one indiscretion to mark a soul." He scratched his chin. "Did you steal your best friend's boyfriend?"

"I wouldn't do that." I picked up the TV remote

and turned on the news, hoping he'd take the hint that I didn't want to talk about my past.

"Had an affair with a teacher?" He paused. "Is that why you've sworn off older men?"

"No! I didn't have an affair with a teacher. Jeez! And you wonder why the guys find you annoying?"

"No, you wondered. I already knew." He leaned toward me. "Who you screwed doesn't matter. I know what put you on Team Lust. What I'm curious about is what else you did to be sent to the pit and not to the Pearly Gates."

Him and me both. I tried to ignore him.

He's trying to trick you into confessing your sins, I told myself and changed the channel to a rerun of one of my favorite cartoons. Wyatt cocked his head to the side, continuing to rub his goatee as he studied me.

"What?" I snapped.

"You've stolen."

A lucky guess, and it was only a tube of lipstick and a bra, not that it was any of his business. I remained on the arm of the couch, pretending to be interested in the show.

"Greed hasn't left a big enough stain on your soul, though." He scooted closer. I acted as if I couldn't see him scrutinizing me. "No, what you did was bigger. Something you regret, but remorse doesn't give one a pass come Judgment Day."

I faced him, tired of the game. "You can leave now."

"But I haven't unraveled the mystery that is Avery, yet." The back of his fingers skimmed my cheek, tucking my hair behind my ear.

He did it so unexpectedly, I didn't have time to

swat his hand away let alone jump up. His fingers wrapped around a few strands of hair as he stared directly into my eyes. His were a warm brown, and he smelled like spring on a rainy day.

I grabbed his wrist. "Wyatt, you need to leave."

He didn't release me, though. Instead, his eyes narrowed. His reply was light, compared to the weight of his gaze. "You have an unusual soul."

The rational part of me screamed to put at least a foot between Wyatt and myself. My curious side won out, though. "How so?" I asked, staring right back at him. The longer I peered into his eyes, the more they reminded me of endless autumn fields. The brown of his irises appeared more gold close up.

His thumb stroked my cheekbone. "The color of a soul changes with a person's mood and can be permanently altered by the decisions they make. When you first came upstairs, yours was dark green, but now it's more of a pale yellow, which is hopeful, and under the circumstances, makes perfect sense."

I had the promise of seeing my family and friends again to keep me optimistic. Not to mention, I hoped I could learn to live with my fate like Cole had learned to live with his.

"What's green?" I asked, hanging on Wyatt's every word.

"Envy." A thick eyebrow rose questioningly.

I *tsked*. "You must have read it wrong because there's nothing in wonderful Woodridge, Illinois, for me to be jealous of."

"If you say so." He shook his head and squinted. "What I find interesting is that if I watch your soul closely, it flickers with streaks of bright pink and murky gray."

"You just said souls are always changing."

"Yeah, but pink is a sign of purity and, well, let's face it, you didn't become a succubus by being abstinent."

No, I became a succubus by allowing a few white lies to spread like wildfire. If the Queen of the Damned hadn't believed me when I'd said I was a virgin, I doubted a nephilim would.

"Avery, how'd you die?"

"What?" His question surprised me. "I…there was a party…Gracie…" A lump formed in my throat. "I can't remember much after halfway through that night. I'd been drinking, and I guess maybe I had too much." Although I'd thought I'd been nursing my beer. "Can you see that type of detail?"

"No, I just get shades."

He smoothed a hand over my hair and then leaned away from me, putting that needed foot between us, but he still appeared to be appraising me. I grabbed the Chicago Bears pillow from the couch and hugged it to my chest.

"You and Cole could tell I hadn't kissed that guy at the restaurant."

"Yes."

"What did my soul look like before Cole shared his stash of energy?"

My lips warmed just thinking about being cradled in Cole's arms, which caused heat to rise in my cheeks. My stomach even did a little jump of excitement. My body's reaction to thinking about kissing Cole—no, kissing a guy—had to be part of being a succubus.

Wyatt squinted, an intrigued expression taking over

his otherwise serious stare. I squared my shoulders, refusing to wither under his gaze. Although, I told myself to stop thinking about kissing guys before my soul burst into some bright, emotion-telling hue that'd give Wyatt even more to ponder. If my soul did change, he didn't say.

"Washed out," he replied. "The colors were so muted, it was hard to tell them apart. That's how I knew that football player didn't even get to first base with you, let alone bang you."

I cringed at his blatant choice of words. Cole and his friends were extremely casual about sex. I didn't know if that was a guy thing or an otherworldly thing, but I was sure I'd never become used to it.

"Stop staring at me," I said as casually as I could— like I had nothing to hide—and turned my attention back to the television.

Several minutes passed. I actually thought Wyatt was watching cartoons with me.

"You killed someone," he announced like a contestant on a game show screaming out an answer that had almost eluded him.

"What?"

But he didn't need to repeat himself. My insides turned to ice, and the air I sucked into my nose didn't make it to my lungs.

"Did I…? Omigod." I killed Gracie.

I dropped my head between my knees and concentrated on keeping my breaths steady.

My wake was Friday—not mine and Gracie's. *Gracie didn't die.* I sat up, pulling my hair away from my face, and glared at Wyatt.

There was this one thing, but I hadn't…and it

120

couldn't be…no, something had happened during the last minutes of my life. An accident.

Yeah, that was it.

I mentally traced my steps on the night of the party. Megan had driven. We'd been late, but we'd planned it that way. We said our hellos to friends on the way to the kitchen. Jared hadn't let us pass without a hug and a beer. Megan's latest crush walked by. That had to be when we went outside. Jared's house had one of those second floor decks. It was a decent size. There had to have been fifteen or seventeen of us outside, and we weren't cramped for space. Gracie had been having the time of her life, joking and laughing with her friends. At one point, she and Karly fell against the banister in a fit of giggles. Then Caleb came over to talk to me.

Or did he come over *before* Gracie's happy outburst?

That was where things got even fuzzier. Caleb reached for me, or did he grab me? Megan screamed. Gracie's eyes were the size of saucers. A loud cracking noise had been swallowed by silence. Lights. Lots of lights. And voices. More screams. Pain.

My fingers flew to my mouth as the missing moments from that night tumbled into place like falling dominos racing to an abrupt end. Faster and faster, until I could see the horrifying last seconds of my life replayed in my mind in slow motion.

"I fell." The words came out in a hushed breath. "The banister gave. My sister's friend, Emily, grabbed Karly, but Gracie wasn't near her. Caleb and I reached for Gracie. My foot slipped. I flew over the edge and must have landed on the broken railing because something pierced my side." My hand went to where

121

the pain had been. My skin was smooth now, no sign of a fatal wound, thanks to Hell. "Cole believes my sister's okay. If he's right, then that means Gracie was saved," I reasoned. "So maybe I pulled someone else to his death." Caleb? Or Karly?

"It wasn't recent," Wyatt said.

"What wasn't?"

"The gray stain on your soul, it's been there awhile." He tipped his head to the side and leaned away from me. "You don't strike me as the murderous type."

"That's because I'm not!"

"I believe you."

"Good."

I lowered myself from the arm of the couch to the cushion and brought my knees to my chest, hugging them. I'd thought knowing would ease my mind, but all I felt was numb. We turned our attention to the television. The lame commercial for the phone company—the one they played so often it became annoying instead of cute—was on.

"You know what I find funny?" Wyatt asked.

"No." And I didn't care. I'd just remembered how I'd died, and I wanted a few minutes to let that newfound knowledge sink in.

"You didn't deny killing someone."

I glared at him, annoyed. "I can't remember all the details from that night."

"It wasn't recent," he repeated.

"Whatever."

But saying that I wasn't the murderous type wasn't wholly true. I had to fight to keep from fidgeting. Wyatt was guessing—I quickly deduced—saying the worst thing imaginable to gauge my reaction. I hadn't killed anyone.

My conscience whispered, *What about Krista?*

But I'd come to the conclusion a long time ago that I wasn't responsible for her death. Had I been wrong in doing so? Was I sent to Hell because I was a murderer? A shiver ran through me just imagining where I would have ended up if it weren't for my fake reputation. I found myself silently thanking the girls in cabin four for starting the lie.

"And you still aren't denying it. Who'd you whack?" Wyatt asked, bringing my thoughts back to the present.

"You're reaching," I said, proud that I'd managed to keep my voice from cracking.

"I've only seen that shade of gray on one other soul, and he was shrouded by death."

"I just died," I pointed out.

"Let me clarify. This other person had knowingly taken another life, as in murdered his wife."

"You really don't know when to drop a subject, do you?" I snapped. "Some things are private, you know. Like who I screwed"—or didn't screw—"and what crimes I committed. Did you drill Cole, too?" I wiped my sweaty palms on my shorts. "No wonder he hates you." I stood, marched over to the door, and threw it open. "Get out!"

Wyatt smirked. "Struck a nerve, have I?"

He stood and casually strolled closer, stopping in front of me so that I was trapped between his body and the wall. "You can lie to me, but you can't lie to yourself." He paused, and I was sure it was for effect. "Do you still want my help or are your panties in too much of a knot to accept it now?"

"You're an ass."

"See you Friday, then?"

He didn't wait for me to answer. I could still hear him laughing when the elevator doors closed.

Chapter 10

I woke the next morning on the couch with a pillow over my head. Muffled noises could be heard coming from the kitchen where Cole was making breakfast. I'd cried myself to sleep before he'd gotten home last night, but I knew he'd come in late. Exhaustion hadn't claimed me until sometime after midnight.

I peeked out from under my shield and realized I was holding one of the pillows from the bedroom. Cole must have given it to me while I slept. I hugged it close and squeezed my eyes shut against the morning light.

Wyatt had rekindled memories I preferred to leave buried. Krista had been one of my closest friends while growing up. We'd gone to the same grade school and were in the same homeroom from third grade until junior high. In junior high, we'd managed to have at least one class together each semester. We rode the same bus, were on the same gymnastics team, hung out at each other's houses. We had thought we'd always be close, but we drifted apart once we hit high school. She'd been set on trying out for the dance team, and I just wanted a break from gymnastics and anything else with a rigorous schedule. She easily secured a spot on the team, which didn't surprise me. Krista had always been quick to learn new moves, and her gymnastics background had helped. So what had gone wrong? Why was Krista dead? I'd convinced myself it was because of peer pressure.

"Hey, sleepyhead," Cole called from the kitchen. "We have work to do today."

"I don't have a job," I replied, pushing Krista and Wyatt from my thoughts. The comforter that had been keeping me warm was ripped off me, letting the air conditioning in the apartment attack my bared arms and legs. I brought my knees to my chest. "Hey!"

"Your job is to learn the ropes of a succubus so Lilith doesn't see fit to visit us."

"I told you, I won't slowly kill someone just so I can live."

He handed me a cup of coffee. He kept the plastic tumbler he'd been holding. "Avery, you're a succubus, but that doesn't have to be all bad. I'm asking you to please give this life another try."

"I don't think I can."

"I didn't think I could ask Wyatt for a favor, but I did. And I don't even want you going to New York."

He would have to point that out. I sighed.

Cole went on. "We'll go someplace where the guys aren't as wholesome as Sport Goofy. And before you say it's not right, a kiss only shortens a human's life by months. Full out sex, two, three years tops. So ask yourself, do you really want to risk Lilith's wrath over that?"

When he put it that way… "No. But I thought a fix from someone who's a player isn't as potent."

"It's not, but the guys where we're going aren't players. They just know how to have fun."

I sipped my drink, moaning with pleasure when the familiar sweetness of hazelnut creamer danced over my taste buds.

He smiled. "I figured Lilith put it in the fridge because it was your favorite."

Cole drank his coffee black, I remembered from breakfast yesterday. He dropped the comforter on the edge of the couch and sat next to me. "Why didn't you put on pajamas?"

I was still in the shorts and tank top from the night before. Cole wore a clean pair of lightly stressed jeans and a dark gray T-shirt. His hair was still wet. I must have slept through him taking a shower.

"I meant to," I lied, not wanting to say I had been busy bawling my eyes out. "I must have dozed off."

"You're a terrible liar." He opened the top of a health shake and chugged a quarter of it. "Your eyes are puffy, and your mascara is no longer on your eyelashes. Want to talk about it?"

"No." I was sure I'd start to cry all over again if I did. I wiped under my eyes. My fingertips came back with the black proof that I looked awful.

"Then get your butt in the shower." I was about to protest, but he held up a hand in the universal sign meaning *I don't want to hear it*. A devilish smile stretched across his face. "Don't make me carry you there."

"Fine." I got up, stopping just outside the bathroom to hold up a cocoa-brown crochet sundress hanging on the doorknob. "What's this?"

"Your outfit for today."

I put a hand on my hip, eyes wide in disbelief. "You're laying out my clothes now?"

"I let you sleep an extra thirty minutes." He passed me on the way to the bedroom. "That dress is perfect

127

for today's events."

The dress was cute, so I didn't argue further about wearing it. "Will Luz be there?" I asked, thinking it would be nice to hang out with her again.

Cole paused near the bed with his back to me, shoulders rigid. "No. Luz would hate me if she knew how fast I went through girls. That's not the type of person I want my human friends to see me as. Besides, you need to focus on the guys and not Luz, remember?"

I tried to see the bright side of what Cole had said. He didn't want his friends to see his incubus side. He wanted them to know the good in him. An unfamiliar tightening in my gut had me wishing that I, too, could only see the kind, caring person who respected girls and not the demon who had countless one-night stands.

****

It took close to an hour to drive to our destination, which turned out to be Raymond's house.

"Raymond's the demon you lived with, right?" I asked.

"Yes."

My gaze roamed over a carpet of red and yellow snapdragons that lined trimmed boxwood bushes. The house was a brick, two-story Colonial with forest-green shutters. Any of the houses on the block could've been on the cover of a home improvement magazine.

Cole opened the front door without knocking. We stepped inside.

"Raymond was a lawyer when he was human," Cole said. "Well, they were called advocates back then."

"How long ago was that?"

"Latter part of the Middle Ages. He lives on Earth

so he can keep current on today's laws."

I stopped in the hallway. "Hell has legal issues?"

"They fight Heaven for souls all the time."

Cole gave a jerk of his head, indicating for me to follow him. We found Raymond in the kitchen. He looked as if he was in his twenties, and he had the body of a swimmer. Two scantily dressed blondes were helping him blend fruit and rum together.

"You made it!" Raymond said when he saw Cole.

The blondes smiled. One wore a peach sundress that emphasized her bronze skin and the other had on cut-off shorts and a thin cotton top.

Cole introduced me to Raymond. His light brown hair was trimmed short, giving him an educated, respectable appearance. However, his clean-cut hair was at odds with the playful twinkle in his cornflower blue eyes and the tattoo of a dragon that climbed his right arm and crawled over his shoulder.

"Is Ian here?" Cole asked.

Raymond shook his head. "He called this morning and said he got tied up in Louisiana. You know how he is."

"Who's Ian?" I asked.

"An old friend from London," Cole replied.

"You've been to London?"

"Lived there for a while."

Maybe one day I might live in another country. The thought made me a little nervous. I'd never been out of the United States.

They chatted as I took in the large black stove and matching appliances. The cabinets were dark wood, but the walls and ceramic-tiled backsplash were shades of light beige. With the exception of the center island where Raymond whipped up drinks, the countertops were bare. No pictures on the refrigerator. I glanced into the adjoining family room and saw a leather couch, a huge flat-screen television, magazines, and a picture of Raymond wearing scuba diving gear.

"Beer and soft drinks are outside, frozen daiquiris inside. Help yourself," Raymond said.

"You thirsty?" Cole asked me.

"A soda would be nice."

Cole placed his hand on the small of my back. The warmth of his fingers seeped through the thin material of my dress. I'd paired it with strappy, bone-colored sandals with a wedge heel. We headed toward the sliding glass door.

"So, is Raymond part of Team Lust?" I asked.

"Nah. He specializes in greed, but he still enjoys the company of a lovely lady."

"Or two." As the girls in the kitchen would suggest.

"True." Cole held the door open.

I stepped outside and found myself on a large brick patio. A group of girls not much older than me sat around a tempered glass table, drinking strawberry daiquiris. A mix of late-teens and early-twenty-somethings were scattered around the yard: some talking, some playing bag toss, others swimming in the in-ground pool.

"Your suit's in the trunk, if you want to jump in," Cole said.

"I own a swimsuit?" Lilith did think of everything.

"Oh, yes. A cute little—I'm talking tiny—bright blue number with white starfish on the bottoms." He bent closer to me. "I'm sure all the guys here would

LOVE to see you in it." He smiled and raised his eyebrows twice, then combed his fingers through his hair. "Not that you need any help—you're beautiful without a string bikini—but if you put it on, I guarantee you'll have the guys here waiting on you hand and foot."

There was no shortage of options: guys that were short, tall, white, black, Hispanic, underwear-model hot to muscular jock. Thing was, Cole's choices were just as plentiful: blondes, brunettes, redheads, skinny, athletic, B-cup to double-D. It was like we'd stepped into a photo shoot for a fashion magazine.

Cole bent down and grabbed a wine cooler from a large ice chest and held it out to me. I surprised myself by taking it without asking if there was any soda. He grabbed himself a light beer.

"Find someone you're attracted to and flirt with him. If he doesn't kiss you, then lean in and kiss him. It'll only take a few seconds for the transfer of energy to start." He chugged half his drink and then asked, "Ready?"

No, but I'd said I'd try the whole hookup thing again. "Sure."

The girls at the table followed Cole with their eyes. I pretended not to notice as I trailed behind him. He wasn't the only one attracting attention. Both girls and guys gave me a once-over. I wished Cole would put an arm around me or take my hand to keep others from ogling. How pathetic was that? I preferred people to think I was with Cole so that they'd stop staring, and he wanted me to hook up with someone at the party? I brought my wine cooler to my lips and drank deeply, needing the alcohol to numb the nerves twisting into knots inside me.

We stopped next to two guys playing cornhole.

"Hey, you made it." A guy in board shorts and leather sandals gave Cole one of those half hugs guys did.

"What's up?" Cole asked. He repeated the half-hug thing with the surfer-looking dude who was playing with Board Shorts Guy.

"Same ol'. Where've you been?" Surfer Dude asked.

"Working." Cole downed the rest of his beer. "This is Avery."

I forced a smile. "Hi."

"She your girl?" Board Shorts asked.

"Nah, just a friend." Cole held up his empty bottle. "I need a refill. You guys want one?"

Board Shorts said no. Surfer Dude said, "Anything but that light crap." I said I'd have another, too. When Cole glanced at the half-full cooler in my hand, I gulped down the rest.

"I'll be right back," he said.

He was talking to all of us but staring at me. His expression said, *pick one.* I had to force myself not to frown. Goliath butterflies invaded my stomach.

"Want to play?" Board Shorts asked. His hazel eyes had a hard time staying on my face. The little macramé dress I wore seemed to shrink by the second.

"No, thanks." I glanced over my shoulder. Cole had his back to us as he chatted with the girls sitting around the table, a fresh beer in his hand. "I'm…yeah." And I walked away.

I tossed my empty bottle in the trashcan and stopped next to Cole. I noticed his new beer was almost empty.

"Hey," I said to the girls in greeting. I received a mix of *hi*'s and waves from the girls.

Cole handed me the wine cooler he'd set on the table and told the girls he'd catch up with them later.

"What happened?" he asked as we strolled toward the pool.

"Not my type."

He opened the beer I was sure was meant for Surfer Dude and sipped it. "What's your type?"

Blue-eyed Hell servants, apparently, because I wanted to lace my fingers through Cole's and get the heck out of there. "Not them."

Cole and I made our way through the partygoers. I met several nice guys. Some of whom I would have flirted with in my old life—guys I'd have loved to hang out with if I were to be honest—but I just wasn't into any of them. I started to think something was wrong with me. That I was no longer attracted to very cute, very sexy guys, but then Cole's arm brushed against mine as he brought his beer to his lips, and a warm, tingling sensation flittered over my skin.

He watched me out of the corner of his eye as he finished off his fifth beer. I pretended I'd heard what the guy with his arm draped over a petite blonde had said.

"I need a drink," Cole announced. "Avery."

He held a hand out for me to go first, which surprised me because grabbing a beer had been his excuse to dump me…I mean, to give me space.

"We've been here two hours. You can't tell me none of these guys are your type," he said, clearly annoyed.

"I have high standards."

"You're not picking a husband."

"I'm not the hookup kind of girl."

He stepped in front of me. I had to crane my neck to see his eyes, but I didn't step back. It was the closest he'd gotten to me since we'd arrived.

"You're a succubus, and you didn't become one by being a nun."

I didn't become one by sleeping around, either. I'd told him and Lilith I was a virgin. It's not my fault they didn't believe me. "I'm not used to chasing guys, and they aren't exactly trying to get with me."

"Bullshit," he hissed. "Half the guys we talked to would love to take you behind the pool house, and you know it. You've been pushing them away. Just pick someone, talk to him a little while, and let nature take its course."

"Is that what you do?"

"Yes, because I'm an incubus and I don't want to end up comatose on my apartment floor. I'd rather steal a few months off someone who won't miss it than become a living corpse. And if you want to go through with this plan of yours to see your family again, you will too."

We got another drink and joined a group of people near an outdoor bar. Cole introduced me to everyone, but I forgot their names almost as soon as I heard them. Jessica or Jennifer—a girl with short, dark hair and a silver stud in her right eyebrow—commented on how she liked my dress. Cole winked at me. She wore a bright yellow tank top with a white miniskirt. It suited her long legs and tan skin. I nursed my drink and noticed Cole doing the same with his. Everyone was nice, and at no time did I feel like an outsider. Slowly, Jessica/Jennifer gravitated toward Cole. A cute guy with spiked blond hair and eyes the color of sage slid closer to me.

"I'm Kevin," Cute Guy said, introducing himself.

I tucked my hair behind my ear. "Avery. It's nice to meet you."

He set his beer down on the bar. "How do you know Cole?"

Out of the corner of my eye, I saw Cole's gaze move from Jessica/Jennifer to me. I replied the same way I had all day. "I'm staying with him for a while."

"Oh." Kevin's gaze flicked to Cole, but Cole was no longer paying any attention to me.

"We're just friends," I added. If I hadn't, it would have seemed as if I were the type of girl who had such low self-esteem she'd watch her boyfriend flirt with another girl and not say anything.

And, okay, it was the truth. Cole and I were just friends, but seeing him whisper in another girl's ear bothered me. I told myself I was being irrational and that I didn't want to rip a chunk of hair out of that pretty head of hers.

Kevin's shoulders relaxed. He rested an elbow on the bar and started to tell me about some band that was playing at a pub this coming weekend. "Most of what they play is original music, but they do sneak in a cover song now and then. Want to come with me?"

"That sounds great, but I'm not twenty-one."

"I can get you in. The bouncers are friends of mine."

Cole was too engrossed in his conversation with Jessica/Jennifer to notice. Kevin trailed his fingers over my forearm, stopping when his hand covered mine. I paid enough attention to him to know he was a sophomore in college and he wrote songs. Although the band he'd invited me to see hadn't bought any of his lyrics yet. I replied with enough enthusiasm to keep him talking, but I couldn't stop myself from glancing at Cole every minute or so. I hadn't thought he'd noticed until he grabbed Jessica/Jennifer and stuck his tongue down her throat. His bright blue gaze was fixed on me as his hand slid to her ass, pulling her to him. She had her fingers tangled in his hair as she tried to slither even closer. A feat that anyone could see was impossible.

I shifted so that I wouldn't have to watch and focused on Kevin's lips. He had a nice mouth—not too thin, not too thick. His voice was deep, and his smile reached his eyes.

Not meaning to, I turned toward Cole and Miss Easy. His eyes were still open. Seeing him kissing her yet watching me caused something inside me to snap. I grabbed the front of Kevin's shirt and pulled him toward me. Rising to my tiptoes, I pressed my lips to his. He only hesitated for a moment, then his arms were around my waist, and he was kissing me back.

His tongue parted my lips as his mouth moved over mine slowly, sensually. His arms held me tight to his body. I felt his belt buckle pushing against my stomach and the hard muscles of his chest pressed to mine. My breath caught, and my pulse raced. I could feel his heart pounding in rhythm with mine. Then that wonderful feeling of liquid sunshine flowed from Kevin into me. His fingers traveled up my back, awakening my senses. Heat soared through me, making me feel as if I could do just about anything. Kevin moaned, a deep guttural groan that snapped my eyes open and caused me to cut the connection that drew his energy into me.

"Wow." He stumbled sideways and leaned on the bar for support. He ran a thumb over my bottom lip and placed it into his mouth as if he wanted one last taste. "So, does that mean you'll think about joining me Friday?"

"Friday?" The band he'd mentioned. "I can't. I have a funeral to attend." When Kevin's smile quickly faded, I added, "A distant relative," so he wouldn't question me more.

I glanced around us. A few people were still huddled near the bar, chatting. If they'd noticed Kevin's and my public display of affection, I couldn't tell. Cole was gone, and so was Miss Easy.

"Another time?" Kevin asked.

"Yeah, I'd like that." And I meant it, but only because I wanted the feeling of life flowing into me to come back. I'm not sure how I'd stopped the current when I had. The sensation had been enticing and addictive. It left me warm and tingling in spots that'd never been warm and tingly before. "Cole," I whispered. He'd given me my first taste of stolen life so that I wouldn't be able to resist, and it was so much sweeter when it came directly from the source.

"What?" Kevin asked.

I was glad I'd spoken softly and that he hadn't heard me. "I'll see you later."

Kevin made sure he got my phone number before he joined his friends. I went to find Cole. After wandering through the partygoers for several long minutes, I started to think I was an idiot for thinking he'd be somewhere outside and not behind closed doors with Miss Easy.

I frowned. Her name is Jessica/Jennifer, I corrected myself. If I continued to call her Miss Easy just because she kissed Cole—who, for all I knew, she might have known for a long time—then I'd have to start calling myself Miss Easy Number Two.

That's when I saw her talking to a girl with short, red hair. The skimpy one-piece Red wore made most bikinis appear modest. I picked up bits of their conversation as I passed them.

"Jessica, you have to tell me what it felt like to be in his arms," Red begged.

"Dreamy," Jessica cooed. "He's going to call me this weekend."

I'd been in Cole's arms before. Dreamy was an excellent adjective to describe the feeling. I kept moving so that I wouldn't reply, "Not if I can help it," to Jessica's statement.

What's wrong with me?

I had a sneaking suspicion I knew the answer and that if Wyatt were here, he'd tell me my soul was a bright green beacon. I couldn't allow myself to have feelings for Cole. Seriously, like a relationship between two people who had to have intimate contact with others could ever work.

I spotted Cole playing cornhole with Raymond and two other guys. Cole's back was to me. His arm swung low at his side, then rose in front of him. He released a small red beanbag. It arched high in the air and landed on the wooden target across from him. The tall, dark-skinned guy next to him saw me heading toward them. He tugged at the bill of his Sox cap, adjusting it on his head as his gaze perused the length of my body to my sandal-clad toes and back up to my face.

"Hello, beautiful," he said when I stopped not far from them.

I half smiled, feeling a little self-conscious when he sucked on his bottom lip while making an *mmm-mmm-mmm* noise. Cole, who'd just tossed his last bag, turned and saw me. He put an arm out, keeping the guy from drawing nearer to me. "Don't even think about it."

On the other side of the playing field, Cole's bag dropped neatly into the hole.

"Nice shot," I commented, nodding toward their target.

"Thanks."

Tall, Dark and Handsome's name turned out to be Chris. I wasn't sure if Chris feared Cole or respected him, but he treated me like a kid sister after Cole's warning. No more goggling or flirting, which was fine by me. I'd already done my hellish deed by kissing Kevin.

Cole acted as if we hadn't just spent the last forty-five minutes with people besides each other. He was an enigma. You know, that guy you just can't figure out: hot one minute and cold the next. I supposed spending decades in meaningless relationships could do that to a person. I remembered something Wyatt had said about Cole not being a poster child for evil. What had he done during his life to earn himself an eternity in Hell?

Across the yard, Raymond took his turn. Cole held out a beanbag to me. "Want to give it a try?"

"Nah. You'd lose your lead."

"It's just a game."

I shook my head. "It's okay. Cole?"

His eyebrows rose, waiting for me to continue.

I wanted to ask him *why Hell? What did you do?* But hadn't I gotten mad at Wyatt for prying into my past? Wouldn't that be hypocritical of me if I did that same thing to Cole?

"Thanks for being nice to me," I said instead. "Not everyone would be so kind after having their life interrupted."

His eyes narrowed as if he knew that wasn't what I'd been about to say. "It's no problem." Sweat glistened on his arms from the afternoon heat. It made his muscles more pronounced when he reached up and scratched the back of his head. "We can leave after this game, if you'd like."

I nodded. We had a long drive home, and after seeing the malicious glares Jessica and her friend threw my way whenever Cole had his back to them, I didn't want to stick around to be the target of their ridicule.

"Cole! Come on!" Raymond called.

"Two minutes," Cole said to me.

As I watched Cole take his turn, I analyzed the moments leading up to my kiss with Kevin, the way Cole's eyes had stared at me while he had another girl wrapped in his arms. It had been the end of my good-girl resolve, but why? If it had been jealousy, wouldn't I have left? Maybe even found a quiet corner where I could break down and cry? The old me certainly wouldn't have kissed the nearest guy. Maybe it was the succubus in me rising to the challenge of Cole's unspoken dare.

That wasn't a comforting thought.

Cole sank his three beanbags effortlessly, making the score twenty-three to seventeen. He acted surprised, as if they were lucky throws, but it made me realize he'd been holding back before.

We thanked Raymond for having us over. Then Cole placed a hand on my lower back—a gesture I was definitely getting used to and liking—and we headed toward the gate leading to the driveway. I couldn't help the grin that spread across my face as we passed a brooding Jessica.

No, Cole wouldn't be calling her anytime soon.

Chapter 11

Morphing into someone else wasn't as easy as Cole had made it appear.

"Try again," he said.

He sat across from me on the couch in our apartment, peering at me through waves of light brown hair. His eyes were now a rich brown. He'd lost his tan, too. It was his third look that morning. Nothing beat the real Cole, though.

"Avery, stop fidgeting." He held my hands in his new, paler ones. "For incubi and succubi, shifting appearances is like slipping into a new pair of shoes. Think five-foot-four blonde with blue eyes and big boobs, and your body does the rest. To shift back, think of your true form and it happens."

Cole guessed I had enough supernatural mojo in me to transform into someone else for a couple of hours—if I ever managed to actually change my appearance. I held a clump of hair up so I could see it and focused. It felt as if I thought *dark-brown hair* forever, but it worked. My hair darkened and became naturally wavy, frizz included.

He frowned. "Shifting into the person you were the day you died doesn't count. Become a sassy redhead with one of those chopped cuts." He waved his hand behind his head at the point where his head met his neck. "Go blue if you want, but the whole idea is to look different."

He was right, of course. I couldn't attend my own funeral resembling the person in the coffin.

I dropped the piece of hair I'd been holding. It had already changed back to its previous color and texture. "Is my body in the morgue?"

"What?" His bushy, brown eyebrows pinched together. They went well with his new Mediterranean features.

"Ew!" I jumped up, shaking my arms as if trying to fling something off them. "Whose body am I in?"

"What?" he repeated, laughing this time. Light brown hair fell over his eyes, and even though they were still brown I could see the real Cole behind them.

I put my hands on my hips to say, *I'm being serious.* I wanted to run, but it wasn't like I could yank my soul out of the skin I was in. I opted for hopping in place, instead. "I need a shower," I announced.

"Wait!" Cole grabbed my arm, obviously fighting back a smile. "You showered this morning."

"I feel dirty!" I gasped. "I can't breathe." I gulped one lungful of air after another.

"You need to calm down." Cole guided me back to the couch. "Put your head between your knees."

My reply came out as short huffs.

"It worked last time."

I did as he said, and it helped, or maybe the aid came from the gentle pressure of Cole's hand caressing my back in a slow circular motion.

"Avery, you're you. The moment your soul was marked as a succubus, you returned to your body. It's the one in the morgue that's not you."

I shook my head, still not convinced. "My parents

know my face. They won't bury a stranger."

"Hell replaced your body with a double." He brushed my hair out of my eyes. "It's the same magic that lets us change our appearance. You're you."

I wiggled my toes. They looked like mine, right down to the crescent-shaped scar I'd gotten climbing on the pier near a friend's lake house. "Promise?"

He used his fingertips to raise my chin. When our gazes met, he said, "I promise."

I rested my cheek on my knee and glanced up at him through a veil of auburn locks. "For someone who doesn't have to breathe, I hyperventilate an awful lot."

"Yes, you do." This time he didn't fight back his smile. "Are you ready to try shifting again?"

I liked the feel of his hand on my back, but I had less than twenty-four hours to pick an alias for my trip back home. I sat up. "Sure, why not."

"Why don't you think of an actress or singer you like and concentrate on shifting into her? It might help to be able to mentally picture the person you're targeting, but don't make it someone famous or you'll have the paparazzi after you."

It was a great idea. Except Gracie and Megan would recognize everyone I could think of. They were my sister and my best friend and had seen all the same shows I had. Turning into Luz wouldn't work because I might be recognized here in lovely Woodridge. So I went with the only other person I could picture in my mind. It wasn't that far of a stretch from my current look, but her forehead was higher than mine, and her skin damn near white. Her eyebrows had a natural arch to them, versus mine that were straighter. Her hair had more red highlights, her cheekbones were high, giving her a sophisticated air, and her eyes were catlike. When Cole scooted backward, letting out a low whistle, I knew I'd done it.

"You chose Chloe, the Reaper?" he choked out.

"She's the only person I could think of that my friends wouldn't recognize." I examined my long, thin fingers. They would take some time to get used to. "Is that bad?"

"No. Only the dead will know her and that's only if she was the one who collected their souls." He pulled me to my feet. "What do you say we give the new you a spin, make sure you can hold it, and top off your energy level while we're at it."

I'd been excited to get out of the apartment until he'd added the last part.

"I'm already chock-full of energy." I felt as if I could run a marathon, and I didn't particularly like to run.

"You didn't spend that much time with what's-his-name." Cole straightened a stack of magazines on the corner of the coffee table, avoiding eye contact. "At least you let him dry hump your leg while you were kissing."

"He did not dry hump my leg!" I said, mortified.

"Yes, he did." Cole grabbed our glasses and went to the kitchen.

I followed. "How would you know? You were busy feeling up Miss Easy." I cringed at how that had to sound—like a jealous girlfriend—but it was too late to censor my words.

"Miss Easy?"

I scratched the back of my head and glanced at the keys hanging on the hook near the door as if they were

145

the most fascinating things I'd ever seen.

Cole placed the glasses in the sink and turned to face me. He didn't quite meet my eyes when he spoke. "Jessica and I kissed. You practically mauled the guy."

Kevin, I silently corrected.

Cole dragged a hand over his hair. "In the beginning, it's hard for us to control our urges once a human's life force starts to flow into us. I suppose he just went with it." Cole passed me, heading toward the bathroom. "What guy wouldn't?"

"What's that supposed to mean?" I stomped after him.

He spun around—one hand on the door and the other on the door jamb—and stared into my flustered gaze. He'd stopped so abruptly, I practically slammed into him.

"It means no straight, single guy will decline the advances of a beautiful girl, and you should be glad he didn't because the more aroused the other person is, the better the fix for us. Raises their level of oxytocin."

"Oxi what?" I asked, interrupting him.

"It's a hormone humans release when they're horny, and he was horny."

I didn't have a comeback for that.

"Were you planning on holding it for me?" He glanced down at his crotch. "Or do you want to give me some privacy?"

"What? Oh! No!" I scurried out of the bathroom.

"You're back to you, by the way," he called after me. "Re-shift and try to avoid moments of extreme emotions."

Like that was possible with him talking about other people, sex, and hormones.

We ended up at a coffeehouse only fifteen minutes from our apartment, Cole resembling an Italian model and me impersonating Death's right-hand girl.

"Stop fidgeting," Cole whispered into my ear after we placed our order. "A younger version of Chloe suits you for this assignment."

Being that succubi could only shift to an appearance within five years of the age we were when we died, I couldn't pull off an exact clone of the Reaper who'd collected my soul. I'd created a damn good image of what she might have looked like at eighteen, though.

In our new forms, we didn't have to worry about being recognized, so we didn't have to drive an hour away to find a potential donor. I ordered a frozen coffee, and Cole got a health shake with protein added. We sat at a table near the window.

"Thanks for the beverage," I said, licking whipped cream off my paper straw.

His mouth twisted to the side as he watched me.

"What?" I asked.

"You're almost too sweet for Hell."

I glanced away. If he only knew.

Cole placed his hand on mine. "Avery, may I ask you a personal question?"

I wet my lips. A yes would mean he could ask me anything, but was I ready to discuss my sins with him? Then again, if he did ask what I'd done to end up in Hell, I'd be able to ask him the same. My desire to know more about him outweighed my hesitation.

"Sure."

"How'd you die?" His thumb drew lazy circles on the palm of my hand, sending tiny shivers through me.

You're here to stalk unsuspecting guys with the singular goal of siphoning months from their lives. This is not a date.

I didn't move my hand, though. Cole's belief in me had me wanting to accept my fate, instead of curling up into a tiny ball and hoping Lilith took mercy on my soul when she punished me for disobeying her.

I told him about the party, how my sister and I had ended up there, about the loose railing.

"You think you died saving your sister?"

"Yeah. For a moment—when Wyatt first told me my soul flickers an odd shade of gray—I thought maybe I'd killed us both. But then I remember we'd only found my obituary, so that has to mean Gracie's alive."

Cole's thumb stopped gliding over my palm. "When did you talk to Wyatt?"

I'd forgotten that I hadn't mentioned Wyatt's visit. It wasn't that I was trying to keep secrets from him. "The other night, after you dropped me off at home. He was waiting outside our apartment when I got upstairs." His hand started to slide from mine, but I tightened my grip. I couldn't figure out if it was jealousy I saw in Cole's eyes or hatred for the nephilim. "We talked. That's it."

He shook his head. "You're a big girl. You can do what you want."

What I wanted was to attend college with my friends, for us to travel to Key West and other fun places, and to eventually marry a nice guy. A pang of sorrow gripped my heart at knowing those things would never happen now that I was a succubus.

I squeezed his hand. "Anyway, from what I can

remember, yeah, I think I kept Gracie from falling off the porch."

"Even if your sister had died, being part of a freak accident wouldn't have made you a killer, Avery. Bad things happen, and sometimes good people die." He slipped his hand from mine and stroked my forearm. "Like you."

He let his eyes shift back to his beautiful ocean-blue ones. Seeing them like that scrambled my emotions, which were already very fragile from talking about my sister.

"Cole…" My voice cracked when I whispered his name. "You can't keep doing that."

His eyes narrowed. "Doing what?"

He still had his hand on my arm. I leaned back because I couldn't think straight with him touching me. "Gazing into my eyes the way you do. Acting like you want there to be more between us." It had to be the incubus in Cole that made me attracted to him. Although you'd think a succubus would be immune to her counterpart's charms. It could also be that he was nice to me, but he couldn't always have been this amiable a person. Not if he'd ended up in Hell. He had to have a darker side. "You've already made it perfectly clear you don't want me that way, so stop flirting."

He laced his fingers behind his head and stared over my shoulder in thought. His eyes were brown again. I sipped my drink in silence. The seconds stretched on.

"I never said I didn't want you." Cole pulled the straw up and down in his cup as he spoke. "I said if you and I were to sleep together, it would be your doing. You're in a vulnerable place right now. I won't take advantage of you, nor will I allow someone else to."

I smiled. "My knight in shining armor who encourages me to have meaningless encounters with strange men."

He chuckled. "We do what we have to do to survive, and I'd prefer if you stuck with teens. Leave the men to Lilith's more experienced employees."

Cole waited for two women to pass.

"Avery, if I could protect you from this life, I would. And I was serious when I said Lilith won't allow you to avoid the job. If you don't mark souls, she'll punish you, and in her twisted mind, the pit would be too generous for a disobedient succubus. She'll exploit your innocent nature by selling your services to the highest bidder, and they aren't attractive millionaires."

From Cole's previous warnings, I'd suspected as much. "Why would Lilith need money?"

"It wouldn't be about the money. It'd be about breaking your resolve. Teaching you a lesson. I know this for a fact."

"Did she…to you?" Was that how he knew so much?

"No, but I've met others like us, and I believe them when they say Lilith isn't a demon to cross."

I nodded. "My turn to ask a question."

"Sure." He spread his arms wide. "I'm an open book."

I thought about asking him what he had done to land himself in Hell, but that would likely lead to questions about why I was there. So instead, I asked, "What was it like when you were alive?"

He sucked in a breath, letting it escape slowly.

"Life was much harder, that's for sure. That's one thing about being around for as long as I have. You can appreciate things like cars and indoor plumbing."

My eyes widened in disbelief. "How long have you been an incubus?"

"Since this country's Civil War."

"That was…" A long time ago. I thought back to my U.S. history class. "In eighteen…" The war had spanned the course of a few years. I tried to remember when it had started. "Sixty-one?"

"Yes. I died in 1862."

I leaned forward. "How old are you?"

"Nineteen. I've just been this age for a long time." His eyes narrowed. "Why are you making a face like you're about to be sick?"

I grimaced. "I kissed an old man."

He threw a stack of napkins at me. "Shut up! Besides, *I* kissed *you*."

"Yes. That was your doing." And yeah, he'd had ulterior motives behind that kiss, but *he* had still kissed *me*.

"Touché." A wicked smirk jerked the corner of his lips upward. "You liked it, and don't try to deny it. I've been around long enough to know."

I lifted a shoulder and let it fall. There really wasn't any point in trying to act as if I hadn't enjoyed our kiss. He had to have felt my heart hammering against his chest and my knees losing the ability to support my weight. I answered by echoing his sentiments. "Touché."

He sipped his shake.

"So you lived in the 1800s. Did you have a big family?" I asked, wanting to know more about his past.

151

"There were seven of us. My parents, of course, then I had an older brother, two younger brothers, and a baby sister."

I could tell his thoughts had drifted far away and that time hadn't allowed him to miss them less. I drank my coffee. Would time be that cruel to me, too? Would I forever long to see my family again?

I already knew it'd be the latter. For me, true death would never come. I'd never meet them in Heaven, and no way did I want to see them in Hell.

"Were you a soldier?" I asked, wondering if he'd died in the war.

"No. My father insisted I stay back and take care of my mother and younger siblings." He tapped his cup on the table as he spoke.

I nodded, waiting to hear how he'd died, but instead of saying more, he stood. "Now's our chance. Follow my lead, and don't let your disguise slip."

There was something about the glint in his eyes that told me he was up to something. Had I known what it was, I wouldn't have followed him.

He tossed his cup out and then addressed a Latino guy waiting near the pick-up counter. "My friend and I have a bet going. I was hoping you'd help settle it." He did this funny wave with his hand that I'd never seen him do before.

"Sure, *hombre*." Latino Guy stuffed his wallet into his back pocket. "What is it?"

"Please don't take offense. You see, we"—Cole pointed to me and him—"couldn't help noticing you when you came into the store, and well, I recently told her I'm not into girls. She either doesn't believe me or thinks it's fun to try to guess my type."

Latino Guy slid back half a step. Cole plunged on, talking quickly.

"I told her you don't play for my team. She bet me I'm wrong. Loser has to kiss you, if you're willing. Either way, I'd appreciate it if you'd tell us who's right so I can rub it in her face for a while."

I fought to not let my jaw hit the sticky floor. Don't get me wrong, Latino Guy wasn't unsightly. He had dark features and from the chest muscles pushing against his T-shirt, he either clocked a lot of hours at the gym or had a physical job. I just couldn't believe Cole would approach a stranger and say he could kiss one of us. Correction—me, because no way was Latino Guy gay.

He smiled. "I'm not gay."

Cole slapped my arm with the back of his hand. Not hard. "I told you," he said in a tone high enough to make Latino Guy believe Cole did like guys. "A bet's a bet. Unless you're chicken or not his type."

"It's okay, man," Latino Guy said. "I'm not one to force a girl to do something she doesn't want to."

Cole nonchalantly kicked my shoe. I needed the extra energy for my trip with Wyatt, which was the only reason I went along with Cole's game.

"I don't make bets unless I'm willing to pay up, and—" I wet my lips. If Latino Guy said no, I'd just have to find someone else. "—I'm glad I was wrong."

He hesitated, seeming to think it over, but Cole and I weren't playing fair. We hadn't turned into ugly people, and Hell made sure that humans were overly attracted to us.

"You're in control," Latino Guy said, and I took that to mean he was letting me decide what type of kiss it would be.

I glared at Cole. "Are you planning to watch?"

"Sorry." He held his hands in front of him. His attention switched to Latino Guy. "She's all yours for the length of one kiss."

I led Latino Guy down the empty hallway toward the bathrooms. He put an arm around my back and pulled me closer. He smelled like the outdoors and musk. It was a pleasant mix on him. "*Chica*," he whispered, "your friend *must* be gay to give you up so easily."

"Yeah, lucky me." I placed my hands on his hips because I didn't know what else to do with them.

If I didn't know Cole was nearby, I'd have allowed myself a moment to admit Latino Guy was sexy. His accent was just thick enough to melt a girl's willpower.

Latino Guy smiled. It was a nice smile. "*Yo nunca trataría a chica así,*" he whispered against my lips. "I would never treat a girl like that."

His mouth met mine. When my lips parted, he kissed me more fully. To my surprise, his hand never wandered from its spot between my shoulder blades. His free hand settled gently against my cheek as our kiss muffled his soft growl. I could feel the flood of his energy streaming into me, awakening my hunger for more, but I didn't press up against him. I wasn't about to have Cole telling me I'd molested another guy. Latino Guy savored our kiss, drawing it out to be something any girl would remember for a long time. Lilith would love him, but I didn't sense that our kiss would leave even the smallest of stains on his soul. Still, his life force was strong, more potent than Kevin's had been.

Latino Guy was the one to break our kiss. I went in for one more peck. My cheeks grew warm, embarrassed that I'd done it. He held me close a moment longer.

"*Un beso de tú y tu amigo sería cambiar equipos*," he said, deep and throaty, and then lowered his voice to a whisper. "One kiss from you and your friend would switch teams." He released his hold on me.

I sheepishly rejoined Cole. He was reading the flyers on the event board near the creamer station. Even though he was pretending to be gay and no one knew who we were, I felt self-conscious. I, Avery Caroline Williams, had just kissed a random stranger and liked it. Okay, Cole seemed to be able to pick desirable potential targets who were not only cute but phenomenal kissers. I supposed over a century and a half of experience would grant a demon that much. What worried me, though, was I couldn't tell if it was my new succubus nature that had me enjoying kissing different guys or if it was simply a guilty pleasure I'd never succumbed to before now.

I glanced back at Latino Guy. He had both hands resting on the counter and shook his head before grabbing his coffee and leaving the store.

Cole bent closer to me. "It'll take a few minutes for his body to adjust to the loss. He'll be fine by the time he hits the main road."

I felt as if I could fly, and he needed a nap. It made sense, if I thought about it.

"He was right," Cole said as we watched Latino Guy get in a slick, white sports car. "You're an excellent kisser. You could make a celibate guy reconsider."

My gaze shot to Cole. "You were listening?"

"He didn't whisper it."

Latino Guy hadn't spoken quietly when he'd spoken in Spanish, but he had when he'd repeated in English. "You speak Spanish?"

"Sí. Y me mata verte en brazos de otro chico, pero hacemos lo que tenemos que hacer para sobrevivir." Cole dug his keys out of his front pocket and left the coffeehouse.

"Hold on! *I* don't speak Spanish." I quickly caught up to him. "I know *sí* is yes, and *chico* is boy. You have to translate the rest for me."

Cole laughed. "No. I don't."

Chapter 12

On Friday, I woke at an ungodly hour, surprised to find myself in a bed. I'd fallen asleep on the couch and wondered if I'd sleepwalked into the bedroom or if Cole had carried me here. The sound of voices drifted into the room along with the mouthwatering aroma of sautéed onions.

I threw on a pair of black jeans and a white shirt, ran a brush through my tangled hair, and went to see who our visitors were. Luz and Nick sat on the stools by the counter that separated the kitchen from the family room.

"Cole, there are some things you just can't keep a secret," Luz said, sipping something pink from a short glass. "Avery!" She hopped off her seat and gave me a hug like we were long-lost friends.

I giggled and hugged her back. I got a "What's up?" from Nick, who yawned.

"Here." Luz handed me a glass with pink stuff in it. "I had Cole make you one, too."

Cole's and my gazes met. I held up the glass and said thanks. He smiled and went back to scrambling eggs with no less than four vegetables mixed in. An empty brown grocery bag lay discarded on the floor next to him. Wyatt would be here in an hour to pick me up for our trip, and Cole was entertaining mortal guests. That wasn't how I'd expected the day to begin.

"Luz brought breakfast," he said, obviously seeing the confusion on my face.

If Cole wasn't worried, then I wouldn't. I tasted my drink. Thick, creamy liquid danced over my taste buds and coated my throat. It was sweet and rich. "This is good. What's in it?"

"Trust me, you don't want to know," Nick replied with a grunt. "Luz unplugged the coffeemaker and insisted our morning jolt come from Cole's health crap. She's lucky she's cute, or I'd have shoved her out of the apartment and made my own damn cup."

That explained why I didn't smell coffee. I realized that every other morning Cole had a cup waiting for me when I woke.

"You like the shake and you know it," Luz retorted, bumping Nick with her shoulder. "He's just crabby because I woke him up and made him drive me over here."

"You called before five. Friends don't call that early," Nick said before I could ask Luz why she wanted to be here so early and Nick why he'd agreed to drive her if he didn't want to be awake.

Nick rested his forehead on the countertop. I could see why Cole liked them. They bickered the way close friends sometimes did. It gave a sense of normalcy in our crazy existence.

Too nervous about attending my own wake to sit, I grabbed a pen and pad of scratch paper from the counter and started to doodle. "Luz, what secret were you talking about?"

"That Ian's coming, of course."

"Why does that name sound familiar?" I asked, trying to recall if Cole mentioned him before.

"I asked about him the other day at the gathering we went to." Cole grabbed plates from the clean dishwasher.

Now, I remembered. Ian was the guy whose detour took him to Louisiana or was it Louisville?

"And he's coming here? This morning?" Silently, I added, when we have plans?

"Yep," Luz said before Cole could answer. "And Cole knows he's my dream-guy."

"He's too old for you," Cole said.

"A girl can fantasize." Luz shook her head. "I heard from Nick who heard from Hunter that he'll be here around six." She checked her cell phone and smiled, showing off her dimple. "That's in, like, ten minutes."

I had to admire her blatant openness about her crush on Ian.

Nick raised his head, peering at us through sandy-blond bangs. "And I'm paying for opening my big mouth." His forehead met the countertop again.

"Serves you right for not knowing better," Cole said, scooping eggs onto a plate and placing it in front of Luz along with a slice of whole-wheat toast. "Avery, want some?"

"No, thanks." With the knots, there was no room for eggs in my stomach.

He glanced at my drawing. "A kitten?"

I shrugged. Since I was eight, the cartoon kitty had been the fallback character I'd draw whenever I was nervous.

Cole made himself and Nick a plate. Cole ate standing up.

How was I supposed to shift into a different person

with Luz and Nick around? I wanted to ask Cole, but it would have been rude to drag him into the bedroom to hold a hushed conversation, so I sipped my health shake instead. It really was tasty and seemed to ease my trepidation a little.

Someone knocked on the door. Luz bounced up and got it before Cole or I could move.

"Luz, what a pleasant surprise," a silky voice said.

Luz giggled as she closed the door.

Ian was tall with broad shoulders and a small waist. He had sun-streaked, golden-brown hair, piercing lapis eyes, and a hint of a mustache and goatee.

He came in and straddled the stool Luz had vacated. "Got a plate for me?"

Cole fixed him one, emptying the skillet. I squeezed by him to the sink and began to wash the dishes as a way to keep busy. Luz snatched the dishtowel from Cole and shooed him out of the way.

"The cook doesn't clean," Luz said. "Ian, take your plate and the guys into the other room."

Like the other room couldn't be seen from the galley-style kitchen.

Luz made sure they were settled on the couch in the family room before whispering, "If only he was twenty years younger, the things I'd let him do to me."

"Luz!" I leaned back and glanced over the counter at Ian's profile.

"Admit it," she whispered, peeking at the guys right along with me. "If you weren't so smitten with Cole, you'd be drooling over Ian with me."

Mortified that Cole might have heard, I quickly turned back to the sink. "I'm not smitten with Cole," I hissed.

"Then you're in denial. It's cool, I had a crush on him when we first met, but he's too nice a guy for me." She paused. "He's the brother I wish I had."

I handed her the skillet I'd just washed. "I thought you had two brothers."

"I do, but I like to pretend we aren't related."

I laughed.

"But Ian." She stepped back to ogle him again, shook her head, and stepped forward. "He's like a god." Wrong end of the supernatural spectrum, but I didn't correct her. "He reminds me of Thor. Did you see the movie?"

I had. I grabbed the last couple of glasses from the counter to give me an excuse to take another look at Ian. He did resemble the actor who'd played Thor, only with short hair.

"Plus, I'm a sucker for a guy with an accent," Luz admitted.

She would have loved Latino Guy. Luz put the last glass in the cupboard. I'd just drained the water in the sink when a warm hand rested on my waist. A dirty dish went in the sink from the other side of me.

"I'll wash it," Ian said.

"It's okay," I told him. "Sponge is still soapy."

"Thanks, luv." He winked at Luz.

Luz's bronze cheeks turned three shades of pink.

When the kitchen was clean, Luz and I joined the guys. Nick scooted over to make room on the couch for Luz to plop down next to him, which she did. He even shifted so that his knee rested against hers. Cole caught me watching them and winked as if the best kept secret of their little group was that everyone except Luz and Nick noticed how well those two fit together.

Luz invited us to go with her and Nick to the beach, but Ian politely declined, saying he was in town on business. Cole made up an excuse for us. Around seven, Nick told Luz they'd interrupted our morning long enough and dragged her to the door.

"So you're the new succubus," Ian said, after the others had left. He sat on the couch with his arms on the back cushion, completely at ease in our small apartment.

I had my legs curled under me on the other end of the couch. "So you're the incubus Cole mentioned."

Ian looked at Cole, who paced back and forth in front of us. "I like her."

Cole glanced out the sliding glass doors as he replied, "Well, don't become fond of her, because if Lilith discovers she's in New York, we'll never see her again."

"If Lilith discovers she's in New York, your arse will be on the fire. You shouldn't have introduced her to that neph."

"It wasn't my idea." Cole went back to pacing.

Ian turned to me, so I said, "Hunter suggested it."

"And told her he'd help her even if I didn't."

"Ah, yes. How is Hunter?" Ian asked.

"Good. Keeping under the radar," Cole replied.

"And throwing his friends into the frying pan," Ian said. "And where is he now?"

"Staying as far away from me and Avery as he can, until after the trip."

Ian shook his head. "Typical cambion. Suggests a dangerous mission and then disappears."

"Do you know a lot of demon offspring?" I asked.

"I've met my fair share over the years. Most have a

reckless side. It's in their DNA. Hunter's not bad. A bit loose with the drinking, if you let him get started, but there are worse vices that a half-demon teen could have."

"Sounds like most the human teens I know." Or was that *knew*?

"True," Ian said. "Tell me, how are you settling into your new role?"

"I just love it." I brought by knees to my chest. "What girl wouldn't want to die young and discover she's become one of Hell's prostitutes?"

Ian chuckled. "I'm definitely going to like having you around, but I prefer to think of myself as Hell's recruiter, corrupting the pure and stealing a few years of life from those who'll never miss them."

"How do you know those years aren't missed?" I asked.

"One can't miss what they don't realize they have." Ian leaned forward and grabbed his glass of juice from the coffee table. "Unless, of course, you choose to drain a person completely and hand deliver their soul to the pit. While ruthless, such an act will win you favors with Lilith."

"Which doesn't interest me," I assured him. Curious, I asked, "Can we kill someone with a kiss?" Because kissing was all I intended to do with strangers.

"No. Kisses are for quick fixes," he said "You can shag 'em to death, if you wanted to. One mind-blowing f—"

"Ian, don't be crass," Cole snapped.

Ian's glare bounced between Cole and me. "How green are you?"

I glanced down at my socks, cheeks on fire.

"She's been dead less than a week, Ian," Cole said. "We haven't gotten to that level of detail, yet."

"It's basic Succubus 101," Ian replied. "Right under the need to be around humans. Kiss and add days to your health, plus gain the ability to alter your appearance. For a bigger, more powerful fix that lasts three times as long, sleep with them. If you want to earn points with Hell, rock their soul right out of their body, and Hell will see to it that you're almost as strong as a second-level demon."

"Is that what you do?" I asked, disgusted. "Or you, Cole?"

Was that why Cole would be out so late? He was screwing girls literally to death.

"Hell would reward him with better accommodations if he were," Ian replied. "And I'm okay with the heightened senses and added strength. I've no desire to go for glory, too."

Cole gave Ian a look that would have had most people backing out of the room. "It took some doing to get Avery to kiss a guy. So do me a favor and refrain from scaring her while you're in New York."

"He's coming?" I blurted, and I didn't care if I was rude. "Why?"

"Because Cole trusts me about as far as he can throw me," Wyatt said from behind us. I hadn't heard him come in. "And you can believe Ian when he says they don't kill people. Their souls would be black."

As reassuring as that was, I had other things on my mind. "Cole, if you don't trust Wyatt, why aren't you coming with?"

I'd have felt much safer with him by my side rather than an incubus I'd just met.

"If both our signatures drop off the grid at the same time, it'd draw attention. Ian's the only incubus I trust not to say anything to anyone."

Ian set the glass down. "Last thing either of you want to reach Lilith is stories of how the newest succubus outsmarted Hell's tracking capabilities."

It was almost seven thirty, the time we were scheduled to leave. I quickly changed into black slacks and a black top. Cole had purchased our tickets and reserved a rental car the day Wyatt agreed to help. The plan was to fly into Westchester County International Airport, drive to Warwick, pop into my wake, and then hightail it back out of New York on the six o'clock flight to Chicago. I'd wanted to stay for the funeral on Saturday, as well, but Cole insisted we limit the trip to one day.

****

Since there was a chance Lilith might notice my signature drop off her radar, Ian felt it would be better if he and I met up with Wyatt away from the apartment and then drove to the airport. That way, should Lilith be waiting for me when I got back, Wyatt still had a chance of remaining anonymous. Ian wasn't worried about the consequence he might face.

"It wouldn't be the first time my actions upset her, and it won't be the last," he'd said with a smile.

Brave words, I thought. But then again, Ian might not have a weakness to exploit like I did.

Wyatt left the apartment ten minutes before Ian and I did. Cole and I stood near the door waiting on Ian, who was in the bathroom.

"Your cell phone's turned off?" Cole asked. "No point in masking your supernatural signature if Lilith can track your whereabouts through today's technology."

I held it up to show Cole it was. "I wish you were coming," I said. It was lame of me, but I had a feeling his quiet strength would have been nice to have around when I saw my family again.

"Me too," he admitted. "You could change your mind and not go."

We'd all worked very hard on this plan to back out now. He must have taken my silence as answer enough.

"Don't turn your phone on until you're back in Illinois."

"I won't." He'd already told me this. If I needed to make a call, I was to use Wyatt's or Ian's phone.

"*Venir a mi casa a salvo.*" Cole cupped my face in his hands, angling my mouth up to his. His lips met mine tenderly. Mine parted without encouragement. I held his wrists, savoring the taste of his kiss until energy started to flow into me.

"Cole, no." My words came out muffled. I put a hand on his chest and tried to push him away. I didn't want to take from him again.

"Don't." His arm slid around my waist. "Please," he pleaded and kissed me more intensely. Urgently. Forcing even more power into me. My body quivered, devouring the energy. I abandoned my protest and leaned into him. Just when I thought I might explode from the forces now in me, he broke our kiss and rested his forehead on mine.

"Cole, what did you say a minute ago?"

"Come home to me safe."

Chapter 13

I almost didn't leave.

Almost didn't let go of Cole.

Almost brought his mouth back to mine.

I hated how pale he was when I'd left the apartment. I tried not to remember him, staggering sideways to lean against the wall for support. He'd given up too much, saying I might need it. I didn't even want to think about what he'd be doing to regain his strength while I was away.

Ian hadn't said anything when he'd come out of the bathroom, but by the way his gaze had traveled from Cole to me, I knew he'd heard our conversation. I wouldn't allow myself to read into Cole's actions or his words. He'd kissed me to force more energy into me. That was all. If I got caught taking this trip, he'd be in trouble right along with me. He was covering his own ass.

That didn't mean my lips weren't still warm from our kiss or that my heart wasn't sprinting through my chest. It didn't keep Ian from giving me a sidelong glance every few seconds. I fidgeted with the butterfly necklace I'd chosen for the trip.

Ian cleared his throat. "Are you okay?"

I folded my hands in my lap. "I'm fine."

"Could've fooled me," he mumbled.

Ian drove us to a small church not far from the

apartment. It was in the opposite direction from the airport. Wyatt's silver coupe was parked in the back. Ian pulled into the parking space next to it and cut the engine.

"First things first. We need to change." As soon as the words were out of his mouth, his golden brown hair morphed into a black crew cut and his olive skin turned dark brown. He chose to resemble an athletic man five years younger than his true form. His gaze—now gray—met mine. "Your turn."

I thought of Chloe and felt the slight shift of my features. I waited a few seconds, knowing my transformation wouldn't be quite as instant as his had been. One look at my bright pink nail polish, and I knew I'd become a younger version of the Reaper.

"Interesting choice," Ian commented. He reached in the glove compartment and pulled out two small pouches and handed me one.

I eyed it curiously, pressing against the burlap. Whatever was in it felt lumpy. "What do I do with it?"

"It's a hex bag. Keep it on you, in your handbag or pocket. It's supposed to hide a person from demons."

"But we are demons."

"If we lose ourselves, we'll know it works a little too well." When I continued to stare at him, perplexed, he added, "I know a girl who's into voodoo. I've seen her do some pretty amazing things: hold off hellhounds long enough to allow a person to get their affairs in order, chase away a spirit, and return souls to their bodies."

"A soul can jump back into its body?" This was exciting news. "Could she help me back into mine?"

"It only works for people who haven't passed onto

the other side, meaning their soul hasn't gone through Judgment, yet. Besides, whose body do you think you're in?"

"Right." I'd forgotten Hell had already shoved me back into mine.

We exited the car. Ian went up to the driver's side of Wyatt's car. "I'm driving."

Wyatt opened his mouth but appeared to think twice about arguing. He got out and trudged to the other side. I climbed in back to avoid any more of Ian's scrutiny. That, and I doubted Wyatt would sit in the back of his own vehicle. As soon as we were seated, Wyatt stretched out his abilities and began to cloak my signature along with his. I felt only the slightest of sensations, like the brush of feathers caressing my skin.

We made the drive to the airport in silence. We got there exactly one hour before our nine thirty flight. That meant we had less than sixty minutes to make it through security and to our gate.

"The hex bag should keep your signature muted should you and Wyatt become separated, but to be safe, try not to be more than a few feet away from him."

Ian waited for me to nod before passing the long, twisting line of travelers waiting to have their personal items x-rayed. He stopped behind a businessman in the much shorter priority line.

I grabbed his wrist. "How will we get past security?" I whispered, panic rising in me. How had we not thought of this?

"Take out your driver's license," he instructed.

I no longer looked anything like my photo. I swallowed, fearing this was the end of our trip. Ian brushed his thumb over my mug shot and then did the same to Wyatt's. I gaped. Staring back at me from my ID was the new me. I couldn't help the smile that graced my lips when I saw the name, Chloe R. Smith from Arlington Heights. I glanced at Wyatt's license. He was now Angel M. Postor. From his scowl, I didn't think he liked his alias.

"It's just an illusion. It won't last long." Ian handed us our boarding passes.

We breezed through security. The plane was loading when we reached our gate, and I had another surprise when we boarded.

"I've never flown first class," I said, sitting in the window seat at Ian's insistence. Wyatt sat behind me, Ian in the aisle seat next to me. He pulled out a book.

I hadn't thought to bring something to read, so I stared out the window and watched the miniature world below us. It was a beautiful day for flying: blue skies with the occasional fluffy white cloud. The air in the plane was stale, but the stench of jet fuel wasn't as strong as it had been while we'd taxied down the runway.

I tried not to think about Cole, but it was hard to forget how his lips had felt against mine. It was the second time he'd kissed me, and both times were to force energy into me. I'd have said he was only doing his job—showing the new succubus the ropes—but his words left me confused. "Come home to me safe." Was he getting used to having me as a roommate? Maybe even developing deeper feelings for me? I mean, it wasn't as if he'd said, "Be safe" or "Get your butt home quickly." Or was he only afraid of having to explain to Lilith where I'd gone if I didn't make it home?

I was sure my disguise would slip if I continued to

analyze Cole's comment, so I thought about my wake and seeing my parents, instead. Soon I'd know if my need to check on Gracie was just the normal concern of a big sister or a deep-seated intuition that she needed to hear what I'd failed to tell her before I'd died.

We were over an hour into the flight when I couldn't take being inside my head any longer. I twisted in my seat so I was facing Ian. "How did you and Cole meet?"

He placed a bookmark between the pages of his novel. "I was his mentor. We lived in London at the time."

That made him Cole's oldest friend. No wonder Cole trusted him so much. With the rumble of the engine and the spacing of the seats in first class, I felt fairly confident we couldn't be overheard. Still, I kept my voice low when I asked my next question.

"May I ask you how long you've been—" I let the sentence dangle.

"Over five hundred years."

My jaw dropped. He'd been an immortal for half a millennium. That was a long time to live. I took a moment to process that and then asked in awe, "Have you spent all of them on Earth?"

"Yes. I suppose I've been lucky. Not many have experienced what I have. I spent a lifetime exploring the Louvre—"

"In France?"

He chuckled. "Is there another? I've seen kings crowned and empires fall."

"Don't you find it lonely?" I asked.

"In our line of work, luv, one is never lonely. Not in the literal sense, anyway. We've got to make human contact every five or six days or die trying. Cole did tell you that if you eat and sleep you burn through energy slower, right?"

"He did. So you've always embraced what you've become?"

"I wouldn't say that." He paused when the flight attendant stopped next to us for our drink orders. He accepted our coffees and cookies, handing me mine so she wouldn't have to reach over him. She lingered a little too long, mesmerized by his mere presence, I think. When she left, he continued. "It didn't take me long to realize there are fates far worse than being expected to keep company with a pretty girl." He paused thoughtfully. "Like being told who to shag."

I remembered what Cole had said about how Lilith deals with difficult succubi and incubi. "You warned Cole about Lilith's punishments."

"Someone had to."

I bent closer. "Were the women that bad?"

The image of a three-hundred-pound woman with black teeth and warts popped into my head.

"Women I could have handled. Girls younger than yourself, stealing their last breath, I could not. I'll tell you the same thing I told Cole when he'd first been changed into an incubus, do not get on Lilith's bad side. She'll know your limits, and that's exactly what you'll face."

My heart went out to those poor girls who'd died decades before they should've, and to Ian for being forced to be the cause of their early demise.

He shrugged. "I can't say I was a saint when I was human. I did bang half the ladies in waiting and several daughters of noble birth, one on her wedding day."

"Ian, you dog." I couldn't stop the giggle that bubbled up from my chest. He sounded so old-fashioned and cliché. "Were you ever caught?"

"Oh, yeah." He took a drink of his coffee. "It wasn't the smartest idea for a knight to bed a lady in her husband's home, but I was young and horny, and she was full of life and willing. Her husband was a stuffy nobleman three times her age from the country to the east. Her marriage was one of convenience. I was doing her a favor."

I smiled at the thought of Ian in chainmail. "I'm sure you were. So what happened?"

"The groom walked in on us. The tosser stood there and watched until we finished. Then he ran me through with my own blade." Ian rolled his eyes. "I learned the hard way never to have my back to the door."

"Isn't stabbing someone in the back considered cowardly?" I asked.

"Very." I got the impression that Ian didn't regret his actions even though they'd cost him his life. He only regretted getting caught. He smiled wickedly. "She was the first person I visited when I returned to Earth, and I didn't bother with a disguise. I took her every night until her husband finally discovered us, and this time, I ran him through with his blade, only I made sure I could see the light leave his eyes."

"Remind me not to piss you off." I tore open my cookies and nibbled.

Ian laughed. "My actions angered the bejeevus out of Lilith. She didn't like that I'd returned home for vengeance."

Not what I wanted to hear on a flight back to my

home.

Ian patted my knee. "We'll be in New York for less than eight hours. Just don't lose that hex bag and stay close to Wyatt." He paused. "Know that, should you be discovered, I'll do whatever's in my power to protect Cole from going down with you."

"Me, too." I didn't even want to think about the partners Lilith would choose for me if I messed this up. "Have you mentored a lot of demons?"

He shook his head. "A dozen or so. Cole is my favorite by far."

"I'm sure it was like stepping into old shoes for him." He certainly had no problem finding a date.

Ian's brows knitted together. "You're assuming Cole deserved eternal damnation. That his actions when he was human were what put him in Hell."

"Isn't that why a soul is sent to the pit?

"I may have enjoyed the company of many a woman when I was human, and you may have committed an unforgivable sin, but that's not the only way to end up in Lilith's clutches." He opened his book. "Do yourself a favor and get to know someone before you pass judgment on them."

I flinched at that. Ian was right. I'd formed an opinion of Cole without learning who he was, but it wasn't like I'd met him in church. He was comfortable with what he was. He didn't appear to be sorry that he embraced being Hell's recruiter. In fact, his ability to select souls who'd provide a substantial fix was scarily impressive. But had I been wrong to assume he deserved his fate? I had to know.

"How did Cole end up an incubus?" When Ian ignored me, I shoved him. It was like trying to shove a century-old oak tree. "Ian, tell me!"

"It's not my story to tell. We'll be there soon."

Chapter 14

We arrived at the funeral home just before two.

"I think it's best if we avoid long conversations," Ian said as I slipped out the back of our rental car. "But if someone asks, you had a class with the deceased."

I had to fight the urge to run to the building. This would be the last time I'd see my friends and family if I didn't find a way to inform them that I was alive. My heart slammed against my chest as I tried to decide who'd take the news about my resurrection the best.

Wyatt grabbed my arm, slowing our pace until Ian was a few steps ahead of us. "Your soul just went from orange, which typically means on edge or worried, to black."

"We're at my wake. Black seems fitting to me."

"It's the color of deception, Avery. The shade a soul takes on when it's planning to do something it knows it shouldn't."

"And according to Hell, we shouldn't be here."

"True, but if that were the case it would have been black when we started the trip. No, I don't think that's the reason for the sudden change." He stopped. "Cole trusts you'll stick to the plan, I'm risking exposure to help you because you have a noble reason to be here, and Ian let himself be dragged into this because Cole's his best mate."

"I know that, Wyatt."

"Then you realize that telling anyone we see today who you really are would be a betrayal of my, Ian's, and Cole's trust. We go in there, you silently say your good-byes to your immediate family and closest friends, deliver your message to Gracie as a friend of a friend, and we leave. Got it?"

"Yes."

I wished the color of my soul hadn't given my thoughts away. The last thing I needed was a speech from Wyatt to make me feel guilty about wanting someone to know the truth.

"Is there a problem?" Ian asked. He'd reached the door.

Wyatt looked at me.

I bit my bottom lip, not really sure what I would do once I saw Gracie or Megan, and replied, "No."

An air of despair hit me the moment we entered the funeral home. We approached the gold and black easel set up in the lobby. Wyatt laced his fingers through mine and gave a reassuring squeeze.

"You can do this," he said.

I forced myself to read the sign.

Avery Caroline Williams

I'd died at the age of eighteen. I'd known this, but reading my name on that board made it real. That girl would never attend college. She wouldn't take fabulous vacations with her friends or get married. She'd never grow up.

I'd been dead a week, yet it wasn't until I read my name on that damned easel that I felt like I'd actually died. I breathed in a ragged breath and swiped at the tears running down my cheeks.

"Careful not to let your disguise slip." Wyatt

rubbed a hand over my trembling arm. "Check the rest of the board. It's just you, Avery. Your sister must be okay."

At the sound of his voice, I allowed my gaze to move downward. Just one more name, Charles Weinstein. I hoped he'd lived a longer life than I had.

Ian handed me a tissue. "Are you ready to go inside?"

I replied with a weak, "Yes."

I knew today would be depressing, but I hadn't prepared myself properly. There was barely a free chair in the room. Music played softly in the background. When we first entered, I didn't recognize anyone, but then I started to truly see their faces: my great aunt and uncle whose names escape me to this day, my next-door neighbors, the parents of the four-year-old I used to babysit every Tuesday, a group of girls in my English class, and Jessica Meyers, who I'd have sworn hated my guts—all either crying or with their heads down.

Wyatt gave a light tug on my hand, indicating we needed to move. The upbeat tune of one of my favorite songs flowed out of the unseen speakers. It was a song I'd listen to whenever I needed to climb out of a funk. I smiled. Just hearing it helped my feet carry me farther into the room. We caught up to Ian, who'd stopped to peruse photographs on a long table. Wyatt and I stepped to his side, away from the aisle so no one would bump into us. My senior-year school picture sat in the middle of the table next to a guest book. To the right of it was a picture of me and Gracie when we were little. It had been taken in front of our favorite castle at the theme park in Florida. She wore a blue princess dress, and I wore a pink one. We both had on glass slippers, which in reality were clear plastic sandals. There was a picture of me with my parents and a collage of Megan and me. Big colorful letters at the top read *Best Friends Forever*. I sniffed and wiped my nose with the tissue. Ian grabbed my free hand for a brief moment. While we hadn't known each other long, the gesture made me glad he was there.

An older woman in a black dress joined Ian as he examined the photos. "She was a beautiful girl."

"Yes, she is," Ian replied. If she caught his use of present tense, she didn't show it.

It took me a moment to recognize the woman as my aunt who lived in Texas and whom I hadn't seen since I was little. She dabbed her bloodshot eyes with a handkerchief and then blew her nose.

"I thought I had myself pulled together the last couple of days, but I guess not." Aunt Marie tucked the handkerchief into her purse. "I can almost feel her presence here. It doesn't seem possible she's gone."

"My granddad used to say our souls sense when our loved ones are near," Ian said.

He glanced at me. I shrunk back from the pointed glare he threw my way. My new position had me pressed against Wyatt's side. Aunt Marie's eyes flicked to the front of the room to where I knew my coffin would be. I couldn't get myself to look at it, yet. But Ian wasn't implying that my aunt's pain was because my body was close. He meant that my aunt could feel my soul.

Lilith had said that would happen. I wished she'd been lying.

Aunt Marie wiped under her eyes with her fingertips and then asked Ian, "How did you know our

Avery?"

I sniffed back more tears.

"I taught world history," Ian replied. "If you'll excuse me, I want to pay my respects."

"Sure, dear." She patted his arm.

I followed Ian and Wyatt to the front of the room. A pearl-white casket sat closed on a pedestal surrounded by several large floral arrangements. Their sweet bouquet reminded me of the park near our house. Eighteen candid pictures had been arranged on top of it—from my baby picture to my eighteenth birthday—one for every year I'd lived.

I'd been a pudgy baby with a thin wisp of caramel-colored hair and bright rosy cheeks. While the girl in each of the photographs grew older, her eyes and big smile remained the same.

"You were adorable with pigtails," Ian whispered, a soft chuckle escaping with his words.

"I was five." And I was sort of cute.

"I'm digging the bell bottoms and big white glasses," Wyatt said quietly. "That smile of yours could light up a room."

I grinned. "That was an amazing day."

His comment referred to a picture of me on my twelfth birthday. The party was at the roller rink. Megan had found the sparkly, white sunglasses. She'd bought three pairs: one for me, one for our friend Krista, and one for herself. Mine were now tucked safely inside the mini backpack I used to carry back then. They were with a few other prized items I'd saved over the years. Small treasures I'd never see again.

My favorite picture was a toss-up between me at the age of three holding Gracie—she couldn't have been more than a few months old, and boy did I look proud to have her in my arms—and me dangling the keys to my first car.

I wiped one cheek and then the other. Ian pulled another tissue from his pocket and handed it to me.

"Thanks."

I liked that my parents had chosen a closed casket. I wanted my friends to remember the Avery in those pictures and not the corpse in the box. I shuddered at the thought of a cold, dead body mere feet from me.

I'd just managed to stop crying when I noticed Mom and Dad sitting in the front row. They had aged ten years in the last week. Mom wore a plain, black dress. Her curly, dark brown hair was pulled into a low ponytail. I had her hair, or I used to, before my change. I'd hated it on humid days because it would frizz something awful. Now, I'd give anything to have those bushy, uncontrollable curls and my parents back.

Dad sat next to Mom, eyes locked on the last picture on top of the casket, the most recent one.

"She's still with us," Mom said, twisting her hands nervously around each other. "I can feel her. Do you feel her?"

Dad put an arm around Mom. "She'll always be in our hearts."

A lump formed in my throat. I must have stumbled because Wyatt moved closer and snaked an arm around my waist, providing support.

"Why don't we offer your parents our condolences while they're sitting alone?" Ian suggested. "You can give them a hug."

"Okay." I drew in a shaky breath. *Hold it together, Avery.*

I didn't argue about Wyatt keeping his arm around me. My legs felt as if I'd walked a thousand miles. We stopped in front of Mom.

"Hi. I was a friend of Ave—" I choked on my tears.

Mom jumped up and hugged me. "Anyone who's a friend of Avery's is someone special in my book."

My tears flowed freely as I held my mom. I didn't want her to ever let go, but too soon she pulled away.

"Thanks for coming," Mom said when we parted. "Avery had so many wonderful people in her life. You being here means a lot to her father and me."

"I'm sorry—" I began, unable to add *for your loss*.

Dad leaned in and gave me a hug, and for a second I felt like his little girl again. A few moments later, Ian squeezed my elbow as if to remind me I should keep my interaction with them brief.

"I know," I whispered out of the side of my mouth. I wouldn't be able to hold a conversation with my parents as someone else anyway.

"Have you seen Cie-Cie?" I asked. "We wanted to say hi before we leave."

Mom cocked her head. "That's what Avery always called Gracie."

Out of the corner of my eye, I saw Wyatt suck in a breath. Ignoring him, I said, "I must have heard Avery say it. Is Gracie here?"

"She is." Mom scanned the room. "She might have gone to the restroom."

I leaned in for one last hug. *Love you, Mom. Love you, Dad.*

That hug had been the hardest hug, knowing it was our last.

Ian, Wyatt, and I made it to the aisle when I heard Megan's voice. I turned in time to see her hand my mom a glass of water.

"Here you are, Mrs. Williams."

"Friend of yours?" Wyatt asked.

"Best." The lump in my throat grew.

Dark circles lined Megan's eyes, but she managed to keep a smile on her face as she talked to my mom. Her gaze met mine, and new tears followed the contours of my nose.

"I'll be right back," I told Ian and Wyatt.

Wyatt tightened his grip on my hand and whispered, "I know you're thinking about doing something stupid. Just remember that for every person who shares your secret, there'll be at least a dozen who are in the dark but who'll sense your soul is close. The holes in their hearts from losing you will keep being ripped open whenever you're near."

I'd planned to run up to Megan, squeeze her tight, and whisper, "It's me." I knew without a doubt that with the arsenal of memories we shared I'd be able to convince her I was me. But then what? She'd want details I couldn't give her without putting my new friends in danger. It broke my heart to keep my existence a secret, but I had to think of the big picture, and that included Cole, Ian, and Wyatt. To betray their trust would be selfish, especially since they'd helped me get this far.

"Wyatt, I promise not to say anything I shouldn't." My gaze dropped to our hands, and he let go. I hurried back to the front row. Ian and Wyatt followed.

Megan's head tilted to the side thoughtfully.

"Hi. I just...um..." I glanced over my shoulder at

my escorts and then turned back to Megan. "I just wanted to say I know you and Avery were good friends—"

"Best," she said, interrupting me. "Avery was the best friend a person could have."

I rubbed her arm, not missing how her voice had hitched when she spoke. "I know she felt the same way about you."

We stared at each other. I didn't know what else to say. *I miss you. Life won't be the same without you. I wish things were different.* Mostly, I just wanted to ask her not to forget me. But none of that would have made any sense to her. I swiped at my wet cheeks. "Take care, Megan."

Her eyes narrowed. "Why do I feel as if I should know you?"

"Because—"

Ian cleared his throat before I could finish my sentence.

Since I couldn't answer honestly, I simply said, "I just wanted to say I'm sorry about Avery."

"Thank you." Megan smiled and turned to talk to my mom.

I'd just taken a few steps away from them when Jared Atkins and Caleb Higgins passed me, stopping in front of the casket. Caleb placed a red rose next to the picture of me at seventeen.

"Figures I'd have to die for him to give me flowers," I whispered, glad to have the distraction from my folks and Megan.

Ian chuckled and shook his head.

"His loss," Wyatt whispered into my ear, making me smile.

When the next song came on, I realized the music was playing from my iPod. It was the playlist I'd listen to when doing homework. I was glad they'd chosen this over the one I played when I was depressed.

"Shall we find Gracie?" Ian asked.

"Yeah." If I stayed at my wake much longer, my eyes would be a swollen mess and I was bound to let my disguise slip.

I dried my face with my fingertips and scanned the rest of the guests on my way out of the viewing room. There was a mix of relatives and friends, some I knew well and some I'd barely spoken to. My old gymnastics squad was there and Tommy and his sister from down the block. The room pulsed with love. How could I have touched the lives of so many people and still been damned in death? It seemed unfair to land in Hell without some horrific, serial-killing event to have sent me there. But like it or not, I was there to stay.

When we reached the hallway, Ian pointed with his chin to the far end of the funeral home. "Restrooms are down there."

The ladies' room was across from a small lounge, where voices drifted out as we passed.

"We'll wait here," Ian said, like he and Wyatt had a choice.

Wyatt placed a hand on the door before I could open it.

"Lilith doesn't know about me," he said. "And she doesn't know you're with Ian. Cole's the one who'll suffer her wrath if she learns you were here, and the more people who know the truth, the higher the odds she'll find out. So if you're thinking of doing a big reveal, don't."

"I know, Wyatt," I snapped, tired of him reminding me of that. "I'm just going to talk to her about Justin. I promise."

"I'm not sure how well my cloaking will work with you in another room, so make it quick." He stepped back, allowing me to open the door.

A moment after I'd entered the restroom, I felt Wyatt's feather-soft protection pull away. I clutched my purse, praying Ian's anti-demon bag really worked. Gracie leaned against the light marble sink. Her two best friends since elementary school, Karly and Emily, huddled close to her. I noticed her so-called new friends weren't there.

Needing a moment, I ducked into a stall and watched them through the gap.

"Gracie, you can't spend the next few hours hiding in the restroom," Karly said.

"We won't leave your side," Emily said. "We promise."

"I can't go back out there." Tears streamed down Gracie's cheeks. She looked like a younger version of me. Though her chestnut-brown hair wasn't as curly as mine had been. Her long locks spilled over her shoulders and halfway down her back. She wore a black top and black slacks that she must have bought for the wake because Gracie never wore black. Normally, she was all about color. My heart pounded, feeling her pain.

"Did I tell you Avery didn't even want to be at the party? Megan and I talked her into it." Gracie wet her lips. "She shouldn't have reached for me."

"You have to stop blaming yourself," Karly pleaded, her face slightly pale.

"She died saving me. How am I supposed to live

knowing that?" Gracie ran her finger along the edge of the sink. "I don't think I ever told her I loved her."

She covered her face with her hands and broke into sobs. Karly wrapped her arms around her.

Emily made it a group hug. "Sweetie, she knew that."

You can do this without falling apart.

I breathed in deeply and exited the stall. A quick glance in the mirror told me my disguise was still in place.

"I'm sorry to eavesdrop," I said as I washed my hands. Three sets of bloodshot eyes met mine. *You can do this,* I silently repeated. "It's a small bathroom; I couldn't help overhearing. You're Gracie, right?"

"Yeah." Gracie swiped at her tears with her fingers.

I plucked a tissue from the box on the counter and handed it to her as I willed my voice to be strong. "Your friends are right. You shouldn't blame yourself for what happened to your sister. Avery wouldn't want you to do that."

Gracie's eyes narrowed. "Did you know her?"

"Um, not super well, but I was at the party and saw her fall. Accidents happen. Blaming yourself isn't healthy."

Gracie's bottom lip trembled.

"Today's been hard for her." Karly put her arm around Gracie. "She's been here all day."

"And the last half hour has been the worst," Emily whispered.

That's how long I'd been at the funeral home. More proof that my family could feel my presence. The sooner I left, the sooner they'd start to heal.

187

"I'm okay," Gracie muttered bravely.

The fact that she refused to leave the restroom said differently.

Tears streaked my face. Standing next to my sister with her unaware it was me was the second most painful experience of my life—the first being saying good-bye to my parents.

Hold it together a little longer.

"I know this isn't the best time," I said shakily. "But I have something to tell you."

Gracie twisted the tissue, waiting for me to continue.

"We have a mutual friend, Justin, and with Avery gone..." Tears welled in my eyes, blurring my vision. Karly handed me a tissue. "Thanks." I blew my nose.

There was a knock at the door. It opened a crack, and Wyatt said we had to go.

"Two minutes," I called back, then faced Gracie again. It was so hard to see her upset, and I hated that I didn't have time to let her grieve before dumping more crap on her. "With Avery gone, Justin needs you."

Gracie sniffed, head tilted to one side. "Why would you say that?"

I glanced at Karly and Emily, not sure how much they knew about Justin's past, but this was my only chance to talk to Gracie. I couldn't back down now.

"He suffers from depression, and Avery once told me she worried about him."

"She never told me that," Gracie said.

I would have if I hadn't died. Thankfully, Gracie stopped crying. It was easier to have this conversation without the tears.

"That's why I wanted to say something. She'd

want you to keep an eye on him, hang out and stuff."

"Justin…you sure?" She paused, seeming to think this over. "That's why…" She bit her lip, thoughtfully. "We don't have anything in common anymore."

That was because her new so-called friends felt girls should spend their free time shopping or doing their nails, not wasting time watching old movies or racing cars around a virtual track.

"He likes video games and comedies," I said, knowing she did, too.

She sniffed. "Does he really suffer from depression?"

I nodded. "He tries to hide it, but I've…Avery's seen him at his worst. She once told me he needs to realize there are people who know what he's been through and are willing to be there when he needs them. You know, to pull him out of funks and stuff."

"I guess I could call him and tell him we're overstocked on Oreos." Gracie smiled. "Our mom buys them for him."

His grandmother didn't keep junk food in the house, and our mom thought sweets solved all of life's problems. I let a small chuckle sneak past my lips. With our mom's love for chocolate, it was a wonder none of us were overweight.

"He was here, earlier," Gracie said. "I didn't really talk to him."

"Time's up!" Wyatt hollered. The bathroom door closed again.

"Okay!" I fought the urge to tell him off. At that moment, I really hated Wyatt for rushing me. "Call him," I urged Gracie as my hand slid into my purse, feeling for the voodoo bag. It had to be working or

Lilith would have shown up by now. "I should…" I pointed over my shoulder to the exit.

Karly ran a hand over Gracie's arm. "Maybe we should get out of here, too."

"Why don't we step outside and call Justin," Emily suggested. "Karly and I will help you keep an eye on him. Three guardian angels are better than one. Right?"

"That would be amazing," I said. And just like that, a weight lifted off my shoulders. Gracie had Karly and Emily, and Justin would have the three of them. Under the circumstances, I couldn't ask for more.

I fumbled with the clasp on the butterfly necklace I wore. When I finally got it off, I held it out to Gracie. "Here. Avery gave me this. I think she'd like you to have it now."

I let the chain fall into her palm.

"Thanks," she said, sniffling.

My vision blurred with tears. "Gracie, try to remember that sometimes it's the small things we do that make a big difference in another person's life. If you do that, I know you'll do incredible things." I jumped forward, giving Gracie a firm hug, and then hastily made my way to the exit. With my hand on the door handle, I glanced over my shoulder. "Take care, Cie-Cie."

I rushed out of the restroom and right into someone too solid to be an average human being.

Chapter 15

Hands closed around my shoulders, keeping me from ricocheting backward from the impact of colliding into another being. I blinked, forcing my tears to spill down my cheeks. My vision cleared enough to see the brown gaze that bored down into me through a veil of dark hair. I breathed in a ragged breath.

"Hey." Wyatt pulled me into a hug, but I didn't want his pity. I wanted out.

I pushed him away and sprinted to the exit. They followed me out of the building.

"I hate to say I told you so," Wyatt began.

"Then don't," I spat. When he opened his mouth, I quickly added, "I'm serious, Wyatt. I don't need one of your righteous lectures right now."

He snorted. "You sound like Cole."

Who owed me a big fat I-told-you-so, also.

I cried the entire ride to the airport. My disguise flickered back to the real me a few times. Each time Ian cleared his throat and told me to pull it together before someone in traffic noticed.

Once at the airport, Ian did that trick with our IDs, and we breezed through security just like we had in Chicago. We sat in first class, again. After a couple of failed attempts at small talk, Ian left me alone. He ordered a soda for me and a rum and coke for himself. As soon as the flight attendant reached the next row, he switched our glasses.

"It'll help settle your nerves," he said.

I sipped my beverage.

The flight had to be the longest two hours of my existence. I walked as if through a nightmare back to Wyatt's coupe. He drove Ian and I back to the church where we'd left Ian's car.

Ian got out, holding the seat forward so I could climb out from the backseat. "Still have that hex bag I gave you?"

I dug it out of my purse and handed it to him.

"Here." He tossed both his and mine to Wyatt. "One for your car and one for your house. Just in case you let your guard down one day. Although I can't guarantee it wards off angels."

Wyatt smiled. "Thanks."

"I don't take lightly the risk you took by helping Cole and Avery. Thank you." Ian patted the roof of the car and shut the passenger door. I was pretty sure I'd just witnessed a rare incubus/nephilim bonding moment.

Ian rolled his eyes. "Wipe that mushy girl expression off your face." When I cracked the first smile since the wake, he added, "Wyatt's actions make him a likable bloke, that's all."

"Uh ha."

"Women." Ian shook his head and unlocked his car with the key fob.

We morphed back into ourselves during the drive to the apartment. Cole was in the kitchen when we got there.

"Right on time," Cole said as he pulled a homemade pizza out of the oven.

Ian checked it out, inhaling deeply before plucking a green pepper from the gooey cheese. "This is what I miss most about having you as a roommate."

Cole shook his head. "Five hundred years and you still haven't learned to cook."

"When I want a home-cooked meal, I date a chef." Ian grabbed a beer from the fridge.

I stood near the doorway watching them. The pizza smelled delicious, but I didn't think I could eat right then.

"How was it, Avery?" Cole asked, turning his attention to me. My gaze met his a moment before he tossed the towel he'd used as a hot pad on the counter. "I knew you shouldn't have gone."

"I'm fine," I replied, knowing my eyes were probably red from crying. Under Cole's sympathetic glare, my waterworks started again.

Ian tried to cover his groan with a cough.

"I'm just going to—" I pointed with my thumb to the bathroom and left.

"Give her some time," Ian said, and I guessed he'd stopped Cole from following me.

I'd underestimated just how bad I looked. My cheeks were blotchy, my eyes swollen, and I had long, black streaks of mascara trailing down my face.

"Nice," I said to my reflection.

I grabbed a washcloth. I'd thought morphing back into myself would have made me presentable. Apparently, it only changed my features. Washing my face with a washcloth was hopeless. *I* was hopeless. My reflection frowned back at me, agreeing.

I stripped, leaving my clothes in a pile next to the tub, and turned on the shower. The hot water felt amazing on my stiff muscles. It had been a long day, most of it spent in a car or on a plane. I didn't want to do that again anytime soon. I tried to tell myself I was glad I'd gone, even if the trip drained me emotionally— that it had been gratifying to see the people I loved— but the ugly truth kept poking holes in my mental pep talk.

I'd died. I'd never be with my family again. Never hang out with my friends again. That life was truly over.

I went through the motions of washing, but even the sweet fragrance of my shampoo and body wash couldn't snap me out of the funk I was in. Finally, when my fingertips resembled prunes, I turned off the water and reached to grab a towel, pausing. Five bright blue towels had been mixed in with Cole's black ones. The way they'd been folded revealed a line of penguins prancing across a white stripe. My fingers brushed one of them, and anger flared in me. I was tired of Lilith thinking she could surround me with nice things to buy my happiness.

With a black towel wrapped around my body, I peeked out of the bathroom. Cole and Ian's voices drifted toward me from the family room along with the sound of gunfire. Whatever battle they watched on television allowed me to take the few steps from the bathroom to the bedroom unnoticed. I then searched Cole's side of the dresser, selected a pair of Chicago Bears' sweatpants and a matching T-shirt and dressed.

"I thought you'd like the blue towels," Cole said from behind me. I hadn't heard him open the door.

I turned to face him. His gaze moved from the damp towel on the bed to me.

"You bought them?" I asked.

He nodded, his brow pinched together as he stared at my outfit. The shoulders of the T-shirt sagged over my skinny biceps and the pants bunched around my ankles. I looked back at him through wet bangs.

"I don't want anything from Lilith touching me." I ran a hand along my waist and hips. "I'm sorry. I should've asked if it was okay to borrow your things."

"So, you don't hate the towels?"

I shook my head. Now that I knew they were from Cole, I loved them.

He smirked and stepped into the room. "You look cute in my clothes."

"I'll wash them tomorrow."

"Avery, it's fine. You can borrow my things anytime." He picked the towel up off the bed. "We're going to put on a movie. I thought you might want a say in what we watch."

"Thanks, but I think I'll stay here," I replied, knowing I wouldn't be good company.

"You sure? There isn't much to do in the bedroom."

"Yeah, I'm just tired."

"Okay." He grabbed a pillow off the bed. "You can sleep in here tonight, I'll take the couch." He turned to leave.

"Cole?" I was on the verge of tears again, and I didn't quite understand where they'd come from. Hadn't I cried every last one of them out of me already? I felt utterly lost and alone. My voice broke when I said, "Don't leave."

He dropped the pillow in the hall and tossed the towel toward the bathroom before crossing the room and wrapping me in a hug. I melted into him, letting him be my knight in shining armor yet again.

"I wish I could've gone with you," he whispered into my hair.

I did, also. "You'd have been in danger if Lilith found out." And Wyatt couldn't cloak all of our signatures.

He pulled away just enough to study me. "You seem better."

Translation: I wasn't a blubbering mess anymore.

"Give me a few minutes and you might take that back." I swiped at my eyes, sniffing back the tears that threatened to return.

Cole's healthy glow had returned. My stomach clenched, knowing he'd spent his day with another girl. I reminded myself that Cole wasn't mine, but when he laced our fingers together and led the way to the bed, I couldn't help feeling like I belonged to him.

His hand slid from mine as he sat down. With his back against the wall, he patted the mattress in front of him. I scooted to the spot he indicated and leaned against his chest. His strong arms encircled me. I nestled into his embrace.

"Thanks," I said, needing the security he offered. Then I realized how self-centered I was being. "What about Ian?"

"He'll be happy to know he has full rein over the television and can have the couch tonight."

"Aren't you going to tell him?" My cheek rested on his arm. He smelled nice, like autumn.

"Ian has awesome hearing, so I'm sure he heard me. Plus I left him a pillow just outside the door."

"Got it," Ian called from the hall. "Thanks. Avery,

hang in there. It gets easier."

Cole squeezed me gently. "He's right, you know."

A disbelieving laugh escaped my lips. "I thought seeing my parents, Gracie, Megan, and everyone one last time would make it easier, but it didn't. They were in so much pain. Gracie's friends said she's not doing well."

"Ian told me you got a chance to talk to her."

I glanced at him over my shoulder. "She's spiraling, Cole."

"She's grieving."

"*Ha!*"

"Avery, your family could sense your presence at the wake. That feeling hinders their ability to move on with their lives."

"My mom said she believed I was near. Do you think she knew?"

"She probably didn't realize how right she was."

"Yeah." I sighed. "It's been a miserable day."

"That's because funerals are sad," Cole replied.

"I went to the wake."

"Not much difference there." He rested his chin on the top of my head. "Hungry?"

"No. Why'd Lilith do this to me?"

"Would you rather be a soul damned to the pit?"

I shuddered. "I'd rather be alive, hanging out with friends, worrying about college and work."

He said nothing. Lilith hadn't killed me. She'd just claimed my soul and turned me into a succubus, damned to spend eternity missing what I'd lost. At that moment, I'd have preferred death to be more final.

"Ian's nice," I commented.

"Best friend an incubus could have," Cole

confirmed.

A muffled *thanks* found us from the other room.

"Stop listening, or I'm kicking your ass out of my home!" Cole called back, but he didn't sound irritated.

Ian turned up the volume on the television.

"Cole, may I ask you what you did to end up on Lilith's team?" After Ian had said there was more than one way to become an incubus, I had to know.

He sighed. "Are you sure you want to hear this?"

"Yeah."

"Well, you know the South and North were at war."

"Yes, but you said you weren't a soldier. Did the enemy attack your village?" I'd seen that in a lot of movies, armies attacking defenseless women and children while the men were away. "Were you left trying to defend your family?"

"Nothing that honorable, I'm afraid."

I turned to look at him. "So the Civil War had begun." When he nodded, I settle against his chest, chin on his forearm. "I won't interrupt again."

"The war had been raging for a year, and at my father's request, I stayed home to take care of my mother, two younger brothers, baby sister, and Thomas's pregnant wife."

"Thomas was your older brother?" I asked for clarification.

I felt his nod against the top of my head. "Thomas was in Tennessee during the Battle of Shiloh. The first day of the battle was a surprise attack. The Confederate Army tried to drive the Union soldiers back. Many lives were lost; Thomas's was one of them."

"Uh huh." I waited, trying to figure out what this

had to do with Cole, expecting a dark secret like Thomas's wife was pregnant with Cole's child or maybe that Cole had gone ballistic when he was told of his brother's death and attacked a soldier, only to be killed himself. After a few seconds, Cole went on.

"A woman showed up at our home the day after we'd heard the news. She found me out back. I'd been taking out my anger on a pile of wood that needed chopping."

"The woman was Lilith, wasn't she?"

"Yes. She said with a snap of her fingers she could return Thomas's soul to his body. His wife wouldn't have to raise their unborn son on her own. All I had to do was trade places with him."

I gasped. "You agreed to die so that your brother could live?"

"In a manner of speaking, except Lilith had said my soul would remain on Earth with my body. She promised I'd never see the inside of a grave. I didn't think of it as dying." He laughed, but there was no humor in it. "I didn't believe her, but I also couldn't find a downside to her offer if she were to be telling the truth. Figuring she'd snap her fingers and nothing would happen, I told her to do it."

"But it did work."

"Obviously. Imagine my surprise when I was suddenly standing on a cobblestone street in front of a palace. I thought she was an angel, and since Thomas was a great guy, good things did happen to good people."

I repositioned myself so that I was sitting facing him with my legs crossed like a pretzel. "She tricked you into making a deal?"

He traced the orange *S* on my sweatpants. "Pretty much."

I quickly put two and two together. If Cole had taken his brother's place that meant his brother's soul, not Cole's, had been marked by lust. "What did your brother do to earn himself a one-way ticket down?"

"The list had been long, but it was his infidelity that made his soul Lilith's property." Cole frowned. "He'd been unfaithful to his wife before he'd left to fight in the war and apparently every chance he got when he was away. If Lilith was telling the truth, and she had no reason to lie, a young woman in Tennessee was to have Thomas's illegitimate child later that year."

"So by your taking his place, he lived out a normal human life and you became an incubus for eternity."

"A young incubus."

Lilith's favorite kind.

"You never actually died, did you? Not like I did."

"No." He dragged a hand through his hair. "Although, for all purposes I ceased being human the moment I made the deal."

I bent forward and asked, "Did you confront your brother?"

"Never had the opportunity. I didn't find out the details of his sordid past until after I'd left with Lilith. By the time he returned home, I was in London. Back then you couldn't hop on a plane." He shrugged. "It's probably better. I would have clocked him one, and he wouldn't even have known why."

"I'm sorry."

"Don't be, I made it work." He nudged my knee with his. "What about you?" He waited a breath. "I've seen you around guys, Avery. Lust may have marked your soul, but you're not exactly loose, yet here you are." He spread his arms wide. "Something else happened, didn't it?"

He'd hate me once he knew the truth, but I didn't feel I could refuse to answer after he'd been open with me.

"I had this friend, Krista. We'd known each other for years. We were in the same classes, on the same cheer squad, gone to the same gymnastics school. We ended up close friends."

Cole's thumb rubbed lazy circles over my thigh in a soothing manner, silently encouraging me to go on.

"One day when we were hanging out, I found a bottle of her mom's painkillers in her dresser. Krista brushed it off as no big deal, claiming she only took one after competitions to help her relax."

"Did you believe her?" Cole asked.

"No. Competitions had been over for a while when I found them, and it wasn't like the bottle had been tucked under her socks. It was right on top as if she'd hastily shoved it into the drawer."

Yet I didn't try to stop her from taking the drugs. Nor did I question her further.

I wrung my hands together and continued. "Her mom eventually noticed the drugs disappearing. When Krista wouldn't fess up, her mom came to my house and asked me."

I still remembered the desperation in Mrs. Hudsen's voice. She'd pleaded for the truth, but what kind of friend would I have been if I'd told on Krista. Cole watched me, not saying a word.

"I looked her mom in the eyes and said that Krista hated people who did drugs. No way would she become one of them."

Cole's thumb stopped its slow, methodical path over my leg. "How old were you?"

"Sixteen. Krista promised me she'd stopped taking the pills, but I knew she hadn't. I could tell. She'd act different. I used to tell myself she didn't have a problem."

More accurately, I'd told myself her problem wasn't my problem, but there was only so much I was ready to admit out loud.

I wrapped my hands in the bottom of my oversized T-shirt and focused on the bright letters running down my leg. "Krista never really fit into a specific group in middle school, and in high school, she sort of got lost in the crowd. Even I lost track of her. She was on the dance team, but I had given up dance in high school. I told myself that our interests had changed, but that wasn't true. I'd been getting invited to parties, and she wasn't. I wanted to go but couldn't bring her."

"Why not?"

I blew out a breath. I could've said it was because Krista didn't know the guys throwing the parties or that they didn't like her. Both were true. Krista and I were hanging in different crowds, and my new friends thought she was weird. In their defense, they'd only seen the Krista on drugs and not the fun-loving girl I'd known.

I'd confessed this much. Now was not the time to start lying. Besides, Cole deserved to know who he was living with. "It was easier to pretend she had new friends than to be the one who showed up at a party with the girl everyone considered a freak. I thought maybe they'd stop inviting me."

Cole remained quiet, waiting, I'm sure, to hear the worst of what I'd done. I continued robotically, as if I wasn't talking about what a horrible person I'd been. "A couple of weekends before we were to graduate, Krista stopped by my house depressed, rambling on about how she hated her life. I could smell rum on her breath, and I could tell she'd taken something." I forced a weak smile. "Krista had beautiful pale-blue eyes and a contagious laugh. The pills dulled both those things. She might have been able to fool most people into thinking she was fine, but not me.

"I hadn't known it at the time, because I hadn't taken the time to ask her, but several of the girls on the dance squad were making her life miserable. She was going through a tough time and needed a friend." I met Cole's gaze. "You know what I told her?"

He shook his head.

"I told her it wasn't a good time for me. Even after she begged me not to leave her alone, I practically shoved her out the door because she was keeping me from getting ready for a party." A tear ran down my cheek. "She left my house and drove her brand-new car into a tree."

Cole inhaled sharply. After a long moment, he said, "That's rough, but Avery, you can't blame yourself for a choice someone else made."

"Yes, I can." How Cole could stand to be in the same room with someone so callous was beyond me. The guilt I'd bottled up since Krista's death caught in my throat, threatening to choke me. "I wasn't honest with her mom. If I had been, she could've gotten Krista help. I could have told someone—my parents, a teacher, another friend—but I didn't. Then, when she needed me the most, I couldn't be bothered. We were friends. I was supposed to be there for her." My voice cracked, but I forced myself to continue. "They found a note addressed to her parents on the passenger seat of her car. She apologized for giving up. It said that even her best friend didn't care about her. She didn't put my name in the letter, but she meant me." I swiped at the new tears running down my face. "I deserved damnation."

Cole pulled me against him. "No, you made a mistake."

"My mistake cost Krista her life."

"That doesn't make you a murderer."

"Really? Judgment Day came and went, and my soul went down. I seriously doubt it was because I stole a pack of gum."

He rested his forehead against mine.

His silence let me know I was right. My reputation as a girl who slept around combined with the small items that fell victim to my five-finger-discount weren't enough to damn my soul. But ignoring a friend, pushing her to kill herself was no different than if I'd driven that car into the tree myself.

"She was a compassionate person," I whispered, stuffing my hands under my legs to stop them from trembling. "She was sweet, you know. She deserved a better friend."

"Is what happened to Krista why it was so important for you to talk to Gracie? You saw her making a similar mistake?"

"Yeah."

We were quiet a moment. I'd never told anyone the truth about Krista, not even Megan. I hated myself for how I'd treated Krista. I'd vowed to be a better friend from the moment I'd heard she'd killed herself. It might have been too late to help Krista, but never again would I ignore a person in need of help. Guess fate had other plans for me, though. Had fate known Hell would suck me up and spit me back into the world or had fate hoped I'd burn for all eternity in the river?

I pulled out of Cole's embrace and wiped my face with the sleeves of my T-shirt. Cole smirked.

"What?" I asked.

"That's my lucky Bears' shirt. They always win when I wear it."

"Sorry." I smoothed the now-wrinkled and damp sleeve. "You must not wear it much."

Cole cocked his head to the side, questioningly.

"I'm not a huge sports fan, but I know the Chicago Bears haven't been in a Super Bowl in, like, forever."

"Hey!" He hit me with a pillow. "Don't down my favorite team."

I suspected Cole was trying to lighten the mood, and I appreciated that. After my confession, I needed to focus on something, anything, except Krista and my wake.

"Let me get this straight," I said, flipping my damp hair out of my eyes with a jerk of my head. "You've been around since the beginning of the sport, and your favorite team is a losing one."

He hit me with the pillow again. "They used to be the best."

"That must have been before my time." I lunged for his weapon.

Cole was quicker. He had the pillow tossed aside and me flipped onto my back, pinned beneath him in a matter of seconds. I squirmed, unable to free myself.

He tickled me unmercifully. "Say you love the Bears."

"Never!" I screamed, giggling and wiggling to no avail.

"Say it!"

He straddled me, making it impossible for me to move far. I tried to knock his hands away, but they were everywhere, tickling my sides until I gasped for air from laughing so hard.

"Okay, okay!" I relented. "I love the Bears!"

He tickled me more. "Mean it!"

"I do. They're the best! Stop!"

Cole grabbed my wrists and pinned them above my head with one hand. He brushed long strands of hair away from me face with the other. "I'm taking you to a game. Once you're at Soldier Field surrounded by fans, you'll see why Chicago has the best football team."

I'd watched his mouth as he spoke, so close and tempting. His eyes held a playful glint to them. He really was gorgeous.

I didn't want to care anymore, and I didn't want to fight what was right in front of me. There was no way for things between Cole and me to end well. I knew that, but I lifted my head and closed the short distance between us, anyway. Our lips touched. My eyes never left his.

He hesitated almost as if he'd just realized he had me pinned beneath him. Then his hands cupped my cheeks, and his lips moved over mine tenderly. My insides warmed, and my heart raced. There was no transfer of energy. It was just Cole and me. My fingers trailed a line from his wrist to his biceps as I enjoyed the taste of his kisses. All I could smell was his spicy cologne and mint on his breath. His hand moved to my waist, over my hip, to the back of my thigh as he pressed me to him. A sigh escaped my lips when his left mine. He kissed my chin, my neck, the center of my chest bone, leaving the skin in those areas alive with fire. I grabbed the back of his head and brought his mouth back to mine. He pulled away, though, and planted one last kiss on my forehead.

"You should sleep." He rolled off me and sat up.

I got to my knees in front of him. "I'm not tired." I slipped my arms around his neck and kissed him again.

He maneuvered away from me, putting several inches of space between us. "Avery, we shouldn't."

"Why? We're damned if we do and damned if we don't, right?" I bent forward and brushed his jaw with my tongue. "We might as well enjoy each other's company." I ran a line of kisses down his neck. I wanted to forget everything—my past, my future—and just live for the moment.

His fingers twisted in my hair as his head fell back, giving me access to his collarbone. His chest.

"You're only doing this because you're depressed," he said in a raspy whisper.

"Do you care?" After all, he slept with girls all the time, and it meant nothing to him.

His body stiffened. In the next moment he was off the bed, combing his fingers through his ruffled dark hair. "This isn't you."

I didn't know who I was anymore. I did know I didn't want to be alone. "Cole…" I crawled across the bed closer to him.

He stepped away from me. "Not like this."

"Why?" I demanded. He had no problem running off and getting his fill of energy from the Devil knew who. What was wrong with me?

"I've told you, I won't take advantage of you." He waved a hand at me and the bed. "And this would be taking advantage of you." Anger and frustration laced his words.

I fell back onto my butt. "Why does it matter?"

Cole pressed the heels of his hands to his eyes and heaved out a sigh. "Avery, you're sweet, and there's a light in you I've never seen in anyone. No matter what put you here, I can tell you're a nice person and a little too innocent for your own good. I won't take that from you."

"Take my innocence? Are you kidding me?" Fury flared in me. "You're the one who pushed me at other guys!"

"To help you gain strength! To keep you safe from Lilith!" He leaned against the wall.

"That's just…" I ran my hands over my thighs. "Messed up."

"Our existence is messed up." Cautiously, he came closer and crouched in front of me and swept my bangs away from my eyes. "I care about you, Avery, and I don't normally care about succubi. They're conceited and heartless." He paused. "They're supposed to be conceited and heartless. But you're different. It's like you don't belong in this world." He drew in a breath, and I found myself watching him closely. His hands curled into fists at my side, and his eyebrows pulled together. An internal struggle could be seen taking place behind his gorgeous blue eyes. "I knew the moment I saw you that you were special."

I let out a disbelieving huff. The only thing special about me was that I was dead yet didn't actually die.

He gave me a disapproving glare and went on. "Part of me wants to dig further into what brought you to me, and the other part is afraid I'll push the wrong buttons and you'll be ripped from my life." He offered me a hint of a smile. "You're a cover hog, and you'd sleep the morning away if I'd let you. As far as I can tell, you don't cook, and you leave wet towels and dirty clothes all over the place, but I sort of…"

I stopped breathing as I waited to hear what he'd say. I couldn't move. I was afraid he'd vanish if I blinked, frightened this moment would turn out to be a cruel dream.

His gaze met mine. "I like having you around, Avery. I don't know what that means. I find it maddening and confusing, to be honest."

The corners of my mouth tilted upward. "I can have that effect on people—the maddening one."

His shoulders relaxed. Apparently he was relieved I wasn't molesting him and that I wasn't on the verge of tears. "If it makes you feel any better, I've taken a cold shower every day since you moved in."

I gave him a narrow-eyed glare.

"Two, some days."

I shook my head. The tiniest of giggles slipped past my lips. "I've only been here a week."

"I know. It's been a long week of cold showers." He faked a shiver.

I didn't know what to say. I probably should've admitted that I liked being a part of his life, too. That I was glad he was my mentor and that his kindness had given me the strength to face eternity. Words escaped me, though. Cole had just admitted he'd thought about being with me. Had my kiss affected him the same way his caused my heart to dance? Or was I just another girl he wanted to sleep with? It couldn't be the latter, or he wouldn't fight me now. He wouldn't care about taking advantage of the situation.

Would he?

I realized he wasn't the only one who was confused.

He placed a finger under my chin and lifted my face until my gaze met his. "Are we okay?"

I nodded. "I don't want to be alone," I admitted, not caring that the confession made me sound fragile. I couldn't stand the thought of spending the night with only my thoughts.

He grabbed the pillow from the floor and returned it to the head of the bed. He then slid under the covers and held them up, indicating for me to slide in next to him. When I did, he lowered the blanket on top of us and pulled my back against his chest.

"Cole?"

"Hmm?"

"Thanks…" For looking out for me. For protecting me. For being a nice guy. Hell, thanks for everything. Though I'd only gotten the one word out, his arms tightened around me, and his lips pressed against the back of my head.

We lay there, listening to the sounds of the television in the next room. At some point, Ian lowered the volume or turned it off, I'm not sure which. I drifted to sleep nestled in Cole's embrace, wondering if I had the right to be grateful that I had him. With my luck, if Lilith discovered he made me happy, she'd rip him from my afterlife and leave me completely and utterly alone.

Chapter 16

I woke to the sound of running water and dishes clanging. I rubbed the sleep out of my eyes and rolled over, hugging the pillow next to me. Cole's spicy cologne greeted me. I buried my nose farther into the pillow and lay there, enjoying his scent until I heard the water in the kitchen stop.

After a quick trip to the bathroom to run a brush through my hair and a toothbrush over my teeth, I went into the other room and paused. Ian—wearing only a pair of navy pajama pants—was wiping the counter. Cole wasn't home.

"It's my fault he isn't here," Ian said.

I turned to face him.

"I'm afraid I mentioned that I haven't had a decent slice of lemon cake since the last time I was here. Cole said he'd fix that, grabbed his keys, and left before I could argue."

I sat on one of the two stools.

"You missed his veggie pizza last night." Ian put the baking stone in the drawer under the oven. It was hard to miss the toned muscles in his arms or how broad his back was. "There's some in the fridge, if you'd like me to warm you a slice."

I quickly moved my gaze to his face and replied, "I thought you didn't cook."

"I don't, but I do help clean up the mess, and I can

manage to reheat leftovers without burning them. Shall I get you some?"

"Not right now. Thanks."

He leaned against the counter across from me, arms folded over his chest, which did nothing to hide his ripped abs or the thin brown hairline that led...well, down. My cheeks warmed with embarrassment that I couldn't manage to keep my eyes at a respectable level.

Ian smirked. "You're a perplexing one."

I rested my elbows on the counter that separated us. "How's that?"

"You traveled across states and not once checked out the men who clearly noticed you. You're a succubus who's embarrassed to be in the company of a man with no shirt. And you've managed to put the type of smile on my best friend's face that I'd thought impossible." He pointed a finger at me. "You're good for him."

"He's just being nice to me because Lilith told him to be." Even after Cole's and my conversation, a large part of me refused to believe his words meant anything more than that we were friends. No different than him and Luz.

Ian grinned, knuckles stroking his chin. "No. Cole doesn't do nice unless it's sincere. Like with his friends. He found that group of misfits and watches out for them because they watch out for him." He paused. "You're the first succubus he's tolerated for more than twenty-four hours, and I get why."

I waited, absorbing what he said.

He pointed at me for a second time. "You're nothing like any succubus I've ever met." He stepped closer, bending at the waist and resting his forearms on the counter in front of me. "No. You're almost... wholesome. How can that be?"

I was only eighteen years old. There should be a level of innocence about me. I half wondered if Ian had the power to see auras like Wyatt did. Did he see how pink mine was? Cole had said an incubus's strength came from how much energy he siphoned from humans. Surely, one who'd been around as long as Ian would have abilities newer demons didn't.

I glanced away from his infinite lapis eyes and traced my finger over a nick in the countertop to give me something besides Ian to focus on.

He laughed. "See, that's exactly what I mean. You blush easily. I bet you're wishing I'd put on a shirt."

I squirmed in my seat. What was taking Cole so long to make a breakfast run? "Cole probably wouldn't mind if you borrowed one of his." Although Ian was bigger in the chest and arms than Cole.

Ian raised a curious eyebrow. "I've plenty of clothes in my suitcase. Besides, I don't think I'd look as cute in his clothes as you. If I didn't know better..." He squinted. "But you can't be."

I didn't like where that conversation was headed, and I didn't know what to say to the statements he'd left hanging.

He straightened, eyes wide. "Blimey!"

"What?" I asked, following his gaze to the door. "Is Cole back?" Was he afraid Cole had heard our conversation?

"Lilith's here," Ian whispered.

I focused all my energy on hearing past the walls of the apartment. I caught the low murmur of children and what sounded like the rumble of a vacuum cleaner.

These were normal sounds for our building.

"How can you tell?" I asked just as quietly as he'd said her name.

Ian grabbed a sheet of paper and a pen from near the phone jack and hastily wrote *I can feel her signature.*

I couldn't, but then I couldn't feel Ian's and he was right in front of me. I took the pen from him and scribbled *Do we lie?*

He shook his head and wrote *Until we find out why she's here, say nothing.*

I nodded.

He scrawled *Act natural and flush this!*

I wasn't sure what *natural* was when in the presence of the Queen of the Damned, but I nodded again nonetheless and hurried to the bathroom with the paper in hand.

"I hope Cole remembered to request a double shot of espresso in my coffee," Ian said conversationally, obviously wanting it to appear as if we weren't panicking.

Too late. I was totally freaking out. My hand shook so badly, I had a hard time lifting the toilet seat. "And a hazelnut latte," I said though the closed bathroom door.

Afraid Lilith could hear our every move, I went through the motions of using the bathroom: sitting and noisily grabbing toilet paper. Before flushing, I dropped the now crumpled piece of paper into the bowl. It disappeared in a swirl of water as I washed my hands. Once I was sure it was gone, I turned off the water and rejoined Ian, who'd dressed and taken a seat in the leather chair in the family room. The television had been turned on to the morning news.

I stood near the couch chewing on my thumbnail, silently chanting, *Crap, crap, crap,* as my left leg trembled uncontrollably. My right leg would have shaken along with it had my knee not been locked into place, holding me upright.

"Stop fidgeting and sit," Ian whispered, indicating the couch with his eyes.

I gladly did the latter. The first wasn't so easy. Each second that ticked by had me jumping in my skin.

Was it ridiculous to ask that Lilith's visit, less than twenty-four hours after my trip home, be a coincidence? I'd been double cloaked: first by Wyatt's nephilim-angelic powers and then by voodoo magic, compliments of Ian.

I couldn't stop shaking. More than anything, I didn't want to face Lilith's wrath. I might have talked a big game before, but truth be told, she scared me shitless.

Ian sat perfectly still—a picture of calm. I wanted to jump up, grab his shoulders, and shake him senseless. His stern expression told me to pull myself together. I slid my hands under my thighs in an effort to keep them steady and breathed deeply.

"So you've only been dead a week," Ian said, motioning with his hand for me to answer.

"To the day." Wow, I hadn't realized that until just now.

"Has Cole been treating you well?"

"He's been great," I replied, praying Lilith was listening to our conversation. "Showing me around, helping me meet new people. I couldn't ask for more." Except maybe to have been allowed to rest in peace, but did I still want that? Was being a corpse in the ground better than being an immortal walking the Earth? I decided I'd give myself more time to answer that question.

Ian mouthed *better*.

I didn't feel better, and I found Ian's don't-have-a-care-in-the-world demeanor astounding.

"How long are you in town?" I asked, keeping the conversation going because it helped keep my mind off Lilith.

"I'm not sure yet. A few days, maybe a couple of weeks."

I closed my eyes and said a silent prayer that Lilith was just checking up on us.

The sound of a key sliding into the doorknob was quickly followed by a faint click of the door being unlocked. Lilith and Cole stepped in.

"We have company," Cole said cheerfully. He was a step behind Lilith, and his eyes immediately found mine. I forced a smile.

"Lilith." Ian strolled over to the Queen of the Damned and kissed her hand. "I thought that was your signature I felt, but Cole hadn't said you'd be visiting."

"Ian, it's been too long," Lilith replied graciously. She wore a violet sundress and gold sandals. Her blonde hair flowed over her shoulders in thick spirals. "I'd forgotten how charming you can be."

He inclined his head. "Won't you have a seat?"

"Thank you." She lowered herself into the chair Ian had vacated.

Ian sat on the couch next to me. Cole set a cardboard cup carrier on the table. He handed Lilith a bottled iced tea and then held a paper travel cup out to me. "Hazelnut latte."

"Thanks." I took it, proud of myself for keeping my hands from visibly trembling.

He handed Ian his cup along with a small bag, which I assumed contained a slice of lemon cake.

"Cole, come sit next to me." Lilith patted the arm of the chair. He did. "Cole and I were just talking about how depressing funerals are."

Ian shifted, pressing his leg against mine in what was most likely a silent message not to lose it. Cole drank from his health shake, not saying a word.

"Did you know Avery's arrangements are this weekend?" Lilith added.

To keep from replying, *You don't say,* I sipped my latte.

"I did know that," Ian said, breaking off a piece of cake and putting it into his mouth.

Lilith ran a hand over Cole's thigh. He stiffened. I wanted to jump over Ian and swat her hand away before she siphoned Cole's energy. She smirked, as if pleased that my jaw had clenched along with the fingers on my right hand, which were now curled into a fist.

Her calculating gaze held mine. "Where were you yesterday?"

"Avery was feeling depressed," Ian began, but stopped when Lilith held up a dainty hand.

"Avery is quite capable of answering for herself." Her scrutinizing glare leveled me.

"I…" am so screwed. I cleared my throat. "I was having a hard time this weekend—I died a week ago today."

"I know when you died." Lilith flicked her perfectly manicured pinkie nail off her equally nice thumbnail.

"Yes." I focused on the carpet and quickly decided to keep my reply as close to the truth as possible. "I wanted to go to church to...ah...pray for my friends and family. Cole doesn't believe in that stuff, but Ian said he wouldn't mind keeping me company." I hoped it was even possible for demons to enter a church without bursting into flames.

Lilith raised a golden eyebrow.

Ian smiled. "I'm always happy to mess with the other side, and what better way to do that than for a demon to visit the house of the Lord?"

"Is that all?" Lilith asked, studying her nails with bored interest.

"I—"

Lilith's green gaze met mine. "Think carefully, because I'd hate to find out you're lying."

Cole hadn't moved a muscle. Ian shifted, his leg bumping into mine, again.

Lilith unscrewed the top on her tea. "Would you like to know what I did yesterday?"

"Yes, ma'am," I replied, hoping that was the end of her inquiry.

She took a sip and set the bottle on the table in front of her. "I attended the wake of my newest succubus. It was quite beautiful: the flowers, friends and family gathered to support each other, easily a hundred pictures showing happier times."

"It sounds very nice." My voice cracked, and I was sure I'd gone white.

"I saw your sister. Gracie, is it?"

My nails cut crescent grooves into my palm. Ian shifted and bumped into me yet again. I wanted to snap at him that I had enough sense not to punch the Queen of the Damned in the face. Instead, I ground my teeth. She knew, but *how* was the question.

She continued. "She had on the most lovely butterfly necklace."

Crap.

"It matches the bracelet you're wearing," Lilith added with a nod to my wrist.

Double crap.

"Now I'll ask you again. Is there something else you'd like to tell me?"

I focused on the edge of the coffee table. "ItrickedIanintotakingmetoNewYork."

She bent forward. "I'm sorry, I didn't hear you."

Louder and slower, I repeated, "I tricked Ian into taking me to New York."

Cole's eyes closed, and his shoulders slumped forward, but what else could I do but tell the truth? Everything I owned I'd gotten from Lilith. She knew the necklace had been mine.

"I'm sorry." I kept my head bowed, hoping by doing so I showed Lilith proper respect. "I just wanted to know if Gracie was okay and to see my parents one last time. I did the shift thing. No one knew it was me."

Lilith's gaze traveled to Cole. His eyes were still closed. She licked her ruby-red lips and returned her attention to me. "What I find interesting is how I didn't sense that you'd been there. See, I've learned to pay close attention to my new charges. Ian helped me realize the importance of that." A sweet smile graced her lips. "Isn't that right, Ian?"

Ian inclined his head in answer, never once flinching. I couldn't figure out how he managed to remain at ease. He casually ate his cake. I wanted to run from the apartment and hide. Instead, I clung onto the one positive thing in what Lilith had said: she didn't know how I'd managed to leave Illinois hidden from Hell and her. It meant she didn't know about Wyatt.

"I had a voodoo bag with me," I replied, saying the first thing that came to mind. "I found out how to make it on the Internet," I added when her eyes narrowed. "You'd be amazed by what you can find these days." *Please don't ask what was in it.*

Lilith was quiet for so long, I started to make up a list of items one might use for such a thing: graveyard dirt, chicken bones, raven's feather, hair. I had no idea if any of those things were correct. I hadn't even known voodoo was real twenty-four hours ago. *If there's a God, please don't let her ask me about the bag.*

Finally, after what felt like an eternity, she clucked her tongue and turned her cold gaze to Cole. "And you allowed it?"

"He didn't know," I blurted. "I knew he'd refuse to let me out of his sight if he even suspected I wanted to attend my wake. That's why I tricked Ian into taking me to church, so that I could get away from Cole long enough to talk Ian into giving me some time by myself. Only Ian's too much of a gentleman to leave a girl crying in a church." I sucked in a breath and then plunged onward with my lie. "When Ian insisted on staying, I decided to play on his kindness and convinced him to come with me."

Lilith's gaze bounced between me and Ian. Out of the corner of my eye, I saw Cole staring at me, mouth agape, but I didn't dare look directly at him. I was afraid of what Lilith might do to him if she didn't believe me. And while I'd just spewed the best lie of my existence, I was afraid it wouldn't fool a fallen angel. I set my latte down before I dropped it.

Ian broke the uncomfortable silence. "I've been around half a millennium and still can't stand to see a lady cry."

"That time has allowed you to forget how much I dislike my employees returning home?" Lilith replied acidly.

"She shifted," Ian said coolly. "Unlike me—who went back home for revenge—Avery wished only to convince her sister to check in on a friend of theirs, and I suspected to say her goodbyes to her parents. A brave thing for such a young lady to do, don't you agree?"

He held Lilith's gaze as if he were a worthy adversary. I was ready to hyperventilate.

That thought almost made me smile, because the memory of Cole telling me to put my head between my knees came rushing back.

"Please don't blame them," I said forcing myself to hold it together. "I'm not a child. I make my own decisions."

Cole jumped up and faced Lilith. "She's—"

"Saving you from the punishment she knows would befall you if I discover you had any part in her trip to New York." Lilith pointed to her iced tea. Cole handed it to her. "Leave us, both of you."

I held my breath. Cole didn't move.

This was it. The last time I'd see him. Possibly my last moments on Earth.

Chapter 17

"As you wish." Ian wrapped a hand around Cole's arm and shoved him toward the door.

I wanted to tell Cole it was okay. I'd known the risk of taking a trip to New York and, despite his warning, still went. I also wanted to hug Ian for forcing Cole to leave. I'd find a way to make it through whatever punishment Lilith dished out. It would be nothing compared to the torture I'd put myself through if Cole had to pay even a minute for my actions.

I remained seated, my back to the arm of the sofa. Lilith waited several minutes before she spoke. Most likely waiting until she could no longer sense Ian and Cole's signatures. This way, they wouldn't hear her say she was sending me to a third world country where it was legal to force girls into a sex trade. I'd be gone without a trace and would have to pray she didn't then punish Cole for failing to keep a close eye on me.

Lilith stood and circled me, placing her hands on my shoulders.

"Did I not make it clear to you that you weren't to return home?"

"You said I couldn't live in New York, not that I couldn't visit." I was so happy she couldn't see my face, because I was sure my nose crinkled as I told that lie.

Lilith's nails dug into my skin like tiger claws,

causing me to wince in pain. "I asked Gracie where she'd gotten her necklace."

I swallowed but said nothing.

Lilith's hands felt like ten-pound anvils on my shoulders. She went on. "Her fingers stroked it tenderly as she replied 'a girl gave it to me.' When I asked her if the girl was still there, she said she hadn't seen her since she was in the restroom."

I had to say something. This time, only the truth would do. "I tried to call Gracie, to hear her voice and let her know our friend needed her now that I'm gone, but you cut me off from everyone I know."

"Everyone in your old life. You are dead, Avery. You're no longer a part of their world."

A tear rolled down my cheek and fell to my knee, leaving a dark spot on my jeans. Did she not understand that for me death meant waking up to a new reality?

I swiped at my cheek, drying the wet streak left behind from my tear.

Lilith sighed. "Despite what you may think of me, I'm one of the more lenient queens."

That news shocked me. "There's more than one?" And she was the nicest?

"There are four, to be exact. Would you like to know how my sisters rule their demons?"

I shook my head. If Lilith's idea of lenient was to punish her demons by forcing them to do the things they most despised, I definitely didn't want to know what her sisters did.

She walked around to the front of the couch and settled next to me with her feet tucked under her.

"Estee and Naamah assign their incubi and succubi specific humans," she replied despite my not wanting to know. "They're experts at finding the pure of heart and those who serve them are proficient at corrupting souls." She picked up her drink again. "Agrat, well, she's just batty if you ask me, insisting her demons personally deliver souls to the pit." I shuddered, remembering what Ian and Cole had told me about succubi who drained humans entirely, killing them. Lilith waved a hand dismissively. "The paperwork alone wastes so much time, and human life is short as it is. Damned souls die on their own every day.

"I prefer to drop my charges into a new life and trust they appreciate my generosity." Her voice was sweet, but there was nothing in her sharp features that could be mistaken for friendly. "Those under my charge are given everything they need to start a new life. In return, I expect them to respect my decisions about where they live, and I expect them to mark souls by doing exactly what they did while human."

"I wasn't a slut when I was human!"

"Your soul was marked by lust, and you weren't invited to pass through the Pearly Gates. It's this." She held her hands wide. "Or the River of Souls to pay for your other sins."

Meaning the murder of Krista, confirming I could've saved her had I tried.

"I didn't mean any disrespect." If true death wasn't an option, then I'd choose living with Cole, stealing months from unsuspecting people over an eternity of torture. "I didn't think—"

"You'd get caught," she said. "What do you think your punishment should be?"

I swallowed and averted my eyes. Ian had never said whether he'd actually done what Lilith had demanded when he was in the hot seat, but no way would I kiss, much less do anything else with, someone younger than me.

"Nick's soul is still unclaimed." Lilith pursed her lips. "If Team Lust were to claim him soon, I'd have yet another young demon in my charge."

"Cole's friend, Nick?" I stammered.

"You've met him?" She smiled. "He's cute. Don't you agree?"

"He's Cole's friend."

"Is that a problem?"

"Yes! He's kind." And I was pretty sure Cole helped to keep him that way. "He's off limits. Cole said so the day I met him." All of Cole's friends were, but that wasn't the reason I'd never kiss him, or Dylan for that matter. They weren't the ones who made my stomach flutter as if a hundred butterflies occupied it. "What do you mean if you 'get him young'?" I asked, her comment just sinking in.

She set her tea down. "Deliver Nick's soul to me, and I'll forget your little trip to New York."

"D-deliver? As in sleep with him and take all of his life force?"

"There are worse ways for a person to die." Like plummeting to her death by falling off a deck or making a deal with a demon, thinking you're talking to one of the good guys. She continued. "Once a succubus sucks the last breath of life from a guy, she is in possession of his soul. You know what they say…"

Possession is nine-tenths of the law. And as Hell's servant, I'd be forced to deliver his soul to Hell.

"I'm not killing Nick." I scooted away from her as if she'd sprouted fangs and talons. Nick was eighteen years old. He had his whole life ahead of him—one I wasn't about to take from him. "I won't."

"You dare to defy my orders a second time?"

Her emerald green eyes turned the color of blood as her enchanting human features desiccated, leaving her skin gray and mummified. I scrambled away from her, stopping when my back was against the television, fearing more than ever that she'd toss me into the fiery river.

"Answer me!" she bellowed.

"No! Yes! I mean, please don't ask *that* of me."

Her glare snapped to the door. "For Satan's sake!"

Please don't let me be about to meet her boss. Anything but her boss.

We were still alone, though.

"Lilith, I swear no one recognized me, and I didn't stay long. No harm was done."

Her eyes remained on the door. Several seconds passed. Then Cole burst into the apartment with a reluctant-looking Ian trailing behind him. Lilith was back to her angelic self. Cole stopped in front of her. She frowned.

"You can't blame Avery for visiting New York," Cole exclaimed.

I jumped between them, my hands on Cole's chest. "Shut up!"

Lilith's gaze moved to Ian. He leaned against the wall in the foyer. "What he meant to say is pardon the intrusion, but he hopes you won't be too harsh on Avery. It was her newness to this life that led her to misinterpret what you would and wouldn't allow."

A red flush crept up Cole's neck. "I meant it wasn't Avery's fault."

"Shut up, Cole!" I'd find the strength to survive whatever new punishment Lilith dished out, but I didn't need the guilt of getting Cole in trouble on my conscience, also. I faced Lilith. "I'm the one who planned the trip and begged Ian to come with me. I didn't tell Ian that I'd already asked you about living in New York," I quickly added so that he wouldn't be the next one in trouble.

"She's new, and she's my responsibility," Cole insisted. "I should've made sure she understood your rules. I'll take her punishment."

Ian closed his eyes. I wished he'd tackle Cole and stuff a sock in his mouth.

Cole had no idea what Lilith had planned for me or that I'd already refused. She hadn't picked Nick to punish just me. She'd done it to also chastise Cole. If she agreed to let him serve my sentence, Cole would have to kill one of his friends.

"No, he won't!" I jumped between Cole and Lilith and pushed Cole toward the door. "For the love of all that is good in you, just go!"

"Well, isn't this an interesting turn of events," Lilith said.

Cole and I froze, our gazes locked on each other's. I was more scared at that moment than I had been before.

"Most incubi and succubi fight like cats and dogs, yet here the two of you are ready to stand before a firing squad for each other." Lilith's words were laced with intrigue.

Snapping out of my panic, I turned to face Lilith. "The two incubi I've met are nice. Stubborn as all heck," I added with a glance at Cole next to me.

Lilith strolled closer. I wanted to place myself between her and Cole, but he put his arm out to stop me from moving.

"I admire loyalty," she said. "For that I'll relent on my earlier punishment." Her gaze bored into me. "In return for me forgiving your insubordination, I expect you to mark a soul by day's end."

Too afraid of what the *or else* would be, I agreed.

"And Cole, you'll clearly explain to Avery what I expect of my demons, or I'll start picking your victims."

He nodded.

"Now that that's settled." She turned to Ian. "Care for a real breakfast?"

"I could eat," he replied. Even if he wasn't hungry, he'd have said yes to Lilith. Only fools like me told her no.

She gripped Cole's cheeks with one hand and brought her lips to his. Their mouths remained closed. Cole's fingers curled into fists as his features turned ghostly. When she released him, he staggered sideways into me.

"Why'd you drain him?" I lowered Cole to the ground. "You're such a bi—"

"Ah, ah, ah," she warned.

Ian hurried forward. "Shall we?" He held out his arm for Lilith to take. When she did, he gave me one of his stern glares. Whether it was to tell me to stop talking before I made matters worse or it was because his friend was in trouble because of me, I didn't know.

"I saw a quaint crêpe place not far from the church," Ian said as he led Lilith to the door. His gaze met mine when he turned to grab his jacket off the kitchen stool. "Help him," he whispered, like I needed to be told that. Then they were gone.

"Cole?" I kneeled next to him. His eyes rolled back into his head as a whisper of a moan passed his lips. I'd never seen him look this bad. I shook his shoulders. "Don't you dare die on me!"

"Can't," he muttered. The corner of his mouth twitched, and I was pretty sure he'd have smiled if he'd had the strength to.

"Shh." I lowered my head and placed my lips on his. I wasn't sure how the sharing of energy worked. With humans, their life force just flowed into me, no thought required. Nothing happened when I kissed Cole. "Come on," I groaned and smashed my lips to his, willing my body to release some of my stolen energy. It was like kissing a sleeping child. Cole lay there, eyes closed and arms next to him exactly where they'd landed when I'd lowered him onto the floor.

Absentmindedly, I ran my fingers through Cole's soft hair and thought, *Please work.* It had to. He needed to refuel with the energy in me, or else I'd have to find someone dumb enough to buy that my hot roommate needed to be kissed by a fair maiden to wake from an enchanted sleep.

It wasn't funny, really, but a small *huff* that was part laughter and part disbelief at the stupid idea escaped my lips before I went back to thinking, *please work.*

I'm not sure how long I kneeled beside him—long enough for my foot to fall asleep from lack of circulation—but I finally felt a weird tingling sensation very much like an army of ants crawling beneath my skin. Seconds stretched past. I fought not to jump back and swat at the unseen creepers. Finally, Cole's mouth started to move with mine, and his hand cupped the back of my head. For a moment, I thought he'd suck all my strength from me. We'd be repeating this process— only I'd be the one nearly passed out, and he'd be saving me. But then the freaky prickling stopped. Cole sat in front of me, his forehead on mine.

"Thank you."

I licked my lips, savoring the last taste of his kiss. "It was the least I could do."

"I hate her visits."

Considering every time he saw Lilith, she drained him, I couldn't blame him. I felt worn out myself.

"What were you thinking, coming back here?" I asked.

"I know how cruel Lilith can be. I didn't want you to face her wrath alone."

"You should be grateful she didn't take you up on your offer." He had no idea what he'd almost agreed to, which seemed to be his downfall when it came to Lilith. He'd make the deal first and ask for the details later. "And thank you, because I was afraid to hear what she'd planned to say before you interrupted us."

He smiled. "You're welcome."

Cole was pale, and the light in his eyes was dim. "We make some pair," he commented, taking me by surprise that he considered us a pair. But in a way, we were: an incubus with a kind heart and a succubus stupid enough to cross a powerful demon. It was a precarious combination. And maybe that was the point. Maybe Lilith wanted us to screw up. A scarier thought was that maybe she'd put me with Cole in the hopes of getting her hands on one of his friends. I'd have to be more careful so that would never happen.

He pushed himself up off the floor. He was slow, his movements almost sluggish, but he managed to make it to the kitchen without assistance or stumbling.

"I'm starting to think Lilith knew exactly what she was doing, when she made me your mentor," he said.

Me, too, but I wanted to hear his reasoning.

He grabbed the orange juice out of the fridge and drank straight from the bottle. "She knew I'd be attracted to you." He rubbed the back of his neck. "She kept her word. It took her over a hundred and fifty years, but she did it." He shook his head. "I didn't see that coming."

I was stuck on the confirmation that Cole was interested in me. He'd lived on Earth for a century and a half. He had to have met girls he liked. Girls he wanted to know. I was trying to make sense of what he'd said when he put the jug on the counter and added, "I'm not sure if I should thank her or slap her."

In the short time it took him to finish rambling, my emotions had ricocheted all over the place. Happiness that he was attracted to me, because I'd wanted to be more than friends since the first time he kissed me. Confusion at the mention of a promise; he'd never told me Lilith had promised him anything. And concern that the thought of liking me had him considering slapping the Queen of the Damned.

My mouth opened and closed a few times. My thoughts were such a jumbled mess that when I finally replied, it was with a high-pitched, "Huh?"

Cole leaned against the kitchen counter, ankles crossed and eyes focused on the slate blue tile. "When Lilith first approached me, she said I could remain on

Earth. She promised me one day I'd find someone special. Once I discovered what I'd become, I figured she'd meant humans I could siphon from. I never thought I'd actually meet someone I'd want to know past a casual acquaintance."

"You hang out with Luz," I said lamely.

His mouth formed a slanted line. "Luz is like a sister to me. Never once have I wanted to kiss her."

I could no longer tell myself that Cole was only tolerating me, waiting for a time when he could pack my stuff into boxes and load them into the back of a cab. Between last night and his current confession, I knew we shared a connection, one that confounded us both. But to believe Lilith meant for us to be anything more than friends was insane. Maybe Cole and I were destined to be a team, sucking life from the living for all of eternity. That was more probable than Lilith playing Cupid.

"You have to have met other succubi."

"Vain creatures that—despite their many suitors— were starved for attention." No wonder Cole liked me. I was a lot of things, but conceited and needy weren't two of them. Compared to other succubi, I was a rare commodity. He walked by me. "I can't believe she kept her promise, and I made one to you, which I plan to keep, even if there are times when your irrational behavior makes it difficult."

"You did?" I pivoted and watched him head toward the bedroom. "Which irrational behavior?" I'd done several foolish things over the past week.

"We should refuel before we're both comatose," he said in lieu of answering my question. "Ian would love to find us down for the count, and I do mean that sarcastically."

I was too busy trying to figure out what promise he referred to, to care about Ian or anything else.

Chapter 18

"Call him or I will," Cole said, exasperated. He sat on the arm of the couch, hands on his knees.

"And what would you say?" I asked incredulously.

"I'll tell him that *Megan*"—Cole put extra emphasis on the fake name I'd given Marcus—"can't stop talking about him, and we'll be at Old Time Bar and Grill in an hour if he'd like to run into you again."

"You wouldn't!"

"Want to bet?" Cole snatched the napkin with Marcus's phone number on it out of my hand and grabbed his phone from the coffee table in one swoop. "Admit it, you liked him or you wouldn't have kept his number."

"Lilith said I had to mark a soul." Saying it out loud caused my stomach to flip in disgust. "Marcus doesn't have a girlfriend, so all I'd be doing is shortening his life."

"He has a girlfriend."

My hands flew to my hips. "How would you know?"

"I heard him telling his friend that he had to call someone by the name of Sasha when he got home, and his friends didn't see what Marcus saw in the girl." Cole turned his phone over and over in his hand as he spoke. "I'll bet he called her after he picked his brother up."

I was about to argue that he couldn't possibly have heard their conversation, but with his heightened senses, he could.

"He's a nice guy, Cole." I grabbed for the napkin, but missed. "If he's dating someone else, he won't care if I call."

"I say he will." Cole tapped the screen of his phone to turn it on. He jumped over the coffee table when I lunged for him, and then dialed.

I went to stop him, moving more sluggishly than I would have had my own energy level not been so low. "Cole, don't!"

Cole planted a palm on my collarbone, keeping his other hand out of my reach.

"Is this Marcus?" Cole said into the phone.

"Hang up!" I hissed, embarrassed.

"This is a friend of Megan's," Cole said into the phone.

I tried to knock it out of his hand, but Cole's arms were longer than mine and I couldn't reach. He was faster than me, too. Every time I moved, so did he.

"Cole, hang up," I begged.

"This is *John*." Cole's frown warned me not to say his name again. "A friend of Megan's." He paused. Defeated, I groaned and stopped fighting him. I did need to mark a soul. If Cole was right about Marcus, then at least I wouldn't be kissing a complete stranger. And if Cole was wrong, I could rub it in his face. Cole went on. "She hasn't stopped talking about you."

"There goes what little dignity I had left," I whined.

Cole grinned and told Marcus that he and I would be at the restaurant later that afternoon.

When he hung up, I sagged against the couch. "Thanks for pimping me out."

"You're welcome." He stuffed his phone into his front pocket.

"I meant that sarcastically."

"I know. Get dressed. We're leaving in five. Oh, and before I forget, the rules for our kind are simple. Do not, under any circumstance, let a human find out you're immortal and mark souls. You already know how."

"Yeah." We'd gone over that. "Well, at least you're back in Lilith's good graces."

I was happy about that.

Cole stepped closer. "I'm not finished. The guidelines most of us live by are, if you even suspect you're about to do something a queen will disapprove of, stop what you're doing at once. The other rule, mark at least thirteen souls a year."

I cringed.

He added, "Marking them doesn't condemn them. It just says that if their actions while alive buy them a one-way ticket down, Lilith gains possession of their soul."

He wrapped his arms around me from behind, pinning mine to my side, and carried me to the bedroom. "Now it's your turn to do as you were told."

"Do you get your kicks out of antagonizing new succubi?"

"You're the first soul I've collected from processing."

Still in his arms, I had to crane my neck to see him. "You never told me that."

"You never asked." He released me but didn't

move away. "From what I understand, you're the first teen sent to this sector of Hell in decades. I think that's why Lilith fought so hard for your soul."

"I don't understand."

Cole rummaged through the closet. "Ian heard your soul could've gone either way, up or down."

And I managed to tip the scales to the dark, wonderful.

"Who'd he hear that from?" I asked, mildly curious if there was an afterlife rumor mill I should know about.

"Ian and Chloe are close." Cole tossed a pair of my skinny jeans onto the bed. "She heard from a low-level demon that Charmian was brought in on behalf of Heaven and Lilith on behalf of Hell. One look at you and Lilith had to have you." A sheer pink top landed on the jeans. "Charmian—who is an angel, by the way— had argued that your sins were minor compared to those of most condemned souls and that you didn't deserve to be sent to the darkest corners of eternity. Lilith agreed that in your case, burning in Hell until the end of time would have been extreme, but not all souls end up in the river. She stressed that yours would be given a useful assignment."

"Marking souls."

Cole nodded. "Most souls go up—what happens to them next is unclear—and the majority of Hell-bound souls never see the light of day again. We're two of the lucky ones."

"Forgive me if I don't consider myself lucky."

"Would you rather just be gone? Your eighteen years on Earth all you ever had?"

I frowned. Seven days ago, I would have said yes,

but now I wasn't sure how to answer that question. Now that I'd seen what I could have, what I did have, I really didn't want death to be final. I wasn't sure if accepting what I'd become made me a bad person. But I liked having my memories, even if it meant I couldn't be part of my family and friends' lives anymore. I liked the idea of attending college. Luz was great, and while I didn't expect her to replace Megan, I could see how she and I could be true friends. Ian, Wyatt, and Hunter weren't the worst supernatural beings I could have in my life. Even Nick and Dylan were nice.

Then there was Cole. No matter what we were to each other—coworkers, friends, or more—I didn't want to lose him.

****

An hour later, we sat at one of the high tables in Old Time Bar and Grill. It was a good thing Marcus had met me in my true form because I didn't have enough sustainable energy to transform into another version of me. Cole had grimaced when he'd seen I didn't put on what he'd pulled out of the closet. Instead I chose an oversized T-shirt, stressed jeans, and sneakers. He, on the other hand, could have passed for a model in his faded jeans and casual, collared shirt. The waitress—a girl in a too-short miniskirt, dowsed in perfume—had just brought us our sodas when Marcus arrived with one of the guys I'd seen him with the other day.

"That's my cue to step away." Cole took a drink of his cola and added, "If you want my advice—"

"I don't."

He set his glass down. "Pretend you're glad to see him, talk for a few minutes, and before we leave give him a meaningful kiss goodbye."

"And what will you be doing while I'm ruining a guy's life?" As soon as the question was out of my mouth, I was sorry I asked because I didn't want to know who he'd be making out with.

"You're not ruining anyone's life," Cole replied with a shake of his head. "Slip in a comment that you won't be here long, okay? I want to be home before rush hour."

Cole moseyed toward the back of the restaurant. A snarl snuck up my throat. Lucky bitch, whoever she was.

The "Hi" that came from my right pulled my attention away from Cole. Marcus stood next to our table every bit as sexy as I remembered.

"Hi." I tucked my hair behind my ear.

Marcus sat in the chair Cole had vacated. "I was hoping I'd see you again."

"Me, too," I lied. "How are you?"

"Good."

His phone rang. He checked the display, staring at it long enough for me to surmise that he was debating whether or not he should answer it.

"I won't mind," I said.

He sucked in a breath and smiled. I sipped my soda.

"Hey," he said into the phone. He was silent as he listened to whoever was on the other end.

I focused my attention on the noises around me and picked up the sound of a girl's voice coming from Marcus's phone. I couldn't catch all her words, though. She said something about finding shoes for cheerleading and watching a movie with friends. I wondered how long it would take for me to get supersonic hearing like Cole and Ian.

"Can't. Dave and I are out."

Dave was currently chatting up one of the waitresses at a table not far from us.

"Yeah, when I'm home." He set his phone down on the table. "Sorry about that."

"No problem." I took another sip of my drink. He squirmed in his seat. Had I not heard bits of his conversation with the mystery girl, I'd have thought his fidgeting was normal meeting-someone-new jitters. "Girlfriend missing you?"

"Ah, no." He glanced at Dave, then back at me. "It was my mom."

I doubted his mother needed shoes for cheerleading.

"She needs help moving some things," he added.

Apparently, Marcus wasn't perfect. His soul was pure, though. I was beginning to understand how Cole could tell. Now that I studied Marcus, I could see a light around him that shimmered. It wasn't as bright as I imagined an angel's would be, and I couldn't see its color like Wyatt could, but a slight haze definitely skimmed his skin like a warm sweater. I glanced around. The waitress's aura was dimmer than Marcus's. And Dave's was so dingy it was as if it was trying to penetrate the grime on a dirty window.

My attention settled back on Marcus. The brightness of his soul must have been what had informed Cole that it hadn't been marked by Hell yet. I was also sure—like, ninety-two percent confident—Marcus wouldn't do anything to condemn his soul later in life.

"Did you get your schedule?" Marcus asked.

"My what?"

"Schedule, for school."

"Not yet," I said, realizing he thought I was a year or two younger than I actually was. "I'm, um, picking it up later this week."

Marcus's fingers brushed mine. "I could show you around, if you'd like."

"Maybe," I said, because I'd already gone with the lie. No need to be rude now.

Marcus told me about football practice, which had already begun. I couldn't help wondering where Cole had disappeared to. The restaurant wasn't crowded. Only a couple of tables were occupied.

After several minutes Marcus paused, head cocked to the side. "I'm sorry, I'm monopolizing the conversation. Do you play any sports?" When I shook my head, he asked, "What classes are you most excited about?"

I wet my lips. I liked Marcus. He was sweet, but I'd already decided there would be no *us* after today. I'd only steal a little of his life this one time to get Lilith off my back.

"Drawing," I replied with a smile. I'd taken Drawing 101 sophomore year but dropped it when the teacher told me my lines were too dark and my shadowing too one-dimensional. I'd used the excuse that I didn't want a bad grade in an elective to bring down my grade-point average. The teacher had tried to talk me into coming back, stating his comments were meant to teach, not discourage. Deep down, I knew that, but homework had been cutting into my growing social life. Dropping art gave me a study hall. I was able to do most my homework at school. Death and the afterlife has given me a new perspective on life.

My cell phone vibrated, letting me know I'd received a message.

Three minutes. It was from Cole.

"I have to go," I said to Marcus. "It was great seeing you again." I leaned toward Marcus. He watched me, his eyes traveling from mine to my mouth and back up. Before I could put too much thought into what I was doing, I brushed his lips with mine. Marcus's hands remained on the table, almost as if he was afraid if he moved I'd back away. A fraction of a moment passed, and then I kissed him. His hand came to rest on the side of my face as his fingers tangled in my hair. He was an excellent kisser, but there were no sparks, for me, anyway. The warm, tingly sensation of his life force fueled my muscles, traveling through me. Like the other times, I knew when to stop the flow and end the kiss.

I stood, grabbing my purse from the back of my chair. "Good luck this season with football."

He gazed into my eyes a moment. "Why do I get the feeling this is the last time I'll see you?"

"You never know." I hoped he lived a long life and that his decisions granted him entrance upstairs. Seeing me again wouldn't help with that.

I had no idea where Cole had been lurking or if he'd been watching or listening, but he and I reached the exit at the same time. As we drove through town, I breathed in deep, savoring the smell of barbecue and fresh-cut grass. I felt invigorated. It was nice to be able to enjoy the scents around me with such clarity. I could've done without the floral fragrance of the waitress's perfume that clung to Cole, though. There were good and bad elements that came with heightened scenes, I supposed.

By the time we got back to the apartment, I'd made peace with what I'd become. It helped to know the alternative was so much worse. And kissing Marcus wasn't bad. Sure, there were no fireworks, but I didn't blame him for that. Fireworks didn't happen with every kiss; even I knew that. The more I pondered it, the more I realized just how innocent our kiss had been.

There was that word again: innocent. I had to be Hell's only succubus who could be described as such. I almost burst into laughter at that thought.

I considered myself lucky that—with the cards I'd been dealt—I'd been surrounded by kind people like Cole and his friends. I could make being a succubus work. No, I *would* make it work. So why, by the time we reached the door to our apartment, did I have an overwhelming urge to slap Cole across the face? Hard, too.

I kicked my sneakers off near the kitchen stools and dropped my purse on the floor.

"What's your problem?" Cole asked. He stood a few feet from me, eyes narrowed.

"Nothing." I breathed in deep, trying to calm myself. The stench of cheap perfume invaded my nostrils. I covered my nose with my hand. "You reek of imitation lavender and…and…onions."

Cole tossed his keys onto the counter. Obvious confusion flittered over his features only to be replaced with the realization that I was referring to the scents of the waitress.

"You're one to talk!" he spit back. "You stink of Sport Goofy."

"Sport Goofy, I mean Marcus, barely touched me."

Cole gave off such a strong odor, I was sure the waitress had put her hands all over him.

Cole stepped closer, placing his hands on the counter on either side of me, caging me in.

"And I barely touched her," he growled. "When a human's life force flows from them to us, our souls grow brighter and—"

"We smell like them," I said, finishing his sentence. He'd told me that once.

"And because our senses become sharper, we know when our kind renews." The blue in his irises was more pronounced than I'd remembered. I bit my lip to keep from asking him if that was because of my heightened vision or because he'd renewed, as he called it. "Now, do you want to tell me what's really bothering you?"

I felt my face warm, and I had to fight to keep my gaze from traveling to his lips. Did I want to admit that I was irrationally jealous that he'd kissed another girl? Nope. So, instead, I said, "Her smell makes me want to puke."

"Eau de Jock is doing the same to me."

"You're the one who called Sport Goofy," I reminded him.

He smiled, clearly happy that I'd called Marcus by the nickname.

"You're the one who pissed off the Queen of the Damned," he countered.

I twitched a shoulder. "I still can't stand how you smell right now."

"Fine!" He grabbed me just under my butt and lifted me over his shoulder. I screamed. He held my legs, keeping me from falling.

"What are you doing?" I grabbed his waist from

my upside down position.

"You think I smell?"

"Reek. And you said I do, too! Now put me down!"

"Let's fix that."

He marched to the bathroom with me slung over his shoulder. The next thing I knew we were standing in the tub. He continued to hold me like a sack of rice.

"Cole?"

He slid me down his chest so I stood in front of him with his arms keeping me from moving.

"Cole?"

He reached behind me.

I glanced up at the showerhead, then to the knob next to me. "You wouldn't!"

"Want to bet?" A glint of annoyed mischief gleamed in his eyes a moment before icy water pelted me.

I screamed, again, but Cole didn't relent. After a few seconds, the spray warmed. Cole kept one arm locked around my waist and reached for the shampoo. The T-shirt and jeans I wore clung to my skin. I wiggled an arm free and caught his wrist as he flicked the cap open.

"Okay, you've made your point!" I conceded.

He held the bottle at the ready. Water followed a path over his dark hair, down his forehead, past his watchful eyes. "I made a promise to you that I'm inclined to break *if* you tell me the truth."

The promise he spoke of came back to me: If he and I slept together, it would be my doing, not his. And while I'd practically attacked him last night, he was too nice a guy to take advantage of me when I'd been so depressed.

"Avery?"

"I might have been…" My gaze jumped from the shampoo bottle back to him. "…just a teeny-tiny bit jealous of Miss Stinky Pants."

Cole set the shampoo down. "I would have liked nothing more than to rip Sport Goofy's heart out of his chest just for looking at you the way he did."

"Then you shouldn't have told him we'd be there."

"We were in a bind, remember? You had to mark a soul." He bent closer so that his lips were a breath away from mine. "I would have felt the same no matter who paid the price."

My heartbeat sped up. Cole's arms around me felt right.

"Cole, how can there be a you and me if our survival requires us to be with other people?"

"I don't know." He smoothed my hair away from my eyes with his fingertips. "But I'm willing to see where this takes us if you are."

Cole being mine sounded good. Maybe it was time I lived in the moment. Took risks. The future wouldn't be easy, but I could enjoy the present.

I melted into Cole's embrace. My lips skimmed his. His right hand caressed my cheek as his left hand found the bare skin of my lower back. My fingers explored his arms and back muscles through his soaking wet clothes. He pulled away, quickly unbuttoned his shirt, and let it fall around his feet. I grabbed the bottom of my T-shirt and yanked it, with some difficulty, over my head. Cole helped to untangle my drenched hair from the thin fabric. His gaze fell to the dusty rose bra I wore. His tongue slowly skimmed his upper lip. The simple gesture caused my heart to skip a beat. I had to be crazy, letting things progress this far with him, but I was past caring. I wanted to feel his body pressed against mine. As if he'd read my mind, he grabbed the cotton of his undershirt at the back of his neck and pulled it off.

My fingers trembled as I tried to undo the button on his jeans. He leaned back and gazed into my eyes. "We don't have to go further if you're not ready."

I was ready, even if a small part of me worried this was happening too fast and that it would hurt. "I want this."

He helped me with the button on his jeans and then, with expert hands, unbuttoned mine. I kissed him again, needing a moment to steady my nerves.

I'd heard mixed reactions from my friends about their first times. Some said it hurt, and others said it felt like a quick prick and then the pain was gone. I hoped my first time would be like the latter.

We shimmied out of our jeans. Then his mouth was on mine again, and my back was against the shower wall.

He broke the kiss, leaving me breathless as his lips traveled over my jaw and down my neck. My skin blazed with delight from his touch.

"I've wanted to taste every inch of you since the day we met," he whispered.

I didn't know how Cole and I could ever work, but I did know I didn't want him to stop. My fingers wrapped around the hair at the back of his head, pulling his mouth back to mine. The water turned off. Cole deepened our kiss, and with one arm wrapped around my back and the other under my knees, he lifted me off my feet. With our wet clothes piled in a heap in the corner of the tub, Cole carried me to bed.

His fingers explored my body, teasing me with whisper-soft touches down my thigh and along my stomach, just under the top of my underwear. The slower he went, the more aroused I got.

I bit my bottom lip as he slowly slid the last of my clothing off. His beautiful eyes never left mine. I couldn't help but think I was playing a dangerous game with my emotions. I liked Cole, and I knew I'd be crushed if we didn't find a way to make us work. I pushed those thoughts aside when Cole's weight settled on top of me as we kissed.

My breath caught when he positioned himself over me. *Please be a brief prick,* I prayed a moment before he slipped inside me. My gasp was swallowed by our kiss. Cole must have noticed, because he stopped moving.

"I'm okay," I quickly said. I was more than okay. The brief pang was already gone. Before he could question me, I covered his mouth with mine and let his kisses steal my heart.

Chapter 19

Ian showed up bright and early the next morning with a box of donuts and news that Lilith had left town. "Apparently, you wasted no time in finding a soul to mark," he said.

There definitely had to be a demon rumor mill out there.

I frowned. "Lilith gave me the day. It wasn't like I had much of a choice."

Cole had felt Ian's presence before he'd knocked. I'd suggested we ignore the door and stay in bed all day. Much to my disappointment, Cole managed to pry himself from my grasp and slip into a pair of jeans. He'd said something to the effect of, "We shouldn't be rude," as he'd put on a T-shirt. I'd been a bit preoccupied with trying to persuade him otherwise to hear his exact comment. By the time I'd managed to untangle myself from the sheet, Cole had already been out of the room. A small amount of blood had stained my inner thigh. Suddenly glad for the interruption, I'd quickly put on a pair of shorts and a cotton eyelet top and ducked into the bathroom to clean up. A few minutes later, I sat on my usual stool near the kitchen.

Ian grabbed a stack of paper plates from the cabinet near the sink and set them on the counter between us. "Trust me when I say you got off easy."

Considering the punishment Lilith had given him

and what she'd first demanded of me, I knew I had.

Cole handed him a mug of coffee. "Extra strong."

"Thanks, mate."

"Extra cream to hide the extra strong," Cole said as he set a mug in front of me.

"Thanks." I counted the number of plates Ian had pulled out. "How many people are you expecting?"

A knock on the door had him grinning. "I give you six months, and you'll be picking up the sounds around you without focusing."

Cole opened the door. Wyatt, Hunter, Luz, Nick, and Dylan filed in, each holding a to-go cup from a fast-food restaurant.

"Hi, Ian," Luz said in a gooey-sweet tone. She plopped down next to me. "Hey, girl. How's it going?"

I held my mug up the way one does when they say cheers and replied, "Wonderful."

She leaned closer. "We ran into Wyatt at a coffee house. He said he was headed over here."

"Did he happen to mention Ian was still here and that's why you came rushing over?" I whispered back, even though I knew Ian and Cole could hear us if they wanted to.

"You can't have them both," Luz teased.

I giggled and chose a chocolate éclair from the box of donuts Ian had brought. She grabbed a glazed donut and followed Cole, Ian, and Hunter into the family room.

"Hi." Nick reached around me and snatched the entire box. He and Dylan joined the others. That left Wyatt standing in the kitchen and me on the other side of the peninsula.

"Ian said your *aunt* visited," Wyatt said,

emphasizing the word aunt. I realized it was code for Lilith. He rested his elbows on the counter as he bent closer. "You okay?"

I nodded. If he'd talked to Ian, he already knew Lilith had found out about our trip. "It was worth it to see Gracie and my parents one last time. Thanks, again, for coming with me."

"You're welcome." He tapped his soda on the counter.

"So, are you and Ian friends now?" I licked at the custard filling spilling out of my donut.

"We share a mutual respect for each other," he replied. *Tap tap. Tap tap.*

Wyatt seemed to be studying me. Thinking I had chocolate on my face, I wiped my mouth with a napkin. He continued to watch me while *tap tapping* his cup on the counter.

"What?" I asked, smoothing a hand over my hair and wondering if I still had the lines from the sheets on my cheek.

"You look different." He tilted his head to the side and continued in a low voice. "Less pink, more red." He squinted. "Bright red."

I shifted, feeling exposed. Damn nephilim and his ability to read auras. "Red and pink are practically the same color."

"No. Pink is a color of purity whereas red is the color of passion."

"Whatever." I forced myself not to squirm under his narrow-eyed gaze. "Didn't your mom ever tell you it's impolite to stare?"

"She also told me I had a gift and not to waste it."

I shook my head and bit into my chocolate éclair.

Maybe if I ignored him, he'd move on to a new topic. I'd just swallowed the last of my donut when Wyatt's eyebrows shot upward. The tapping ceased.

"Holy crap! You lost your virginity," he blurted.

"Shh!" I hissed, but from the sound of someone choking behind me, I knew everyone had heard. I pivoted in my seat. Ian and Hunter were patting Cole's back, trying to dislodge the food he was choking on. Dylan and Nick exchanged stupid smirks. Luz was frozen mid-sip of her coffee.

I groaned, turned back to Wyatt, and covered my face with my hands. Why did the apartment have to be so small, and why did Wyatt have to announce *that* to the world? I peeked through my fingers to see Wyatt holding out a handful of paper towels, which Luz grabbed.

"I knew you guys liked each other," she whispered into my ear.

When she returned to the adjacent room, I told Wyatt, "Thanks. I could've gone my whole existence without everyone knowing that."

"You did? But you're a...how could you be..." He glanced past me to someone in the other room. "Is that possible?"

The next thing I knew, Ian was ushering the others to the door.

"But we just got here," Dylan protested, coffee in one hand and a long john in the other.

"Yes, and thanks for coming," Ian said as he opened the door. "But I need to talk to Wyatt and Cole alone."

Luz ran up to me and gave me a hug good-bye. "I'm so happy for you," she whispered. "I want to hear how it happened. Lunch, soon." She smiled at Ian as she flounced out the door.

Hunter, who'd lagged behind the others, said, "I'm sticking around to hear this one."

I didn't want to discuss it, so I slipped on my sneakers, grabbed my purse, and went to follow Luz. I had one foot out of the apartment when Ian grabbed my arm.

"I don't think so," he said.

"Call me!" Luz disappeared down the hallway.

Ian closed the door. "Cole, you couldn't tell?"

Cole scrubbed his face with his hand. I got the feeling he was replaying snippets of last night in his mind: Specifically, how nervous I'd been and my initial reaction to him being inside me. I was sure if Cole hadn't been in a hurry to get the door this morning, he would have seen the blood and known.

"Do we have to talk about this now?" My cheeks burned from embarrassment. It was bad enough they knew I was a succubus and what that meant. Them also knowing I'd lost my virginity was more than I could bear.

Cole got up. Ian, Wyatt, and Hunter seemed to take that as their cue to move into the family room, which didn't give Cole and me much privacy. They milled around the patio window, not bothering to sit.

Cole grasped my hands in his and spoke quietly. "When you winced." He closed his eyes. "I should've stopped, but I convinced myself you were only nervous. I'm sorry."

I met his worried gaze. "You did stop. I told you to keep going."

My first time had been special, and I didn't want

that to change. And I didn't want Cole to regret it.

Wyatt lowered himself onto the couch. "I should've realized sooner, but you're a succubus and normally succubi are experienced. Hell, it's in the job description. It never crossed my mind that you could've been a virgin." He let out a low whistle.

Hunter laughed. "Dude, you popped a succubus's cherry. That has to be a first."

Ian smacked him in the back of his head.

Cole's eyes narrowed. "What I don't understand is that if you never…how did you end up a succubus?"

I shrugged. "I was marked by lust." When he just continued to stare at me, I told them—the others were listening just as intently as Cole was—about camp and the little white lies that followed.

Ian shook his head. "That wouldn't mark your soul."

"Think," Cole said softly. "Did you date a friend's boyfriend? Purposely break up a relationship?"

I thought about the guys Lilith had ticked off the day we'd met. Nothing whatsoever had happened between me and Eddie Grenier, the hot counselor at camp. Frank Lutz did kiss me on the cheek. That was hardly a Hell-worthy moment.

The guys appeared to be holding their breath, waiting to hear the ugly truth about my past, but the lies that had spread like wildfire were much more entertaining than reality. That was why no one had wanted to believe me when I'd said nothing had happened. Take Adrian Bloom, for instance. He and I had spent seven minutes in a coat closet, discussing my best friend's secret crush on him. And Tom Cooper and I had had nothing more than a romantic stroll down the beach. There was flirting and a little kissing. It was actually romantic, and if it hadn't been for Nina Dionne—

"Oh."

Cole's eyes widened, waiting for me to elaborate.

It had been early spring with unseasonably hot weather. A group of us had decided to hang out at the beach one evening. I'd gone with Megan, but when Adrian had shown up, I'd felt like a third wheel. So I'd decided to give them some privacy and wandered by the shore. That was how I'd bumped into Tom. He'd been skipping rocks over the water. Tom was one of those guys everyone got along with.

"Give it a try," he'd said, holding out a flat stone. His white shirt had been unbuttoned and flapped in the breeze, revealing a lean chest and abs. His pale-gray eyes had caught the light of the moon, and his smile had urged me to hang out with him awhile.

I'd sucked at skipping rocks, but Tom had made it his mission of the night to teach me. He'd stood behind me, one warm hand on the bare skin of my waist and the other one holding my wrist. It'd been hard to concentrate with his hot breath tickling my neck. We must have tossed a dozen stones before one had finally hopped over the water. Satisfied that his work was done, Tom had asked if I'd like to go for a walk. One thing had led to another. We'd held hands, stopping every now and then to toss a stone into the ocean. He'd splashed me. I'd splashed him. It hadn't taken long before we were play fighting and then kissing.

That night had been perfect and, like a dream, gone by morning.

Tom and Nina had been the on-again, off-again

couple at school. Everyone knew when they were off because Nina would turn into a major bitch and Tom would drown his newfound freedom in beer bongs and keg parties, claiming life was better when he was a bachelor. That night, Tom hadn't been drunk, and the only reason Nina hadn't been there was because she'd had some family event to attend—a wedding or baby shower; I couldn't remember which. The point was, I'd known Tom had a girlfriend and I'd willing kissed him. By doing so, my soul had been marked by lust. It didn't matter that we hadn't planned to run into each other on the beach or that we hadn't planned on making out.

Nina had found out the following Monday and had broken up with Tom. She'd forgiven him a month later. Like I said, they were the on-again, off-again couple. Our class had even voted them most likely to end up married.

"Tom Cooper." I told them the short version.

Hunter broke the silence that followed. "Have you ever met a succubus who hadn't screwed half the football team?"

Metaphorically speaking, I assumed.

Ian and Cole shook their heads.

"Shagging comes with the job," Ian said.

"It's a necessity." Cole dragged a hand through his hair. "How could Lilith?"

"How could Lilith jump on the chance to make a teenager a succubus?" Wyatt asked in a tone that said *Think about it.*

"You know most souls have already been marked by another sin before lust touches them," Ian said. "Young succubi are rare."

"Lilith had to have been salivating at the jowls

when Avery died," Hunter added.

"So much so that she fought for Avery's soul." Cole looked at me. "Your soul should have gone up."

I wasn't sure if the bite in Cole's words were caused by sympathy, anger, or sorrow. Maybe it was a bit of all three. But what did it mean to go up? No one knew. Not for sure. Even if Heaven did send souls back to Earth, I doubted I'd come back as me with the memory of my family and friends intact.

"Ian, is there a way to find out?" Cole asked.

"Raymond knows about a lot of Hell's legal issues. He might know. And if it's true, there's a possibility that Avery could file an appeal."

Cole sank down onto the stool next to me. "Has that ever been done?"

"I'm sure someone at some time has." Ian pulled his phone from his pocket.

"Who are you calling?" I asked. I needed time to digest this news.

"Raymond," Ian replied.

"Ask him if he'll help us with her defense," Cole said.

I crossed the room and took the phone from him just as a gruff voice said hello. "Wrong number. Sorry." I hung up.

Ian frowned. "He has caller ID."

"What if I appeal and lose?" I asked, not sure if I wanted to take that risk. My troubled gaze met Cole's. "Do you think Lilith would just let me continue living here? She'd find a way to punish me for going behind her back, again." Really, how many times could I piss her off before someone we knew paid the price?

"Avery, you could get out of Hell," Cole said.

"Why didn't you appeal?" If it were such a marvelous idea, wouldn't Cole have argued that Lilith wasn't upfront about their deal?

"Because I willingly made a binding agreement with Lilith." When I opened my mouth to argue that point, he quickly added, "Ian and I discussed this in detail a long time ago."

"That's true," Ian interjected. "We even brought it up to Raymond at one point."

"In his words," Cole said, "'it wasn't Lilith's fault I didn't ask to read the fine print.'"

I leaned against the arm of Ian's chair, staring at the edge of the coffee table. I didn't want to be a demon. I didn't want to survive by siphoning life from the living. But I also didn't want to lose any more than I already had. Surprisingly, it wasn't the centuries-old incubus who figured that out.

"Maybe Avery doesn't want to give up what she has now," Hunter said.

"If she has a chance to break free of this life, she has to take it," Cole argued.

Ian's gaze traveled between me to Cole. A look of understanding settled into his features. He rubbed my arm, but his attention turned to Cole. "What do you think will happen next?"

All eyes settled on Cole. He pressed the heels of his hands to his eyes.

"I don't know the inner workings of Hell," Wyatt said, "but if her succubus card is revoked, I doubt she'd be allowed to stay here."

"Or on Earth," Hunter added.

Ian took his phone from me, got up, and indicated with a nod for Wyatt and Hunter to follow. He stopped next to Cole and gave his shoulder a squeeze. "You stand a good chance of losing her if she pursues this, mate."

Wyatt and Hunter left without another word.

Ian stopped at the door. "Avery, I'll back you whatever you decide."

"Thanks."

And then it was just Cole and me. A part of me thought I should jump for joy. I had a chance to rest in peace. Wasn't that what I'd originally wanted? Yet now that seemed so final. Absolute. I'd be gone. My story over. My hesitation wasn't because of a boy. Although, having more time to figure out if Cole and I shared a connection that could stand the test of time was what'd had me smiling when I'd fallen asleep last night.

"Avery, I know what you're thinking, but if you have a chance to change things…"

I shook my head, unconvinced. "Lilith didn't push me off that deck. I'm dead, and nothing will change that."

He moved into the family room, sat in the leather chair, and pulled me onto his lap. "You'll be in Heaven instead of in this hellhole."

I glanced around us. "It's not so bad here." It was a misfit crowd—two incubi, a half demon, and one of Heaven's unwanted children, with a few humans thrown in for normalcy. But despite their flaws, they were caring individuals.

I'd hoped to get Cole to crack a smile with my comment, but he was stone-faced. I rested my cheek against his shoulder, letting myself be cradled in his arms. "No one knows what happens to souls in Heaven, except that they never see Earth again. Not as the person they were when they died."

"The popular theory amongst demons is that souls are reborn," he replied. His fingers caressed my arm in a slow, steady pattern, up and down.

"As someone different." Did I want to be a different person?

"They're given a fresh beginning, but they're still the same soul."

"With no memory of their past life." Or was that lives?

"I know you're scared, but if you can get out of this existence—"

I pulled away from him. "You keep saying that, but maybe I don't want to be a corpse in the ground."

His hand stopped moving. "That's the way it's supposed to be, Avery, and you'd be fine with it if you hadn't seen anything different."

Frustrated, I jumped up and paced zigzags around the family room. "I wouldn't be *fine,* I'd be dead." I shook my head. "Maybe I don't want to forget my parents or my sister. Maybe I don't want to be a soul caught in the loop of living and dying. Maybe I don't want to discover that version of Heaven is a fairytale and there's nothing left after death except to wait for my friends and family to join me. How morbid an existence is that?" I grabbed my bangs and held them at the back of my head. "I need time to think."

"Avery, it's the circle—"

I pinned him with a glare that had him swallowing the rest of his words. "Don't you dare finish that sentence! If you want me out of your life, just say that. But don't you dare start quoting lame clichés."

I'd gone to sleep the night before feeling as if I was

on top of the world, only to find myself in a new nightmare the very next day.

"Avery." Cole stood in front of me. He moved to put his arms around me, but I stepped back, tears welling in my eyes. Gingerly, he placed his fingers under my chin and guided my head up so that he could see my eyes. "I'm just starting to know you. The last thing I want is for you to leave, but I can't be that selfish. We're talking about your soul here. You could be free from Hell's fury. Free from Lilith's reign."

Free from this lifetime. Free from me.

I didn't want to lose me.

Or Cole.

And I'd promised Luz we'd do lunch.

Plus, I sort of had a guardian angel—half angel. Okay, an aura-reading nephilim who needed to learn what to blurt and what not to.

And Ian had said he'd back me no matter what I decided.

I rested a hand on Cole's arm. "I've already accepted what I've become."

His fingers curled into fists at his side. I stepped closer, sliding my hands over the ball of his palms. He unclenched, letting me lace my fingers through his.

"I've already lost my family and my friends. Appealing my sentence won't change that. Don't ask me to now risk losing you and our friends."

His shoulders slumped forward. "You shouldn't have to live like this."

I crouched so I could see his eyes. "We do what we have to do to survive," I said, echoing what he'd told me.

"Until you find another way."

He was so infuriating, but I could tell by the sorrow in his gaze and the way the corners of his mouth tugged downward that he wanted what was best for me.

"We're supposed to find a way to make what we are work. Remember?"

He sighed, resting his forehead on mine. "You're going to keep throwing my words back at me, aren't you?"

I smiled. "Well, you can be pretty smart when you want to be."

He closed his eyes. "I don't agree with your decision."

"It should be my choice."

He pulled me into his arms. I inhaled his spicy scent. When he looked at me, his eyes were glossed over. Then his mouth was on mine, kissing me more passionately than he had the night before.

The way I saw it, I had time to think about my future. Staying for eternity on Earth with Cole or risking the unknown of Heaven wasn't a choice I had to make that day.

I slipped my hands under Cole's T-shirt, tracing the strong muscles in his shoulders down to his waist. He backed me up, lowering me onto the couch.

His lips caressed a path to my ear. "*Dejarte ir será lo más difícil que tengo que hacer.*"

"Cole, tell me what you said."

He kissed me, then replied, "Letting you go will be the hardest thing I ever have to do."

"Then don't, and we'll see where this leads us."

Chapter 20

"Oh no!" Luz said as she weaved through the tables at the local deli. "I haven't had a boyfriend in months, which means I'm living vicariously through you until I get one." She slid into a booth. "I want the juicy details about you and Cole. What are his kisses like?"

Dreamy. Addictive. Hungry.

"You hesitated." Luz crinkled her button nose. "Too much tongue? Not enough?" She made a face like she'd just sucked on a lemon. "He's not one of those guys who slobber all over your face, is he?"

"No!" I set my tray down on the table and scooted into the booth across from her, fixing the spaghetti strap on my tank top so it was on my shoulder again. "He's an amazing kisser."

I'd have liked very much to have been home kissing him and not at the mall with her, but Ian had stopped by, which meant Luz wasn't far behind. I swear she had a tracker planted on him. She always knew when he'd be at the apartment. This time she'd shown up with Nick's car and not Nick.

"Working" had been her explanation when I'd asked where he was.

Ian had wanted to steal Cole for a while, which had Luz psyched for our girls' lunch date. It was for the better. I needed time to think about what I'd learned the night before. Was Cole right? Had Lilith interfered with my Judgment? Should my soul have gone up? Cole and I still disagreed about what I should do. I hoped Ian would talk to Cole, help him see the bigger picture.

"Whew," Luz exclaimed, bringing me back to the present. "You almost ruined the image I'd drawn of Cole in my head: strong, sensitive, the kind of guy who takes the time to make sure a girl's toes curl."

"Luz!" I glanced around to make sure no one was listening. My toes had not only curled, my pulse had raced and his touch had sent pleasant waves of heat coursing through me. But Luz and I were in the middle of a restaurant, for goodness' sake.

She dumped a few packets of sweetener into her iced tea. "Dish. Who made the first move?"

"It just sort of happened."

She sipped her tea and tore open another packet of sweetener.

"I knew you two would hook up, even when you both claimed to be 'just friends.' " She paused in her stirring to make air quotes around the last two words.

I pointed a forkful of salad at her. "Says the girl who doesn't know when the right guy is standing in front of her."

"I would, too," she replied through a mouth full of food. "Sure, I've dated plenty of losers, but I can spot the type now." She swallowed. "I think that's why I tried things with Dylan. I knew he'd never use me. We'd either work or we wouldn't."

"Too bad you dated the wrong friend."

"What's that supposed to mean?"

For a moment, I thought she would throw her sandwich at me.

"Nick's the guy you should be dating," I replied, not letting her evil glare deter me. "He's the one you mesh with." It was so obvious. I was surprised Miss Observant didn't see it.

"I've known Nick since he was a snot-nosed brat who threw worms on unsuspecting girls."

"And were you the recipient of these worms or were you his partner in crime?" I crunched down on lettuce.

She burst out laughing. "Partner in crime. How'd you know?"

"You guys fit together."

"As friends."

I grinned.

"You think he likes me?"

"Oh, yeah. Only a guy who is into you wakes up at the crack of dawn to be your chauffeur, and guys don't loan out their cars lightly."

She was quiet for a minute, which was incredible considering how much she'd been chatting before Nick's name had come up. "He got up early to drive me to Cole's to see Ian."

"Who he knows is too old for you and therefore not a threat."

She bit into her sandwich, chewed thoughtfully, and swallowed. "You think he likes me?"

"Yes, Luz. He's totally into you."

"Me and Nick?" She giggled and stuck a chip into her mouth. "Hey! You changed the subject."

"What subject?" I asked innocently.

"You and Cole, and since at the moment I'm still boyfriendless, you owe me the steamy details." She waved a chip at me. "Don't make me beg. Besides, best friends are supposed to tell each other everything, and if you're hanging out with us, then that makes you my best friend."

I grinned. Luz reminded me a little of Megan in that she said what was on her mind. I couldn't believe I was talking about my first time with a girl I barely knew, but Luz was so likable and easy to talk to. I gave her the highlights, telling her just enough to satisfy her curiosity without betraying Cole's and my privacy.

"I'm glad you were thrown into Cole's life." Luz's hand flew to her mouth. "Oh, Avery! That was heartless of me. I'm sorry about your family. Cole told me you lost them recently."

"It's okay, Luz." And I meant it. I missed my parents and Gracie. Boy, did I miss them. My throat tightened just thinking about them, but seeing how torn up they'd been at my mere presence gave me the strength to admit I couldn't be a part of their lives.

"No. I'm sorry," Luz said. "My brothers drive me nuts and my parents can be overbearing, but I can't imagine them not being around." Cole had told me Luz felt her family was a little too apple pie, but sometimes that was okay. "If you ever want to talk about them, I'm here for you."

"Thanks." Maybe one day I'd take her up on that.

"Before, I just meant that Cole's a great guy, and he deserves someone who makes him smile."

I tilted my head to the side. "You think *I* make him smile?"

Sure, Cole smiled a lot, but I'd thought that was part of his personality.

"Duh! Yes! I mean, he's always joked and laughed, but when he's with you, he means it. It's real."

I grinned. Surely Cole's desire to have me around would override his insistence that I should file the appeal.

"What do you say we do a little shopping?" I wiped my mouth with a napkin.

"Sexy lingerie?" Her eyebrows rose and fell in rapid succession.

I cracked up laughing as I peeled my bare legs from the vinyl seat. "Luz, you're bad."

Besides, I already had plenty of sexy lingerie at the apartment, compliments of the Queen of the Damned.

****

Luz had to pick up Nick from work, so she didn't come up to the apartment after our shopping trip. I'd bought a sketchpad and some drawing pencils. I wanted to register for an art class. I was okay with outlines, but always screwed up the shadowing. With a little guidance, I was sure I could learn what I was doing wrong, and I had plenty of time to get it right.

Cole had beaten me home. He sat on the chair in the family room, elbows on his knees and head in his hands. It took me a moment to realize he had his phone pressed to one ear. He acknowledged my entrance with a slight nod and went back to staring intently at the carpet.

I sat on the couch and pulled out my new art supplies. Whoever it was Cole chatted with had to be doing most of the talking. Cole occasionally added a "How much," "Got it," or "I'm sure."

With my legs tucked underneath me, I flipped to the first page in my sketchpad. I meticulously worked on the shape of Cole's face, trying to capture the angle of his head and his set jaw.

He glanced at me, mouth in an expressionless line and eyes devoid of emotion. I worked on my drawing, adding a line here and a curve there. The nose came out too short, and the eyebrows had too much of an arch. I tore the sheet out of the pad, crumpled it into a ball, and started over. I had Cole's head, eyes, and nose outlined and was working on his lips when I heard a curt, "Just do it."

He tossed his phone onto the coffee table. "You know you have a sketch book in the bedroom."

"Lilith got me that one." I continued drawing. "I wanted to buy my own." Which wasn't much different from using the one in the bedroom, since the new one was purchased with money I'd found in the wallet Lilith had given me. "I should find a job."

When Cole didn't reply, I glanced at him.

"Yeah. Next week," he said, though it was obvious his thoughts were elsewhere.

"And I promise to pull my weight around here. Help with the bills and cleaning." I'd have to learn to cook. Right now my skills in the kitchen were limited to boiling water and popping prepared food into a microwave.

I bit my bottom lip as I carefully drew eyebrows. Better.

He scooted to the edge of the chair. "What are you working on?"

"You." I'd always liked sketching people, although I was slow and had more half-drawn sketches than I did completed ones. People tended to move before I could finish.

He ran his hands over his face.

"Are you okay?" I asked.

"Yeah. Long day."

"What did you and Ian do? And where is he?" I'd expected him to be here for dinner.

"We went to talk to old friends. Ian stayed with them."

I nodded. If people were two-dimensional outlines, I'd actually be pretty good. I chuckled at that thought, tilting my head to the side as I tried to decide if I should stop or attempt to add the shadows that would bring the drawing to life.

Cole got up and came to sit next to me. "Not bad."

I shrugged, erased a line. "It needs work. I figured I'd take a class or two. When's registration?"

"We have time."

We couldn't have that much time, but I didn't push.

It was hard to concentrate with my subject now lounging next to me, tracing lazy figure eights on my leg, instead of sitting across from me where I could see the contours of his cheeks and the length of his neck. I set the pad on the table and settled my back against his chest. "How was your day?"

"Exhausting." He put an arm around me. "Yours?"

"It was nice. I needed a girls' day out."

"I've heard it's a must."

Cole buried his nose in my hair and breathed in deep.

I craned my neck to the side to see him. "Are you sure you're okay?"

"Yeah."

That was the third *yeah* since he'd hung up the phone, and Cole didn't say *yeah*. He was better at articulating his thoughts than that. I studied him. He cupped my face with his hand and gently stroked my cheek. I was sure something was bothering him, but before I could press him to tell me what it was, his mouth covered mine with the sweetest kiss. His tongue skimmed my lip and sent an elated shiver through my entire body a moment before he pulled me closer. His hands were on my back, my waist, my thighs, never stopping for long. My fingers twisted in his hair. When I came up for air, Cole's mouth followed my neck down to my collarbone.

I could've kissed Cole for an eternity. Only, he leaned back against the couch, leaving my mind a bit mushy and my body aching for his touch.

"Let's get out of here," he said.

I glanced at the bedroom. After a kiss like that, I was fine with staying in. He chuckled and pulled me off the couch.

****

We ended up in Evanston, following the path along Lake Michigan. A Mediterranean-blue sky stretched down from the heavens to meet the glistening water below. A mix of motorboats and sailboats cruised the lake. Cole held my hand in his as we followed the paved path along the shore.

"If you love the water so much, why don't you live on the coast or in the tropics?" I asked. Cole wore a faraway expression whenever he gazed out at the lake. He didn't need to say he loved the water for me to know.

"I've lived in Sicily, Cabo San Lucas, and Riviera Maya before this."

All places I'd never been. "Riviera Maya's in Mexico, right?"

He nodded. "Right on the water."

"If you liked it there, why move?"

"It's part of being what we are. We can't stay in one place a long time or people notice we've stopped aging. I say I'm sixteen whenever I start over. That way I can stick around longer."

"Can't you just morph into an older you?"

"I top out at twenty-four, so I still stop aging. I can get away with my looks remaining the same for six to eight years." He paused. "I guess, if I wanted to stay, I could change my appearance altogether. But if I did that, I'd still have to build a new life. The energy it would take for me to sustain a new disguise wouldn't be worth it, because I wouldn't be able to keep the same friends and job."

"So you might as well move," I said.

I swallowed. I wouldn't have to give up everyone, though. I'd always have Cole and Ian. Wyatt's angel blood and Hunter's demon blood slowed their aging. They'd live at least twice as long as Luz and the others. A lump formed in my throat, and I forced myself not to think about that. I'd deal with losing them when I had to.

"Being immortal isn't so glamorous anymore, is it?"

It was a little depressing to know I wouldn't grow old with the people around me and to know I'd constantly have to say goodbye to friends. No wonder so many succubi were cold, unfeeling creatures. Decades of losing those closest to them would have chipped away at their hearts until they were made of ice.

A warm breeze cut over the water, moving my hair

and caressing my neck as if to say I'd be okay.

"I wouldn't have chosen this life if I'd known the truth," Cole said.

I stopped. "But you've found a way to make it work."

"I had to," he said, slipping the strap of my tank top back onto my shoulder.

I couldn't deny there were disadvantages to being a demon, and there were some big ones, but nothing was worse than not existing at all. Cole believed all Heaven-bound souls were reborn in time. My favorite theory was that a soul remained in Heaven one year for every year lived on Earth. On the final birthday, his or her soul was given new life. It was a beautiful assumption, but it didn't change the fact that, if souls were reborn, memories of their previous lives were lost. My memories were all I had, and I didn't want them taken from me.

Not liking the direction the conversation was headed, I decided to point out the positive. "So you spent the last three or so decades in warm places. Were you in school?"

"Nah," he said as we strolled toward the end of a pier. "I was a waiter in Sicily and a beach bum in Cabo."

"Do we need Lilith's permission to move?"

"We have to have Lilith's blessing before we relocate—more to keep peace between her employees than because she cares where we live. If you pick a place close to another incubus or succubus, she'll have you pick somewhere else. If she agrees, she makes sure you have what you need: new alias, a roof over your head, and money in your pocket."

"And what did you do in Riviera Maya?"

"Took tourists scuba diving. That was fun."

"I bet you looked hot in a dive skin." I bumped his shoulder with mine. "Maybe you could teach me."

We reached the end of the walkway. Cole sat on the wooden planks and indicated for me to sit in front of him. He wrapped his arms around me and kissed the side of my neck. "This is how I want to remember you."

His kisses tickled in a pleasant way. I smiled. "With windblown hair and smelling like summer."

He nibbled my ear. "You look sexy."

Had to be the cutoff shorts or maybe the way the strap of my tank top kept slipping from my shoulder.

We fell silent as we watched the sailboats make their slow journey over the lake. Maybe one day I'd learned to sail and purchase a boat of my own. It would have a red sail, one that could be seen from miles away, and I'd spend countless days relaxing on the water somewhere tropical. I'd like that.

****

Cole and I stopped outside our apartment. He held the key an inch from the doorknob, eyes focused on the lock.

"Avery, I want you to know I care about you more than I've cared about anyone in a very long time."

He didn't need to tell me that. His actions had shown it. I hoped one day mine would do the same for him. I stepped closer and rested a hand on his arm. "I care about you, too."

His eyes closed a moment, then he peered at me through dark stands of hair. "I'll always do what's best for you. I want you to know that."

"I do."

"I'm glad." He unlocked the door. "*No me odies.*"

I stepped in front of him, wrapping his arms around my waist and then draping mine over his shoulders. "You're teaching me Spanish."

He smiled, pulling me closer. "In your next life."

"The way I see it, that's now." I kissed him. A quick peck. "*Sí?*"

He chuckled, although his smile fell short.

"You're special, Avery." He kissed me deeply. "*No puedo dejar que secrifiques tu alma solo porque tiene miedo de lo desconocido.*"

"What did you say?" I nuzzled closer to him. Kissed his neck just below his ear. "Come on, tell me."

"I'd rather do this."

His lips were on mine again. Tenderly. Stealing my breath. He continued kissing me as he opened the door and backed me into the apartment. When he pulled away, a single tear ran down his cheek.

"Cole, what's wrong?" I wiped the tear with my thumb.

"I'm sorry, but it's for your own good." He quickly left, closing the door behind him.

Chapter 21

"What's for my own good? Cole!" I grabbed the door handle, immediately snatching my hand back when the metal seared my skin. "Son of a bitch!" I exclaimed, kicking the door. I shook my hand as I marched into the kitchen to get a hot pad, pissed that Cole had ditched me and pissed that he'd turned the doorknob into a red-hot iron, both without warning. It wasn't until I was back near the door that the aroma of rose and jasmine found me. My heart lodged in my throat, and my hands trembled. Shaking my head, I mumbled, "No, no, no. He wouldn't."

But then a faint prickle tugged at my subconscious, and I knew I wasn't alone in the apartment. If only I'd have picked up Lilith's signature sooner.

What would I have done? Run screaming down the hall? Cole was faster than me. He'd have stopped me before I reached the elevator. Not to mention that if Lilith wanted an audience with me, she could probably snap her fingers and transport me to anywhere in this world and beyond.

"Avery, why don't you have a seat?" Lilith said calmly.

I preferred not to, but I turned from the door, anyway. I tossed the hot pad onto the counter and did as she'd asked. Lilith was dressed in a sleeveless, cream-colored mock turtleneck, matching slacks, and stilettos.

Her golden blonde hair was pulled to the side in a ponytail that tumbled over her shoulder.

My hand stung something fierce. It was a constant reminder of Cole's betrayal.

I forced a smile. "What brings you back so soon?"

"I'm pretty sure you know." Lilith cocked her head to the side. "Would you like to know what Cole said when he spoke in Spanish?"

Of course she'd been listening to our conversation. My stubborn side didn't want anything from Lilith. My curious side, however, was dying to know what he'd said. Conflicted, I curled my fingers over my stinging palm and sat a little straighter, refusing to ask, yet hoping she'd offer the information anyway.

"He asked you not to hate him, and then he said he wouldn't allow you to sacrifice your soul because you're afraid of the unknown."

I liked that he wanted what was best for me. I was sad that we didn't agree on what that was.

"Is he right? Are you afraid of the unknown?" she asked.

I forced myself to hold her gaze. "I like to think of the unknown as an adventure waiting to be explored."

That was a total lie. I was terrified of what I couldn't see or touch.

Lilith nodded as if she approved of my reply. "You and Cole seem to have hit it off."

"We're making our living arrangements work." At least, I'd thought we were.

"That boy has always been one of my favorite souls," Lilith said with a sigh. "He has such a kind heart."

"That's because he didn't deserve to go to Hell," I

said through clenched teeth.

Lilith studied her blood-red nail polish. "He made the deal of his own free will, and before you try to say he didn't know what he was agreeing to, I never lied."

"You didn't tell him he was making a deal with the Devil either," I retorted.

Lilith might have a porcelain complexion and an angelic appearance, but she was far from an angel. She seduced humans with offers of the impossible. She told them what they wanted to hear in order to persuade them to trade their soul for a loved one's. She was the worst kind of monster, preying on the bereaved.

Lilith laughed a whimsical chortle. "I'm hardly the Devil. And you must admit Cole hasn't had a bad existence. He lives on Earth in a location of his choosing. He has friends. I kept my promises."

"And I'm your way of fulfilling one of those promises." The taste of bile climbed up my throat and rested on my tongue.

"You're a young soul who died a tragic death and was placed in my care."

After you fought to get me, I interjected silently.

"Did I believe you and Cole would enjoy each other's company? Yes. Did I know he'd want to keep you in his life? I suspected as much. Did I place you with Cole to fulfill a promise? No. I placed you with Cole because it suited my needs and because I knew he'd be able to help you adjust to your new life."

"I am adjusting." And I did have Cole to thank for that. Without him I'd have curled up into a ball, waiting for a death that would never come. It was obvious why Lilith was here. Cole wouldn't have left me alone with her unless he'd known what she was up to, but I needed to hear her say it. "You're not here to see how I'm doing, are you?"

"No. Cole filed an appeal on your behalf. He's requested Heaven and Hell reevaluate your sins. And I've been sent here to bring you back for Judgment."

She didn't appear happy about that, and her tone made it perfectly clear that she didn't like to be *sent* anywhere. I hugged myself. I wasn't an evil person when I was human. Yes, I'd made mistakes, some bigger than others. And if I could've gone back in time and done things differently, I would have, but time didn't work that way. When our actions hurt someone, we're left living with the memory of the pain we'd caused. But we did have a choice to do better from that moment forward. I did do better, I'd thought.

I wrung my fingers together, ignoring the throbbing in my hand. "Is he right? Am I in Hell because you fought for my soul?"

"You're on Earth because I fought for your soul."

A second chance with a catch, I almost laughed hysterically. Instead, I asked, "What's on the other side?"

"Paradise, if you believe the Bible."

"You were once an angel. You have to know what happens to souls in Heaven. Do they remain there waiting for their loved ones to die and join them, or are they sent back to Earth to live new lives?"

"This is the unknown Cole spoke of, and I can't give you the answers you seek. Even I must abide by the rules set by higher powers." She stood. "We should go."

I jumped up and quickly put the coffee table between us. "I don't...I won't...What if I refuse to leave with you?"

Her eyes narrowed. "If you don't show for your hearing, your appeal will be thrown out, and you'll remain in my service for all of eternity."

Suddenly, forever seemed like an impossibly long time to be bound to the Queen of the Damned. "What if I withdraw the appeal now, couldn't I file a new one later?"

"Perhaps," Lilith said thoughtfully. "But twice now, Cole has broken the trust I placed in him when I made him your mentor: first when he let you slip to New York, and then again when he filed the appeal. It is only because he is one of my favorite souls that he remains here on Earth in this cozy apartment, and it is because you are not only new to this life but also so young that I forgave your discrepancies. But I will not allow either of you to cross me a third time without ramifications. Other demons will think I've become soft, and I will not have that.

"So while I can't stop you from filing in the future, know this: should that happen, someone will be tossed into the River of Souls on mere principle. And since you'll be expected back in Judgment, that someone will be Cole." She clapped her hands together once. "The moment of truth, Avery. You can have your appeal, or you can accept your original judgment. No going back. No changing your mind. Choose now."

Chapter 22

The wait was excruciating. I could hear the *tick* of the Chicago Bears wall clock announce every blasted second that crawled by. It was that quiet in the apartment. My mouth went dry, knowing what I'd done, but there was no turning back. Lilith had made that very clear. Part of me hoped I would forget this afternoon so I could never second-guess my decision.

What's done is done, I told myself as I yanked the clock off the wall and turned it over. A Phillips head screwdriver was needed to remove the batteries. *Tick*—pause—*tick*—pause—*tick*. It was maddening. I dropped the clock on the floor and slammed my heel into its face. It took several solid stomps before it sighed its last breath.

I reminded myself that Cole believed the appeal was in my best interest. It wasn't that he hated me or that he wanted to see me leave. He'd done what he thought was right. If I had a chance at Heaven, he thought I should take it. Truth be told, I'd have been the first to encourage someone else to do that very same thing. Only a fool would choose Hell.

I wondered if Cole regretted filing the appeal. What was more important to me was whether or not he'd be disappointed by the choice I made.

But I had friends in this lifetime, and I wasn't ready to give them up. Nor did I want to risk losing my memories. They meant the world to me. Plus, I liked the idea of Cole and me figuring things out.

Lilith had left hours ago, yet Cole hadn't returned home. My calls to him went straight to voice mail. Wherever he was, he didn't want to be disturbed.

On the second day of being alone in the apartment, Wyatt and Hunter stopped by; only I didn't open the door. I peered through the peephole, immediately disappointed it wasn't Cole. I didn't know if they'd helped Cole with my appeal, and I wasn't ready to face them. I didn't need Wyatt reading my aura, and I wasn't in the mood to explain myself to them.

By the third day, I began to wonder if Cole was coming back. What if Lilith forbade it? What if he had already started a new life somewhere else? What if I was wasting my time, waiting for him? My stubborn side refused to give up hope. Afraid of missing him if I stepped out, I remained locked in the apartment. Waiting. Wondering. Left drowning with my thoughts.

On day five, I sat on the leather chair in the family room, legs dangling over the arm as I flipped through one of Cole's car magazines for the umpteenth time. Hunger nudged at me, and not the type that could be satisfied with half a box of cereal or a frozen waffle. I'd already finished the leftover pizza and what little else had been in the fridge. This hunger was more of a thirst—pure need for life essence. I tried to remember the last time I'd fed. Six, seven days ago?

I regretted not letting Wyatt and Hunter in and kicked myself in the butt for not getting Ian's number. I thought about calling Luz but decided against it since I couldn't tell her what had happened. The last thing I wanted was for her, Nick, and Dylan to stop by.

I paced, plopped down onto the couch, stared blindly at the television, not seeing what was on, dozed off only to awaken startled by a car backfiring or the neighbor's door slamming shut. On the seventh day, I finally heard keys jingle just outside the apartment door. A sinking feeling stopped my heart. What if it wasn't Cole? What if it was the landlord, coming to clean the place out?

Then Cole walked in. Eyes haunted by dark shadows and hair disheveled. His incredible blue gaze met mine. It should be a crime to have eyes that extraordinary. A mix of relief and dread filled me as I took in his hooded expression.

"Hey," I said, not moving from where I'd been staring out the patio window, watching the day pass.

His eyes narrowed in obvious confusion. "You're here? But…is this Lilith's doing? Did she stall the hearing?"

"No." I had hoped for a warmer greeting from him, and I couldn't get a read on if he was happy or disappointed to find me here.

"Then you must be here to say goodbye." He hung his keys on the hook next to mine, wet his lips, and faced me again.

"Only if you want me gone." Luz might let me move in with her until I found a job and could afford my own place. "I declined the appeal."

"Avery…" Cole raked a hand through his hair. "You have a way out of this life."

"Cole, I was serious when I said I didn't want to lose my memories of my parents and sister, of my past. That I don't want to give up the friends I have now. You have to be able to understand that." A week's worth of anxiety came crashing down on me, threatening to crush me beneath its weight. Afraid I'd collapse from emotional and physical exhaustion, I settled a hip against the wall. "I wasn't sure you were coming back."

"I wasn't planning to." He picked up the notepad I'd drawn the cartoon kitty on. "I figured you'd be gone—Lilith was supposed to take you to the hearing, and Raymond was sure you'd win." Cole shrugged. "I couldn't stand the idea of being here alone with so many things to remind me of you. Only Lilith sent me a text this morning, telling me to go home before she had me reassigned to a permanent position in Hell." He put the notepad down and glanced around. "I was expecting her to be here ready with my punishment."

One line in what he said resonated above the others. "You stayed away because you'd miss me being here?"

"Is that so hard to believe?" Despite the fact that he tried to have me sent away, no, it wasn't. He crossed the room, cupped my face in his hands, and pressed his lips to mine. When he broke the kiss, he said, "We should enjoy what time we have left together, because Lilith will have my head for trying to free you."

That thought sobered me up again. "You weren't worried about my head when you left me alone with her."

"She wouldn't hurt you before the appeal, and like I keep saying, you would have won."

"Maybe, but you would have been in the hot seat." I shook my head. "What were you thinking?"

He kissed the top of my head. "That you deserve better."

"She likes you. She said you were one of her favorite souls."

"That won't stop her from making an example of me. Wait! What did you mean 'I *would have* been in the hot seat?' Please tell me you didn't make a deal with her."

"I'm already in her service, remember?" I shrugged. "We have an agreement: I forget the appeal, and she forgets you filed it. Oh! And we're to never mention this incident to anyone. She has a reputation to uphold of..." I paused to remember her exact words. "An evil bitch who's not to be crossed."

But I'd seen through her hard exterior. She might have been powerful, and she might have been ruthless, but she cared for the souls who reported to her. I decided that had to be due to the angel in her.

"You must hate me."

"I'm angry with you. You shouldn't have gone behind my back." Although, seven days of wondering if I'd ever see him again gave me the time I'd needed to understand why he'd done it. "But I don't hate you."

He combed his fingers through his hair. "Choosing to remain a succubus has to be the dumbest thing you've ever done."

"That might be debatable." I smiled. "Cole?"

"Hmm."

"The next time we disagree, talk to me about it. Don't do it, anyway."

He gave me a squeeze. "Deal."

****

Now that I'd turned down my one chance to let my physical body rot in the ground, and instead chose to have my soul remain right where it was, living out eternity in my own personal Hell on Earth—knock my analogy all you want, but it was easier to believe I'd made the right choice when I worded it that way—I decided to start living. I enrolled at the local college. Cole did too. Although his schedule included advanced classes, and since I'd see him every morning and every evening anyhow, I didn't pretend I'd be able to keep up. I chose similar classes to what I'd have had in New York. Plus, with a little help from Cole's friend, Raymond, I managed to slip into the already-full art class I wanted.

I chose living to not existing. Death sucked, no two ways about it, but I'd been given a rare and definitely unorthodox second chance, and I planned to make the best of it. I'd find a way to keep an eye on Gracie. Granted, I'd do it without pissing off the Queen of the Damned. I was thinking I could stalk my sister on social media or maybe ask Ian to check in on her from time to time. I hadn't worked out the details, but where there was a will, there was a way. I'd already proven that.

Luz, Nick, and Dylan had gained another guardian demon.

Hunter and Wyatt had gained an ally.

Ian now knew a succubus who wasn't vain and conceited, and he vowed to make sure I didn't change.

And Cole, well, I had no idea if we could make our romance work for the long-term, but I hoped we could, and I was excited to see where tomorrow led.

Acknowledgments

Here we are, at the end of the book and one of my favorite parts of the writing process: thanking the people I've been blessed to have in my life. This book had a long journey from first draft to publication. If I missed anyone, please forgive me.

Thanks to Eilidh MacKenzie, my wonderful editor at The Wild Rose Press, who ushered *Damned When I Didn't* through its many stages of edits. Additional thanks to the many others at TWRP who had a hand in bringing this book to you.

Much appreciation to my closest author friends, Kym Brunner, Katie Sparks, Allan Woodrow, and Kathleen Reitmann, for their continued encouragement and insight. And to Beverly Keough Nickelson and my Wednesday night critique group whose comments and advice were greatly appreciated.

On the home front, I would like to thank Vince. He encouraged me so many years ago to write down the stories I talked so much about, and he's remained my sounding board, offering encouragement when I need it and keeping me writing even when times are rough. To my boys, Kyle, Cory, William, and Ethan, for their continued support. And to Kate, whose excitement about my stories is contagious and whose reassurance seems to come at just the right time.

I'd also like to thank my readers. You're awesome, and I hope you enjoyed *Damned When I Didn't.*

A word about the author...

Cherie Colyer is the author of *Challenging Destiny* and the *Embrace* series. When she's not getting the fictional people in her life into trouble, she can be found solving network issues at work, spending time with family and friends, reading, or exploring the great outdoors.

Cherie lives in Illinois with her family. To learn more about Cherie and her novels visit:

www.CherieColyer.com

Thank you for purchasing
this publication of The Wild Rose Press, Inc.

For questions or more information
contact us at
info@thewildrosepress.com.

The Wild Rose Press, Inc.
www.thewildrosepress.com